THE CHINESE MAZE MURDERS

Judge Dee Mysteries Available from Chicago:

THE CHINESE MAZE MURDERS

A Chinese detective story
suggested by three original ancient Chinese plots

by

ROBERT VAN GULIK

*With nineteen plates
drawn by the author in Chinese style*

THE UNIVERSITY OF CHICAGO PRESS

THE CASE OF THE MURDER IN THE SEALED ROOM

THE CASE OF THE HIDDEN TESTAMENT

THE CASE OF THE GIRL WITH THE SEVERED HEAD

The University of Chicago Press, Chicago 60637
The University of Chicago Press, Ltd., London

Library of Congress Cataloging-in-Publication Data

Gulik, Robert Hans van, 1910–1967.
    The Chinese maze murders : a Chinese detective story suggested by
three original ancient Chinese plots / by Robert Van Gulik ; with
nineteen plates drawn by the author in Chinese style.
        p.   cm.
    "A Judge Dee mystery."
    ISBN 0-226-84878-7 (alk. paper)
    1. Dee Jen-Djieh (Fictitious character)—Fiction.   2. Judges—
China—Fiction.   I. Title.
PR9130.9.G8C54   1997
823'.914—dc21   97-1028
                                                           CIP

⊗ The paper used in this publication meets the minimum
requirements of the American National Standard for
Information Sciences—Permanence of Paper for Printed
Library Materials, ANSI Z39.48—1984.

AFTER the appearance of my translation of the old Chinese detective novel 'Dee Goong An'* I was asked to search for other Chinese novels of that kind. However, such books are now rather scarce and moreover it proved difficult to find one that appeals equally to modern Chinese and Western taste. As a matter of fact, 'Dee Goong An' is an exception. As a rule style and contents of ancient Chinese crime and mystery stories differ so much from modern ones that they are of slight interest to the present-day Oriental reader, and even less to the Westerner.

On the other hand old Chinese crime stories contain many clever plots and much material relating to the detection of crime. I thought, therefore, that it would be an interesting experiment to write a Chinese-style detective story myself, utilizing plots found in Chinese stories from bygone times.

I engaged upon this experiment mainly in order to prove to present-day Chinese and Japanese authors that it is possible to write a detective-novel in traditional Chinese style that yet appeals to the modern Oriental reader. I thought this all the more worth while since at present the

---

* *Dee Goong An, three murder cases solved by Judge Dee.* An old Chinese detective novel translated from the original Chinese with an introduction and notes, by R. H. van Gulik, Litt.D.; one illustrated vol. publ. Tokyo 1949.

book-market in China and Japan is flooded with bad translations of third-rate foreign thrillers, while their own ancient crime novels are practically forgotten. When I had completed my English manuscript of 'The Chinese Maze Murders', it was translated into Japanese by Professor Ogaeri Yukio, and published in 1951 by the Kodan-sha in Tokyo, under the title *Meiro-no-satsujin*, with a preface by the well known Japanese mystery writer Edogawa Rampo. Then I myself prepared a Chinese version, which was published in 1953 by the Nanyang Press in Singapore, under the title *Ti-jen-chieh-chi-an*. Both editions were favourably received in the Chinese and Japanese press. Encouraged by this success I wrote two more 'Judge Dee' novels, 'The Chinese Bell Murders' and 'The Chinese Lake Murders', of which a Chinese and Japanese version is now in preparation.

Having thus attained my main object, it occurred to me that also Western readers might perhaps be interested in this new type of crime novel. Therefore I decided to publish my English text of 'The Chinese Maze Murders', an additional motive being that the Chinese element has been introduced so often by Western writers of detective stories that I thought that the reader might be interested in seeing how it looks in genuine Chinese garb.

For information on the background of the present novel and the Chinese sources utilized the reader is referred to my Postscript at the end of the book. Here it may suffice to say that I borrowed three plots from ancient Chinese sources, rewriting them as one continuous story centering round the famous ancient Chinese master-detective Judge Dee. I retained the typical features of old Chinese detective novels, such as the prologue which gives some idea of the main events of the story itself, the chapter headings in two parallel lines, the peculiar Chinese device of letting the detective solve a number of cases simultaneously, etc., and in general tried to preserve as much as possible Chinese style and atmosphere.

The scene of my story is laid in Lan-fang, an imaginary border town of China during the seventh century A.D. The reader will find a Chinese map of that city on page xiv of the present publication. The plates were drawn by me in the style of book-illustrations of the Ming Dynasty.

All the credit of what may be found satisfactory in this novel must go to the ancient Chinese writers who evolved the plots. All its shortcomings must be blamed on the present author.

The Hague, spring 1956

ROBERT VAN GULIK

It should be noted that in Chinese the surname, here printed in capitals, precedes the personal name.

Main Characters:

DEE Jen-djieh, newly appointed magistrate of Lan-fang, a town district on the Northwest border of the Chinese Empire. Referred to as 'Judge Dee', or 'the judge'.

HOONG Liang, Judge Dee's confidential adviser and sergeant over the constables of the tribunal. Referred to as 'Sergeant Hoong', or 'the sergeant'.

MA Joong
TAO Gan   } the three trusted lieutenants of
CHIAO Tai   } Judge Dee

Persons connected with 'The Murder in the Sealed Room':

DING Hoo-gwo, a General living retired in Lan-fang. Found murdered in his own library.

DING Yee, a Junior Candidate of Literature, his only son. Referred to as 'Candidate Ding', or 'Young Ding'.

WOO Feng, son of Commander Woo of the Board of Military Affairs in the capital. A Junior Candidate of Literature and amateur painter.

Persons connected with 'The Hidden Testament':

Yoo Shou-chien, an ex-Governor who died while living retired in Lan-Fang.

Mrs. Yoo, *née* Mei, the Governor's young second wife.

Mrs. Lee, a painter, friend of Mrs. Yoo.

Yoo Kee, the Governor's eldest son by his first wife.

Yoo Shan, infant son of Mrs. Yoo.

Persons connected with 'The Girl with the Severed Head':

Fang, a blacksmith. Later appointed headman of the constables of the tribunal, and hence referred to as 'Headman Fang' or 'the headman'.

White Orchid, his eldest daughter.

Dark Orchid, his second daughter.

His son.

Others:

Chien Mow, the local tyrant who usurped power in Lan-fang.

Liu Wan-fang, his eldest counsellor.

Corporal Ling, a deserter from the regular army, reinstated by Judge Dee.

Orolakchee, an Uigur chieftain. His real name is Prince Ooljin. His false name 'Orolakchee' means *agent* or *representative*.

The Hunter, accomplice of Orolakchee.

Tulbee, an Uigur girl.

Occurs in Chapter XIX only:

Master Crane Robe, an old recluse.

LIST OF ILLUSTRATIONS

CONTENTS

SKETCH MAP OF LAN-FANG

1. *Tribunal*
2. *Temple of the City God*
3. *Temple of Confucius*
4. *Temple of the War God*
5. *Bell Tower*
6. *Drum Tower*
7. *Pagoda*
8. *Northern Row*
9. *Southern Row*
10. *Chien Mow's Mansion*
11. *General Ding's Mansion*
12. *Eternal Spring Wineshop*
13. *Hermitage of the Three Treasu*
14. *Mrs. Lee's House*
15. *Former Yoo Mansion*
16. *Yoo Kee's Mansion*
17. *Watergate*
18. *Execution Ground*

First Chapter

Heaven created an immutable pattern for ten thousand ages,
Regulating sun and stars above, mountains and rivers below;
Thereafter the sages of old did model our sacred social order,
Taking Heavenly Justice as warp, and man-made Law as woof.

A wise and honest judge is Heaven's unerring instrument,
The people's father and mother, both compassionate and stern;
In his court the oppressed obtain redress of all their wrongs,
No criminal there escapes, despite base fraud and guile.

UNDER the present illustrious Ming dynasty, in the Yoong-lo era, our Empire is at peace, crops are plentiful, there are neither droughts nor floods, and the people are prosperous and content. This fortunate state of affairs is due entirely to the August Virtue of His Imperial Majesty. Naturally in this blessed time of peace crimes are few, so that the present provides scant material for the study of crime and detection. Rather than the present one must turn to the past for accounts of baffling crimes, and their marvellous solution by perspicacious magistrates.

Finding myself with ample leisure for the pursuit of my favourite study, I diligently search old records and dusty archives for famous ancient criminal cases, and I have made it a habit always to listen carefully to my friends and acquaintances when, gathered in the tea house, they start discoursing on the astounding crimes solved by famous judges of past centuries.

The other day, late in the afternoon, I strolled through the Western Park to admire the lotus flowers that were in full bloom. I crossed the carved marble bridge that leads to the island in the center of the lotus pond, and found myself an empty corner table on the open terrace of the restaurant there.

Sipping my tea and nibbling dried melon seeds I enjoyed the beautiful view over the lake all covered with lotus flowers. I observed the motley crowd and, as I often do, amused myself by trying to deduce from the appearance of some passers-by their personality and background.

My eye fell on two remarkably beautiful girls who passed by walking hand in hand. Their strong resemblance suggested at once that they were sisters. But evidently their characters were entirely different. The younger one was gay and vivacious who talked all the time. The elder, on the contrary, was reserved and shy who hardly answered the other. Here face bore an expression of deep sadness. I felt sure that somewhere there was a deep tragedy in her life.

As the two girls disappeared among the crowd I noticed that they were followed by an elderly woman; she had a slight limp, walked with a cane and seemed intent on overtaking the girls. I took her to be their duenna. But as she passed in front of the terrace I saw such an evil leer on her face that I hastily transferred my attention to a handsome young couple that came walking along.

The young man wore the cap of a Candidate of Literature, the girl was dressed demurely as a housewife. They walked apart but from the fond looks they gave each other it was clear that they belonged together. I concluded from their furtive air that theirs must be an illicit love affair.

2

Just when they were passing in front of me the girl made to take the young man's hand, but he hastily withdrew his and shook his head with a frown.

Letting my eyes rove over the guests assembled on the terrace I noticed a plump, neatly-clad man who was sitting alone just like myself. He had a round, pleasant face, I placed him as a member of the landed gentry. Since he seemed the talkative type I hastily averted my eyes fearing that he would mistake my intent gaze as an invitation to strike up an acquaintance. I preferred to be left alone with my own thoughts, all the more so since I had seen a glint in his eyes that made me wary. I reflected that a man with that cold, calculating look that so belied his friendly face might well be capable of committing a dark, premeditated deed of evil.

After a while I saw an old gentleman with a flowing white beard slowly come up the steps of the terrace. He was clad in a brown robe with wide sleeves seamed with black velvet, and a high cap of black gauze on his head. Although he wore no insignia of rank, he had a most distinguished appearance. He stood for a moment leaning on his crooked staff, surveying the crowded terrace with piercing eyes from under bushy white eyebrows.

Since a person of such venerable age cannot be left standing, I hastily rose and offered the newcomer a place at my table. He accepted with a courteous bow. While drinking our tea we exchanged the usual polite inquiries and it transpired that his family name was Dee and that he was a retired prefect.

Soon we were engaged in an agreeable conversation. My guest proved to be a man of wide learning and elegant taste, time passed unnoticed while we discoursed on prose and poetry, in between looking at the gay crowd that milled along the water front.

I had noticed that my guest spoke with the accent of Shansi Province. So during a lull in the conversation I asked whether by any chance his family was related to the old Dee clan of Tai-yuan, the capital of that province, which centuries ago, during the Tang dynasty, had produced the great statesman Dee Jen-djieh.

Suddenly the old gentleman's eyes blazed. He angrily tugged at his long beard.

"Ha!", he exclaimed, "my family is indeed a branch of the Dee clan from which issued the great Judge Dee, and very proud I am to count him among my ancestors. Yet at the same time this fact is a source of continuous vexation. Whenever I am eating my bowl of rice in a restaurant or sipping the fragrant brew in a tea house, as often as not I will hear the other guests tell each other stories about my illustrious ancestor. It is true that what they say about Dee Jen-djieh's brilliant career at the Imperial Court is usually substantially correct; moreover such facts can be verified by referring to the official annals of the Tang dynasty. Mostly, however, those ignorant persons will bandy about bizarre tales about the earlier part of Dee Jen-djieh's career when he was serving as district magistrate in the provinces, and as 'Judge Dee' became famous for having solved many a mysterious criminal case. In our family the truthful account of most of those cases has been faithfully transmitted during untold generations. It greatly annoys me to have to listen to all those spurious stories told in the tea house, and I usually leave without finishing my meal."

The old gentleman shook his head and angrily stamped his staff on the stone flags.

I was delighted to learn that my guest was indeed a descendant of the famous Judge Dee. I rose and bowed deeply in front of him to show my deference for his distinguished family. Then I spoke thus:

4

"Venerable Sir, know that I am a keen student of true accounts describing the feats of detection performed by the eminent judges of our glorious national past. Far from being an idle gossip, however, I delight in a careful analysis of those ancient records. For do they not serve as a mirror for us who live in this late age, warning us by showing our own foibles and defects? Those accounts not only improve the morals and ameliorate the customs, they also act as a powerful deterrrent for all wicked people. Nowhere can be found more eloquent proof of how closely the net of Heavenly justice is woven, and of how no evil-doer in the long run ever succeeds in slipping through its mazes.

Now in my opinion antiquity has no detective that can compare with Judge Dee. For many years I have been sedulously collecting notes about the cases solved by his brilliant mind. Now that a propitious fate has granted me this meeting with you, Sir, who are a fount of information on this subject, I wonder whether it would be presuming on your kindness if I humbly requested you to give me the benefit of hearing a few lesser known cases from your own lips."

The old gentleman readily agreed, and I invited him to join me in a simple supper.

Twilight was falling and the guests had left the terrace for the restaurant inside where the servants had lighted candles and coloured paper lanterns.

I avoided the main hall with the chattering dining crowd and led my guest to a small side room overlooking the lake, now bathed in the red glow of sunset.

I ordered two dinners of four courses and a pot of warm wine.

When we had tasted from the dishes and drunk a few rounds, the old gentleman stroked his long whiskers and said:

5

"I shall relate to you three astonishing criminal cases which my revered ancestor Judge Dee solved under most unusual circumstances. At that time he was serving as magistrate of Lan-fang, a far-away district on the Northwestern border of our Empire."

He then set out on a long and complicated narrative.

Although what he told was not without interest, he proved much given to lengthy digressions and his voice was as indistinct and monotonous as the humming of a bumble bee. After a while I found my attention flagging. I emptied three cups in succession to clear my mind but the amber liquid only made me still more drowsy. While the voice of my guest droned on and on I seemed to hear the spirit of sleep rustle in the close air.

When I woke up I found myself alone in the chilly room, bent over the table with my head resting on my folded arms.

A surly waiter was standing over me and told me that the first nightwatch had been sounded; did I perchance mistake this restaurant for a hostel where people stay overnight at will?

My head was heavy and I did not immediately find the right phrase to put that boorish yokel in his place. Instead I inquired after my guest, describing his appearance in some detail.

The waiter answered that earlier in the evening he had been serving another section of the restaurant, and anyway did I think that he had time to look up and down every single guest? Presently he produced a bill for two six course dinners and eight pots of wine. I could do nothing but pay, although by then I greatly doubted whether my encounter with the old gentleman had not been a dream, and whether that rascal of a waiter was not taking advantage of my confusion to overcharge me grossly.

I left feeling I had been ill-used and walked home through the deserted streets. My page was fast asleep huddled in a corner of my library. I did not wake him but tiptoed to the bookshelves. I took down the annals of the Tang dynasty, the Imperial Gazetteer and my own notes on Judge Dee. Poring over these volumes I found that although the general features of the old gentleman's story accorded well enough with historical fact, there existed no such place as Lan-fang on the Northwestern border. I thought that possibly I had misheard the name and resolved to visit the old gentleman next day to ask him for further elucidation. Then I found to my dismay that although I clearly remembered every word of the story he told me, try as I might I could not recollect one single personal detail concerning him; I had forgotten both his full name, and his present place of residence.

I shook my head, moistened my brush, and that very night committed to writing the entire story he told me, laying down my brush only when the cock started crowing.

The next day I made exhaustive enquiries among my friends but no one had ever heard about a retired prefect by the name of Dee living in our town; neither did subsequent investigations as to his whereabouts bring to light more information. Still this fact did not dissolve my doubts. The old gentleman might well have been only passing through, or he might be living somewhere in the countryside.

Thus I now make bold to offer this story as it is, leaving it to the better judgement of the discerning reader to decide whether my encounter on the lotus lake was dream or reality. If this tale of three mysterious crimes should distract the reader for a few moments from the cares and anxieties of daily life, I shall not grudge the coppers extorted from me. For no matter what actually happened, that waiter evidently was a mean rascal; it is quite inconceivable that one, or even two gentlemen of refined taste ever should consume eight pots of wine at one single sitting.

Four horse carts were slowly wending their way through the mountains east of the city of Lan-fang.

In the first cart Judge Dee, the new magistrate of Lan-fang, had made himself as comfortable as was possible on such an arduous journey. He was sitting on a bed roll, and leaned his back against a large package with books. His faithful assistant, the old Sergeant Hoong, was sitting opposite him on a bale of cloth. The road was rough and these precautions provided scant protection from the continual bumps.

The judge and the sergeant both felt tired, for they had been on the road for several days on end.

After them followed a large tilt cart with silk curtains. Here Judge Dee's three wives, his children and the maids were trying to snatch some sleep, curled up among pillows and padded quilts.

The two other carts were loaded with luggage. Some of the servants were sitting precariously perched on top of the bales and boxes, others preferred to walk by the side of the horses which were covered with sweat.

Before dawn they had left the last village. Thereafter the road had led through a desolate mountain region. The only people they had met were a few wood gatherers. In the afternoon their progress had been retarded for two hours by a broken wheel and now dusk was falling, making the mountains seem even more forbidding.

Two tall fellows rode at the head of the procession. Broad swords hung down their backs, each had a bow fastened to the pommel of his saddle, and arrows rattled in their quivers. These two were Ma Joong and Chiao Tai, two of Judge Dee's loyal lieutenants. They acted as the armed escort of the group. Another of Judge Dee's lieutenants, a lean man with a slight stoop, called Tao Gan, brought up the rear together with the old house steward.

Arrived on top of the mountain ridge Ma Joong reined in his horse. The road ahead descended into a wooded valley. Another steep mountain rose up on the opposite side.

Ma Joong turned round in his saddle, and called out to the coachman:

"An hour ago you said that we were approaching Lan-fang, you dogshead! And here is another mountain to cross!"

The coachman grumbled something about fellows from the city always being in a hurry, then said sullenly:

"Don't worry, from the next ridge you will see Lan-fang lying at the foot of the slope."

"I have heard that bastard speak about a 'next ridge' before", Ma Joong observed to Chiao Tai. "How awkward that we arrive in Lan-fang at so late an hour! The departing magistrate must have been waiting for us since noon. And what about the other dignitaries of the district administration and their welcome banquet? By now their bellies must be as empty as mine!"

"Not to speak of a dry throat!", Chiao Tai added. He turned round his horse and rode up to the judge's cart.

"There still is one valley to be crossed, Your Honour", he reported, "but then we shall at last reach Lan-fang."

Sergeant Hoong suppressed a sigh.

"It is a great pity", he remarked, "that Your Honour was ordered to leave Poo-yang so soon. Although two major criminal cases came up directly after our arrival there, all in all it was a pleasant district."

Judge Dee smiled wryly and tried to settle his back more comfortably against the book package.

"It would seem", he said, "that in the capital the remnants of the Buddhist clique joined forces with friends of the Cantonese merchants, and effected my transfer long before my term of office in Poo-yang had expired. Yet it will be most instructive to serve as magistrate in such an outlying district as Lan-fang. Doubtless we shall find there interesting special problems that one will never meet with in the larger cities of the interior."

The sergeant agreed that that was so, but he remained gloomy. He was over sixty years old, and the discomforts of the long journey had worn him out. Since his early childhood he had been a retainer of Judge Dee's family. When Judge Dee had entered official life, he had made him his confidential adviser, and at every post where the judge had served he had appointed him sergeant over the constables of the tribunal.

The coachmen cracked their whips. The cortège passed over the top of the ridge and descended into the valley along a narrow winding road.

Soon they found themselves down in the valley, where the road was darkened by high cedar trees that rose from the thick undergrowth on both sides.

Judge Dee was just thinking of ordering his servants to light the torches, when he heard confused shouting ahead and behind.

A number of men, their faces covered with scarves of black cloth, had suddenly emerged from the wood.

Two men took hold of Ma Joong's right leg and dragged him from his horse before he had time to draw his sword. A third had jumped from behind on Chiao Tai's horse, and had pulled him down to the ground by a strangle hold on his neck. At the end of the cortège two other robbers were attacking Tao Gan and the steward.

The coachmen jumped down and disappeared in the

JUDGE DEE ATTACKED BIJ TWO ROBBERS

wood. Judge Dee's servants ran away as fast as they could.

Two masked faces appeared before the window of Judge Dee's cart. Sergeant Hoong was knocked unconscious with a blow on his head. The judge could just dodge a spear that was thrust inside. He quickly gripped the shaft with both hands. The other pulled from outside to wrench it loose. The judge first held on tight, then suddenly pushed it in the direction of the pulling man. His assailant tumbled backwards. Judge Dee pulled the spear from his hands and jumped out of the window. He kept his two attackers at a distance by whirling the spear round and round. The robber who had hit Sergeant Hoong was armed with a club, the man with the spear had now drawn a long sword. Both attacked the judge fiercely, and he reflected that he would not be able to hold out long against these two determined opponents.

The two ruffians who had dragged Ma Joong from his horse were ready to cut him down with their swords while he was scrambling up. Unfortunately for them, however, they were up against a formidable fighter, who only a few years back had himself been a famous highwayman. Until Judge Dee had caused their reform, both Ma Joong and Chiao Tai had been 'brothers of the green woods'. Thus there were very few things about roadside fighting that Ma Joong did not know. Instead of trying to get up he twisted his body round, gripped the ankle of one attacker and jerked him off his balance. At the same time Ma Joong placed a vicious kick on the other man's knee. This double move gave him time to jump up. He felled the stumbling man with a terrible fist blow on his head. Turning round like lightning he gave the man who was clasping his crushed knee a kick in the face that made his head snap back and nearly broke his neck.

Drawing his sword Ma Joong rushed over to Chiao Tai

who lay on the ground wrestling desperately with a man clinging to his back. Two others stood ready with long knives to stab Chiao Tai as soon as they got the chance. Ma Joong ran his sword right through the chest of one robber. Without taking the time to withdraw his sword he went on to the second and gave him a kick in his groin that doubled him up on the ground. Picking up the robber's long knive Ma Joong thrust it under the left shoulder of the man fighting with Chiao Tai.

Just when he was helping Chiao Tai up, Ma Joong heard Judge Dee call out: "Look out!"

Ma Joong swiftly turned round, and thus the club of Judge Dee's assailant who had ran up to help his comrades, missed Ma Joong's head. It landed with a thud on his left shoulder. He sank down with a curse. The robber lifted his club to brain Chiao Tai. The latter had drawn his knife, he dived under the robber's raised arm and plunged his knife to the hilt in the other's heart.

Judge Dee, now only faced with the swordsman, made quick work of him. He made a feint with his spear at his attacker who raised his sword to parry the blow. Then Judge Dee suddenly practised the fencer's trick known as 'the tumbling flag pole'; he turned the spear round in the air and brained his opponent with a blow of the shaft.

Leaving it to Chiao Tai to truss up the robbers, Judge Dee ran on to the luggage carts. One robber was sprawling on the ground, clutching frantically at his neck. The other, with a knobstick in his hand, was looking under the cart. The judge laid him out by hitting him over the head with the flat of his spear point.

Tao Gan came crawling out from under the cart, with a thin rope in his hand.

"What is happening here?", the judge inquired.

Tao Gan answered with a grin:

"One of these yokels knocked down the steward, the other hit a glancing blow on my head. I let myself fall down with a horrible gasp, and did not move. They thought that I was laid out and started to tear down the luggage. I rose and from behind slipped my thin noose over the head of the nearest ruffian. Then I dived under the cart, pulling the cord as tight as I could. The other robber could not follow me there without exposing himself, and his club was of no use. He was just debating with himself what to do, when Your Honour solved his dilemma for him."

Judge Dee smiled, then hurried back to where he heard Ma Joong cursing roundly. Tao Gan took a length of catgut from his sleeve and securely bound the hands and feet of the two robbers. Then he loosened the noose round the neck of the man who by now was nearly suffocating.

These two robbers had been deceived by Tao Gan's inoffensive appearance. Tao Gan was of middle age, not much of a fighter, but an extremely wily person, who for many years had earned his living as a professional swindler. Once, Judge Dee had extricated him from an ugly situation, and made him one of his lieutenants. Owing to his intimate knowledge of the ways and by-ways of the underworld he had proved very useful for tracking down criminals and collecting evidence. And, as the robber with the blue face had good reason to know, Tao Gan was full of unexpected tricks.

When he came to the head of the cortège, Judge Dee found Chiao Tai in a hand-to-hand fight with one of Ma Joong's first attackers who had recovered from the blow on his head. Ma Joong himself was crouching on the ground, his left arm lamed by the blow on his shoulder. With his right he tried to fight off the attacks of a little robber, who danced round him with amazing agility, brandishing a short dagger.

The judge raised his spear. Just then Ma Joong succeeded in catching his opponent's wrist. He twisted his arm in an iron grip till the robber let the dagger drop. Then Ma Joong forced him down and put his knee on his stomach.

The robber let out a pitiful cry.

Ma Joong rose to his feet with difficulty, while his captive hammered his head and shoulders with fistblows from his free hand. These, however, did not seem to bother Ma Joong. He said panting to the judge:

"Would you remove the mask, Your Honour?"

Judge Dee pulled down the scarf. Ma Joong exclaimed: "May Heaven preserve us! It's a wench!"

They looked into the blazing eyes of a young girl. Ma Joong let go her arm in sheer astonishment.

Judge Dee hastily pinned her arms behind her back and said sourly:

"Well, on occasion one will find an abandoned woman among these robber bands. Tie her up as the others!"

Ma Joong called out to Chiao Tai who by now had subdued and trussed up his opponent. Ma Joong remained standing there scratching his head in perplexity while Chiao Tai bound the girl's hands behind her back. She did not say a word.

Judge Dee went to the tilt cart with the women. His First Lady was crouching in the window with a dagger in her hand. The others were cowering under the quilts in a dead fright.

The judge told them that the fight was over.

Judge Dee's servants and the coachmen had emerged from their hiding places. They hastily set to work to light torches.

In the flickering light Judge Dee surveyed the results of the battle.

On their own side there was little damage. Sergeant Hoong had regained consciousness, and had his head bandaged by Tao Gan. The old steward had suffered more from fright than from the robber's blow. Ma Joong was sitting on a tree trunk stripped to the waist. His left shoulder was purple and swollen, and Chiao Tai was massaging it with medicinal oil.

Ma Joong had killed two robbers, Chiao Tai one. The six others were all more or less the worse for wear, only the girl was entirely unhurt.

The judge ordered his servants to tie the robbers on top of one luggage cart, and the dead bodies on the other. The girl would have to walk.

Tao Gan produced a padded basket, and the judge and his lieutenants drunk a cup of hot tea.

Ma Joong rinsed his mouth, spat contemptuously and said to Chiao Tai:

"All in all, it was an amateurish attack. I don't think that these fellows are professional highwaymen."

"Yes", Chiao Tai agreed, "with ten men they could have done a better job."

"They did well enough for my taste", Judge Dee remarked dryly.

They silently drank another cup of tea. All were exhausted and no one felt inclined to say much. One only heard the whispering voices of the servants, and the groans of the wounded robbers.

After a brief rest the cortège set into motion again. Two servants with lighted torches led the way.

It took them well over an hour to cross the last mountain ridge. Then the road came out on a broad highway, and soon they saw the battlements of the northern city gate of Lan-fang silhouetted against the evening sky.

JUDGE DEE OPENS THE FIRST SESSION OF THE TRIBUNAL;
HE DISCOVERS IN THE ARCHIVES AN UNSOLVED PROBLEM

CHIAO TAI looked amazed at the formidable gate surmounted by a high gate tower. Then he remembered that Lanfang was a border town where one had to reckon with sudden attacks from the barbarian hordes of the western plains.

He knocked with the hilt of his sword on the iron-studded gate.

After considerable time the shutters of a small window in the gate tower opened. A gruff voice called out from above:

"The gate is closed for the night. Come back tomorrow morning!"

Chiao Tai gave a thunderous knock on the gate. He shouted:

"Open up, the magistrate has arrived!"

"What magistrate?", the voice asked.

"His Excellency Dee, the new magistrate of Lan-fang. Open the gate, you fathead!"

The shutters slammed shut.

Ma Joong rode up to Chiao Tai. He asked:

"What is all this delay?"

"The lazy dogs were asleep!", Chiao Tai said disgustedly. As he spoke he let his sword again rattle on the door.

They heard the clanking of chains. At last the heavy doors opened a few feet.

Chiao Tai forced his horse through, and nearly trampled down two slovenly clad soldiers wearing rusty helmets.

"Throw the gates wide open, lazy dogs!", Chiao Tai barked.

The soldiers looked impudently at the two horsemen. One opened his mouth to say something, but seeing the fierce look on Chiao Tai's face he thought better of it. Together with his colleague he pushed open the gate.

The cortège passed through and moved south along the dark main street.

The town presented a desolate appearance. Although the first nightwatch had not yet sounded most of the shops were closed for the night with solid wooden shutters.

Here and there small groups of people clustered round the oil lamps of the street vendors. When the cortège passed by they turned round and looked for a moment indifferently at the horse wagons, then turned again to their noodle bowls.

No one came to meet the new magistrate and there were no signs of welcome.

The cortège passed under a high ornamental archway that spanned the street. Here the main street divided to left and right, running along a high wall. Ma Joong and Chiao Tai took this to be the rear wall of the tribunal compound.

They turned east and followed the wall till they came to a large gate. Over its archway there hung a weather-beaten wooden board with an engraved inscription reading:

"The Tribunal of Lan-fang"

Chiao Tai jumped from his horse and started to knock on the door with all his might.

A squat man clad in a patched robe opened the door. His ragged beard was dirty with grease and he had a horrible squint. Lifting up a paper lantern he surveyed Chiao Tai. Then he snarled:

"Don't you know that the tribunal is closed, soldier?"

This was too much for Chiao Tai. He gripped the man by his beard and violently shook his head; it bumped against the doorpost with dull thuds. Chiao Tai only released him when the man started crying for mercy.

Chiao Tai said peremptorily:

"His Excellency Magistrate Dee has arrived. Open the door and call the personnel of the tribunal!"

The man hurriedly pushed the double doors open. The cortège passed through and came to a halt in the main courtyard, in front of the large reception hall.

Judge Dee descended from his cart and looked around. The high, sixfold doors of the reception hall were barred and locked, the windows of the chancery opposite shuttered. Everything was dark and deserted.

Folding his hands in his sleeves Judge Dee ordered Chiao Tai to bring the gate keeper before him.

Chiao Tai dragged him along by his collar. The squat man hastily knelt.

Judge Dee asked curtly:

"Who are you, and where is the outgoing magistrate, His Excellency Kwang?"

"This insignificant person", the man stammered, "is the warden of the jail. His Excellency Kwang left early this morning by the southern city gate."

"Where are the seals of office?"

"They must be somewhere in the chancery", the warden answered in a quavering voice.

Judge Dee's patience gave out. He stamped his foot on the ground and shouted:

"Where are the guards, where are the constables? Where are the scribes, where are the clerks, where is everybody in this accursed tribunal?"

"The headman of the constables left last month. The

senior scribe has been on sick leave for the last three weeks, and . . ."

"So there is nobody but you", the judge interrupted him. Turning to Chiao Tai he continued: "Throw this warden in his own jail. I shall find out for myself what is wrong here!"

The warden started to protest but Chiao Tai boxed his ears and bound his hands behind his back. He turned the warden round, gave him a kick and barked:

"Lead us to your jail!"

In the left wing of the compound, behind the empty quarters of the guards, they found quite a capacious jail. Evidently the cells had not been used for a long time; but the doors looked solid enough and the windows had iron grates.

Chiao Tai pushed the warden into a small cell and locked the door.

Judge Dee said:

"Let us now have a look at the court hall and the chancery!"

Chiao Tai took up his paper lantern. They found the double gate of the court hall without difficulty. As Chiao Tai gave the door a push it swung open with a creaking of rusty hinges. He lifted his lantern.

They saw a large, empty hall. A thick layer of dust and dirt covered the stoneflags and cobwebs hung from the walls. Judge Dee walked up to the dais and looked at the faded and torn red cloth that covered the bench. A large rat scurried away.

The judge beckoned Chiao Tai. Then he stepped up onto the dais, walked round the bench and pulled aside the screen that covered the door opening leading to the magistrate's private office, behind the court hall. A cloud of dust descended on the judge.

The office was empty but for a bare, ramshackle desk, an armchair with a broken back, and three wooden footstools.

Chiao Tai opened the door in the wall opposite. A dank smell assailed them. The walls were covered with shelves supporting rows of leather document boxes, green with mould.

Judge Dee shook his head.

"What fine archives!" he murmured.

He kicked open the door to the corridor and silently walked back to the main courtyard, Chiao Tai with his lantern leading the way.

Ma Joong and Tao Gan had locked their prisoners in the jail. The three dead robbers had been deposited in the quarters of the guards. Judge Dee's servants were busy unloading the luggage under supervision of the house steward. The latter informed the judge that the magistrate's living quarters in the back of the compound were in excellent condition. The departing magistrate had left everything there in good order; the rooms had been swept, the furniture was clean and in a good state of repair. Judge Dee's cook was lighting the kitchen fire.

Judge Dee heaved a sigh of relief; at least his family had shelter.

He ordered Sergeant Hoong and Ma Joong to retire. They could spread their bed rolls in a side room of his own quarters. Then the judge beckoned Chiao Tai and Tao Gan to follow him, and went back to his deserted private office.

Tao Gan placed two lighted candles on the desk.

Judge Dee lowered himself gingerly into the rickety armchair. His two lieutenants blew the dust off the footstools and sat down.

The judge folded his arms on the desk. For a while no one spoke.

They presented a queer spectacle together. All three were still clad in their brown travelling robes, torn and muddy from the fight with the robbers. Their faces were drawn and haggard in the uncertain light of the candles.

Then the judge spoke:

"Well, my friends, the hour is late and we are tired and hungry. Yet I would like to have a consultation with you about this queer state of affairs we have found here."

Tao Gan and Chiao Tai nodded eagerly.

"This town", Judge Dee continued, "baffles me completely. Although my predecessor was in residence here for three years and kept his living quarters in excellent condition, he apparently never used the court hall, and sent home the entire personnel of the tribunal. Although a courier must have duly informed him of my arrival scheduled for this afternoon, he went away without even leaving a message for me, entrusting the seals of office to that scoundrel of a warden. The other officials of the district administration simply ignored our arrival. How do you explain all this?"

"Could it be, Your Honour", Chiao Tai asked, "that the people here are planning to rebel against the central government?"

Judge Dee shook his head.

"It is true", he replied, "that the streets are deserted and the shops closed at an unusually early hour. But I did not notice any sign of unrest and there were no barricades or other military preparations. The attitude of the people in the street was not antagonistic, they were just indifferent."

Tao Gan pensively pulled at the three long hairs that sprouted from a mole on his left cheek.

"For a moment", he remarked, "I thought that maybe the pest or some other dangerous epidemic disease had ravaged this district. That, however, does not tally with the fact that there were no signs of panic, and the people were partaking freely from the food of the street stalls."

Judge Dee combed with his fingers some dry leaves from his long side whiskers. After a while he said:

"I would rather not ask that warden for elucidation. The fellow has all the marks of a consummate rascal!"

The steward entered followed by two of Judge Dee's servants. One carried a platter with bowls of rice and soup and the other a large tea pot.

The judge ordered the steward to have bowls of rice brought to the jail for the prisoners.

They ate in silence.

When they had finished the scratch meal and drunk a cup of hot tea, Chiao Tai sat for a while in deep thought, twisting his small moustache. Then the spoke:

"I fully agree with Ma Joong, Your Honour, when out there in the mountains he said that the robbers who attacked us were no professional highwaymen. How about questioning our prisoners about what is going on here?"

"An excellent idea!", the judge exclaimed. "Find out who their leader is and bring him here!"

After a while Chiao Tai came back, leading by a chain none other than the robber who had tried to stab Judge Dee with his spear. The judge gave him a sharp look. He saw a strongly built man with a regular, open face; he seemed more like a small shopkeeper or a tradesman than a highway robber.

As he knelt in front of the desk Judge Dee ordered curtly:

"State your name and profession!"

"This person", the man said respectfully," is called Fang. Until recently I was a blacksmith in this city of Lan-fang, where my family has been living for several generations."

"Why", Judge Dee inquired, "did you, engaged in

an old and honourable trade, prefer the despicable life of a street robber?"

Fang lowered his head and said in a dull voice:

"I am guilty of assault with murderous intent. I fully realize that the death penalty awaits me. I confess my guilt which needs no further proof. Why should Your Honour bother to make further inquiries?"

Deep despair rang from his words. Judge Dee said quietly:

"I never sentence a criminal until I have heard his full story. Speak up and answer my question!"

This person", Fang began, "has been a blacksmith for over thirty years, having learned the trade from his father. I and my wife, one son and two daughters were strong and healthy, we had our daily bowl of rice, and now and then even a slice of pork. I considered myself a happy man.

Then, one unfortunate day, Chien's men saw that my son was a sturdy young fellow, and they pressed him into their service."

"Who is this Chien?", the Judge interrupted him.

"What", Fang replied bitterly, "is Chien not? Since more than eight years he has usurped all power in this district. He owns half the land and nearly one-fourth of the shops and houses in this town. He is magistrate, judge, and military commander, all in one. He regularly sends bribes to the officials of the prefecture, five days on horseback from here. He has convinced them that if it were not for him, the barbarian hordes from over the border would long have overrun this district."

"Did my predecessors acquiesce in this irregular state of affairs?", Judge Dee inquired.

Fang shrugged his shoulders. He answered:

"The magistrates appointed here soon found out that it was easier and much safer to be satisfied with a shadow existence, leaving all real power in the hands of Chien. As long as they acted as his puppets Chien gave them rich presents every month. They lived in peace and comfort while we of the people suffered."

"Your story", Judge Dee said coldly, "sounds absurd to me. Unfortunately it is true that occasionally a local tyrant usurps power in an outlying district. And sadder still, sometimes a weak magistrate will accept such an unlawful situation. But you cannot make me believe, my man, that for eight years every magistrate who was appointed here submitted to the man Chien."

Fang said with a sneer:

"Then we of Lan-fang were just unlucky! There was but one magistrate who, four years ago, turned against Chien. After two weeks his body was found on the river bank, his throat cut from ear to ear."

Judge Dee suddenly leaned forward. He asked:

"Was that magistrate's name by any chance Pan?"

Fang nodded.

"Magistrate Pan", Judge Dee continued, "was reported to the central authorities as having fallen in a skirmish with invading Uigur hordes. I was in the capital at that time. I remember that his body was forwarded there with military honours and that he was posthumously promoted to the rank of prefect."

"That was how Chien covered up his murder", Fang said indifferently. "I know the truth, I myself saw the body."

"Proceed with your story!", Judge Dee said.

"Thus", Fang went on, "my only son was forced to join the band of ruffians that Chien keeps as his private guards, and I never saw him again.

Then a wretched old crone who acts as procuress for Chien came to see me. She said that Chien offered ten silver pieces for White Orchid, my eldest daughter. I refused.

Three days later my daughter went to the market, and never came back. Time and again I went to Chien's mansion and begged to be allowed to see her, but everytime I was cruelly beaten and chased away.

Having lost her only son and her eldest daughter my wife began ailing. She died two weeks ago. I took my father's sword and went to Chien's mansion. I was intercepted by the guards. They fell over me with their clubs, and left me for dead in the street. One week ago a band of ruffians set fire to my shop. I left the city with Dark Orchid, my youngest daughter who was also caught tonight, and joined a band of other desperate men out in the mountains. Tonight we made our first attempt at holding up travellers."

Deep silence reigned. The judge was going to lean back in his armchair but remembered in time that the back was broken. He hastily placed his elbows on the desk again. Then he spoke:

"Your story has a very familiar ring. It usually is some such tale of woe that robbers dish out in the tribunal when they have been caught in the act. If you lied, your head will fall on the execution ground. If it turns out that you have spoken the truth I shall reserve my verdict."

"For me", the blacksmith said dejectedly, "there is no hope left. If Your Honour does not have my head chopped off, Chien will certainly kill me. The same goes for my comrades, who are all victims of Chien's cruel oppression."

Judge Dee gave a sign to Chiao Tai. He rose and led Fang back to the jail.

The judge left his armchair and began to pace the floor. When Chiao Tai had come back, Judge Dee stood still and said pensivily:

"That man Fang evidently told the truth. This district is in the power of a local tyrant, magistrates are nothing

26

but powerless figureheads here. That explains the queer attitude of the local population."

Chiao Tai hit his large first on his knee.

"Must we", he exclaimed angrily, "bow to that scoundrel Chien?"

The judge smiled his thin smile.

"The hour is late, he said, "you two had better retire and have a good night's rest. Tomorrow I shall have much work for you. I shall stay here for an hour or so and have a glance at those old archives."

Tao Gan and Chiao Tai offered to stay up for assisting the judge but he firmly refused.

As soon as they had left Judge Dee took up a candle and entered the next room. With the sleeve of his dirty travelling robe he rubbed the mould from the labels of the document boxes. He found that the most recent file was dated eight years before.

The judge carried this box into his office and spread out the contents on his desk.

It took his experienced eye but little time to verify that it were mostly documents relating to the routine of the district administration. On the bottom of the box, however, he found a small roll, marked "The Case Yoo versus Yoo". Judge Dee sat down. He unrolled the document and glanced through it.

He saw that it was a law suit concerning the inheritance of Yoo Shou-chien, a provincial governor who, nine years before, had died whilst living in retirement in Lan-fang.

Judge Dee closed his eyes and cast his thoughts back fifteen years, when he was serving in the capital as a junior secretary. At that time the name Yoo Shou-chien had been famous all over the Empire. He had been an exceptionally able and scrupulously honest official; devoted to the state and the people, he had earned fame both as a benevolent administrator and a wise statesman. Then, when the Throne appointed him Grand Secretary of State, Yoo Shou-chien had suddenly resigned from all his offices; pleading poor health he had buried himself in some obscure border district. The Emperor himself had urged him to reconsider his decision but Yoo Shou-chien had steadfastly refused. Judge Dee remembered that at that time this sudden resignation had created quite a sensation in the capital.

So Lan-fang had been the place where Yoo Shou-chien lived his last years.

Slowly Judge Dee unrolled the document once more, and read it carefully from beginning to end.

He found that when Yoo Shou-chien settled down to a life of retirement in Lan-fang, he was a widower of over sixty. He had an only son called Yoo Kee, then thirty years old. Shortly after his arrival in Lan-fang the old governor had remarried. He chose as his bride a young peasant girl of barely eighteen, of the surname Mei. Out of this unequal marriage there was born a second son, called Yoo Shan.

When the old governor fell ill and felt that his end was drawing near, he called his son Yoo Kee and his young wife with her infant son to his deathbed. He told them that he bequeathed a scroll picture he had painted himself to his wife and his second son Yoo Shan; all the rest of his possessions was to go to Yoo Kee. He added that he trusted that Yoo Kee would see to it that his stepmother and his half-brother would receive what was due to them. Having made this statement the old governor breathed his last.

Judge Dee looked at the date of the document and reflected that now Yoo Kee must be about forty, the widow nearly thirty, and her son twelve years old.

The document stated that as soon as his father had been

buried, Yoo Kee expelled his stepmother and Yoo Shan from his house. He had said that the last words of his father evidently implied that Yoo Shan was an illegitimate child and that he was not bound to do anything either for him or for his adulterous mother.

Thereupon the widow had filed a complaint with the tribunal contesting the oral will, and claiming half of the property for her son, on the basis of common law.

At that time Chien had just established himself as the ruler of Lan-fang. It seemed that the tribunal had done nothing to settle this suit.

Judge Dee rolled up the document. He reflected that at first sight the widow did not have a strong case. The last words of the old governor together with the disparity in age of him and his second wife seemed to suggest that Mrs. Mei had indeed been unfaithful to her husband.

On the other hand it was curious that a man of such high ethical standards as the great Yoo Shou-chien had chosen this peculiar way of proclaiming that Yoo Shan was not his son. If he had really discovered that his young wife deceived him one would expect that he would have quietly divorced her, and sent her and her son away to live in some distant place, thus protecting the honour of himself and of his distinguished family. And why this queer bequest of the picture?

It seemed strange also that Yoo Shou-chien had not left a written testament. A man of his long official experience ought to have known that oral testaments nearly always engender bitter family quarrels.

This case had several angles that deserved a careful investigation. Perhaps it might also bring to light the key to the mystery of Yoo Shou-chien's sudden resignation.

Judge Dee rummaged through the documents but he could find nothing else that had a bearing on the case

Yoo versus Yoo. Neither did he find any material that might be used against Chien.

The judge replaced the documents in the box. He remained sitting in deep thought for a long time. He pondered ways and means to oust the tyrant Chien, but time and again his thoughts reverted to the old governor and his curious bequest.

One candle spluttered and went out. With a sigh Judge Dee took up the other one and walked to his own quarters.

Third Chapter

THE JUDGE WITNESSES A QUARREL ON THE MARKET; A YOUNG MAN FORECASTS HIS FATHER'S MURDER

THE next morning Judge Dee found to his dismay that he was late. He had a hurried breakfast and then went immediately to his private office.

He saw that the room had been thoroughly cleaned. His armchair had been repaired and the desk polished. On its top all Judge Dee's favourite writing implements had been laid out with a care in which the judge recognized the hand of Sergeant Hoong.

The judge found the sergeant in the archives room. Together with Tao Gan he had swept and aired the dank place; now it smelled pleasantly of the wax they had used for polishing the red leather document boxes.

Judge Dee nodded contentedly. As he sat down behind his desk he ordered Tao Gan to fetch Ma Joong and Chiao Tai.

When all his four lieutenants were assembled before him the judge first inquired how Sergeant Hoong and Ma Joong were doing. Both said that they were none the worse for the fight of the night before. The sergeant had replaced the bandage on his head by a plaster of oil paper and Ma Joong could move his left arm again although it was still somewhat stiff.

Ma Joong reported that early that morning he and Chiao Tai had inspected the armoury of the tribunal. They had found a good collection of pikes, halberds, swords, helmets and leather jackets, but everything was old and dirty and needed a thorough polishing.

Judge Dee said slowly:

"Fang's story offers a plausible explanation for the strange situation here. If all he said is true we must act quickly before Chien has found out that I am going to turn against him and steals the first move. We must attack before he knows what is happening. As our old proverb says: 'A dangerous dog bites without first baring its teeth'!"

"What shall we do with that warden?", Sergeant Hoong inquired.

"For the time being we shall leave him where he is", the judge replied. "It was a lucky inspiration that made me lock up that rascal. Evidently he is one of Chien's men. He would have run immediately to his master to tell him all about us."

Ma Joong opened his mouth to ask something but Judge Dee raised his hand. He continued:

"Tao Gan, you will now go out and collect all information you can get about Chien and his men. At the same time you will make inquiries about a wealthy citizen called Yoo Kee. He is the son of the famous Governor Yoo Shou-chien who about eight years ago died here in Lan-fang.

I myself shall now go out with Ma Joong to obtain a general impression of this town. Sergeant Hoong shall supervise affairs here in the tribunal together with Chiao Tai. The gates shall remain locked and no one is to leave or enter during my absence except for my house steward. He will go out alone to buy food.

Let us meet here again at noon!"

The judge rose and put on a small black cap. In his simple blue robe he looked like a scholarly gentleman of leisure.

He left the tribunal with Ma Joong walking by his side.

First they strolled south and had a look at the famous pagoda of Lan-fang. It stood on a small island in the middle of a lotus lake. The willow trees along its banks were waving in the morning breeze. Then they walked north and mingled with the crowd.

There was the usual coming and going of an early morning and the shops along the main street did a fair amount of business. But one heard little laughter and people often talked in a low voice, quickly looking right and left before they spoke.

When they had reached the double arch north of the tribunal Judge Dee and Ma Joong turned left and strolled to the market place in front of the Drum Tower. This market presented an interesting scene. Vendors from over the border clad in quaint gaudy costumes praised their wares in raucous voices, and here and there an Indian monk lifted up his almsbowl.

A group of idlers had gathered round a fish dealer who was having a violent quarrel with a neatly dressed young man. The latter apparently was being overcharged. Finally he threw a handful of coppers into the fishmonger's basket, shouting angrily:

"If this were a decently administered town you would not dare thus to deceive people in broad daylight!"

Suddenly a broad-shouldered man stepped forward. He jerked the young man round and hit him in his mouth.

"That will teach you to slander the Honourable Chien!", he growled.

Ma Joong was going to intervene but the judge laid a restraining hand on his arm.

The spectators hurriedly dispersed. The young man did not say a word. He wiped the blood from his mouth and went his way.

Judge Dee gave Ma Joong a sign. Together they followed the young man.

When he had entered a quiet side alley, the judge overtook him. He said:

"Excuse my intrusion. I happened to see that ruffian maltreat you. Why don't you report him to the tribunal?"

The young man stood still. He gave Judge Dee and his stalwart companion a suspicious look.

"If you are agents of Chien," he said coldly, "you can wait long before I incriminate myself!"

Judge Dee looked up and down the alley. They were alone.

"You are greatly mistaken, young man", he said quietly, "I am Dee Jen-djieh, the new magistrate of this district."

The young man's face turned ashen, he looked as if he had seen a ghost. Then he passed his hand over his forehead and mastered his emotion. He heaved a deep sigh and his face lit up in a broad smile. He bowed deeply saying respectfully:

"This person is the Junior Candidate Ding, the son of General Ding Hoo-gwo, from the capital. Your Honour's name is quite familiar to me. At long last this district has got a real magistrate!"

The judge inclined his head slightly to acknowledge the compliment.

He vaguely remembered that many years ago something untoward had happened to General Ding. He had fought a victorious battle against the barbarians across the northern border. But when he had returned to the capital the general had been unexpectedly compelled to resign. Judge Dee wondered how the general's son came to be in this distant place. He said to the young man:

"There is something very wrong in this town. I would like you to tell me more about the situation here."

Candidate Ding did not answer immediately. He remained in thought for a few moments. Then he spoke:

"These things had better not be discussed in public. Might I have the honour of offering the gentlemen a cup of tea?"

Judge Dee assented. They went to the tea house on the corner of the alley and sat down at a table somewhat apart from the other guests.

When the waiter had brought the tea young Ding said in a whisper:

"A ruthless man called Chien Mow has all the power in his hands. There is nobody here who dares to oppose him. Chien keeps about one hundred ruffians in his mansion. They have nothing to do but loaf about this town and intimidate the people."

"How are they armed?", Ma Joong asked.

"Out in the street these rascals have only clubs and swords with them, but I would not be astonished if in Chien's mansion they kept quite an arsenal."

Judge Dee asked:

"Do you often see barbarians from over the border in this town?"

Candidate Ding shook his head emphatically.

"I have never seen a single Uigur here", he replied.

"Those attacks Chien reported about to the government", Judge Dee observed to Ma Joong, "are evidently but an invention of his, to convince the authorities that he and his men are indispensable here."

Ma Joong asked:

"Have you ever been inside Chien's mansion?"

"Heaven forbid!", the young man exclaimed, "I always avoid that entire neighbourhood. Chien has surrounded his mansion with a double wall, with watchtowers on the four corners."

"How did he seize power here?", Judge Dee inquired.

"He inherited great wealth from his father", young Ding

replied, "but none of his eminent qualities. His father was a native of this town, an honest and diligent man who became rich as a tea merchant. Until a few years ago the main route to Khotan and the other tributary kingdoms of the west ran through Lan-fang and this town was quite an important emporium. Then three oases along the desert route dried up and it shifted a hundred miles to the north. Chien then collected a band of ruffians around him and one day proclaimed himself master of this city.

He is a clever and determined man who could easily have been successful in an official military career. But he will obey no one, he prefers to govern this district as the undisputed ruler, responsible to no one in the Empire."

"A most unfortunate situation", Judge Dee commented. He emptied his tea cup and rose to go.

Candidate Ding hurriedly leaned forward and begged the judge to stay a little longer.

The judge hesitated but the young man looked so unhappy that at last he sat down again. Candidate Ding busied himself with refilling the tea cups. He seemed at a loss how to begin.

"If there is anything on your mind, young man", Judge Dee said, "don't hesitate to speak!"

"To tell Your Honour the truth", young Ding finally said, "there is a matter that weighs heavily on my mind. It has nothing to do with the tyrant Chien. It concerns my own family."

Here he paused. Ma Joong shifted impatiently on his chair.

Candidate Ding made an effort and continued:

"Your Honour, my old father is going to be murdered!"

Judge Dee raised his eyebrows.

"If you know that in advance", he observed, "it should not be difficult to prevent this crime!"

The young man shook his head.

"Allow me to tell the whole story. Your Honour may have heard that my poor old father was slandered by one of his subordinates, the wicked Commander Woo. He was jealous of my father's great victory in the north and although he could never prove his false accusation the Board of Military Affairs ordered my father to resign."

"Yes, I remember that affair", Judge Dee said. "Is your father also living here?"

"My father", young Ding replied, "came to this distant place partly because my late mother was a native of Lan-fang, and partly because he wished to avoid the larger cities where he might be embarrassed by meeting former colleagues. We thought that here we would be able to live in peace.

One month ago, however, I began to notice that suspicious looking men often loitered in our neighbourhood. Last week I secretly followed one of them. He went to a small wine shop in the northwest corner of the city, called 'Eternal Spring'. Who can describe my astonishment when I learned from another shop in that street that Woo Feng, the eldest son of Commander Woo, is living over that wine shop!"

Judge Dee looked doubtful.

"Why", he asked, "should Commander Woo send his son here to annoy your father? The commander has ruined your father's career. Any further mischief would only land him into trouble."

"I know what his plans are!", Candidate Ding exclaimed excitedly. "Woo knows that my father's friends in the capital have discovered evidence that the commander's accusation is pure slander. He sent his son here to kill my father and thus save his own wretched life! Your Honour does not know that man Woo Feng. He is a confirmed drunkard, a most dissolute person who likes nothing better than indulging in acts of violence. He has hired ruffians to spy on us and he will strike as soon as he sees his chance."

"Even so", Judge Dee remarked, "I don't see how I could intervene. I can only advise you to keep an eye on Woo's movements and at the same time to take a few simple precautions in your own mansion. Is there any indication that Woo is in contact with Chien Mow?"

"No", the young man answered, "Woo apparently has made no attempt at enlisting the support of Chien. As regards precautions, my poor father has been receiving threatening letters ever since he resigned from the service. He rarely goes out and the gates of our mansion are locked and barred day and night. Moreover my father has had walled up all doors and windows of his library save one. That door has only one key which my father keeps always with him. When he is inside, he pushes a bar across the door. It is in that library that my father spends most of his time, compiling a history of the border wars."

Judge Dee told Ma Joong to note down the address of the Ding mansion. It was located not far from there, beyond the Drum Tower.

As he rose to go the judge said:

"Don't fail to report to the tribunal if there are any new developments. I have to go now, you will realize that my own position in this town is not too comfortable. As soon as I have settled with Chien I shall make a further study of your problem."

Candidate Ding thanked the judge and conducted his guests to the door of the tea shop. There he took his leave with a deep bow.

Judge Dee and Ma Joong walked back to the main street.

"That young fellow", Ma Joong observed, "reminds me f the man who insisted on wearing an iron helmet day and night because he was in constant fear that the vault of Heaven would crash down on his head!"

The judge shook his head.

"It is a very queer affair", he said pensively. "I don't like it at all."

Fourth Chapter

TAO GAN REPORTS ON A MYSTERIOUS OLD MANSION;
AN INGENIOUS TRAP IS SET IN THE DARK TRIBUNAL

MA JOONG looked astonished but Judge Dee vouchsafed no further comment. Silently they strolled back to the tribunal. Chiao Tai opened the gate for them and informed the judge that Tao Gan was waiting for him in his private office.

Judge Dee had Sergeant Hoong called in. As his four lieutenants seated themselves in front of his desk the judge gave a brief account of his encounter with Candidate Ding. Then he ordered Tao Gan to report.

Tao Gan's face was even longer than usual as he began:

"Matters don't look too good for us, Your Honour. That man Chien has established himself in a powerful position. He has drained the district of its wealth but he has been careful to leave alone members of influential families who came here from the capital, in order to prevent them from sending unfavourable reports about him to the central authorities. This applies to General Ding whose son Your Honour just met, and to Yoo Kee, the son of Governor Yoo Shou-chien.

Chien Mow has been clever enough not to turn on the screws too tightly. He takes a generous percentage of all business conducted in this district, but leaves the merchants a reasonable margin of profit. After a fashion he also maintains the public peace; if a man is caught stealing or brawling he is beaten half to death on the spot by Chien's henchmen. It is true that these men eat and drink in restaurants and inns without paying a copper. On the other hand Chien spends freely and many of the large shops have a good customer in him and his men. It are the small shopkeepers and tradesmen that suffer most from his tyranny. On the whole, however, the people of Lan-fang are resigned to their fate and reason that it could easily be worse."

Are Chien's men loyal to him?", the judge interrupted.

"Why should they not be?", Tao Gan asked. "Those ruffians, about one hundred in all, spend their time drinking and gambling. Chien recruited them from the scum of the city and picked up quite a number of deserters from the regular army. Chien's mansion, by the way, looks like a fortress. It stands near the western city gate. The high outer wall has iron spikes all along its top and the main entrance is guarded day and night by four men who are armed to the teeth."

Judge Dee remained silent for some time, slowly caressing his side whiskers. Then he asked:

"Now what did you learn about Yoo Kee?"

"Yoo Kee", Tao Gan replied, "lives near the Watergate. He seems to be a man of retiring habits who lives very quietly. But people tell many stories about his father, the late Governor Yoo Shou-chien. He was an eccentric old man who spent most of his time on his large country estate at the foot of the mountain slope, outside the eastern city gate. That country mansion is an old, dark house surrounded by a dense forest. People say that it was built more than two centuries ago. At the back the governor constructed a maze that covers nearly one acre. The path is bordered by thick undergrowth and large boulders which form an impenetrable wall. They say that this maze abounds in poisonous reptiles; others aver that the Governor laid many a weird man-trap along the path. Anyway this maze is so perfect that no one except the old Governor himself has ever ventured to enter it. He, however, used to go there nearly every day and stayed inside for hours on end."

Judge Dee had followed Tao Gan's words with great interest.

"What a curious tale!", he exclaimed. "Does Yoo Kee often visit that country mansion?"

Tao Gan shook his head.

"No", he replied, "Yoo Kee left there as soon as the old Governor had been buried. He has never gone back there since. The mansion is empty but for an aged gate keeper and his wife. People say that the place is haunted and that the ghost of the old Governor walks about there at night. All give the estate a wide berth, even in broad daylight.

The Governor's town mansion was located just inside the eastern city gate. But Yoo Kee sold it soon after his father's death and bought his present house, right at the other end of the city. It stands on an empty plot of ground in the southwest corner, near the river. I had no time to go there myself, but people say that it is quite an imposing mansion, surrounded by a high wall."

Judge Dee rose and started pacing the floor.

After a while he said impatiently:

"The overthrow of Chien Mow resolves itself into a purely military problem and I for one find but small interest in such problems. They resemble too much a game of chess, the opponent and all his resources are known right from the beginning, there are no unknown factors. I am greatly intrigued, on the other hand, by two most interesting problems, namely the ambiguous last will of old Governor Yoo, and the murder of General Ding that is announced in advance. I would like to concentrate on these two matters which I find of absorbing interest. Instead I must first dispose of this miserable local tyrant! What an annoying situation!"

The judge tugged angrily at his beard. Then he rose and said:

"Well, I suppose that it can't be helped. I shall now have my noon meal. Thereafter I shall open the first session of this tribunal."

Judge Dee left his office. His four lieutenants walked over to the empty guard house, where the steward of the judge had prepared a simple meal for them.

As they were entering Chiao Tai gave a sign to Ma Joong. The two remained standing together for a moment in the corridor outside.

Chiao Tai whispered to Ma Joong:

"I fear that His Excellency underrates the problem we are up against. You and I have military experience, we know that we have not got a chance. Chien Mow has one hundred well-trained men, the only fighters we have are, except for our judge himself, just you and me. The nearest military post is three days on horseback from here. Should not we warn our judge not to act too rashly?"

Ma Joong twisted his short moustache.

"Our judge", he replied in a low voice, "has all the data we have. I take it that he has evolved a scheme to deal with the situation."

"The most clever scheme", Chiao Tai observed, "is of no avail against such superior strength. It does not matter for us, but what about our judge's wives and his children? Chien will have no mercy on them. I think it is our duty to propose to the judge that we first pretend to submit to Chien and thereafter work out some plan for attacking him. We could have a regiment of our army here in two weeks."

Ma Joong shook his head.

"Unbidden advice is never welcome", he said. "Let us wait awhile and see what happens. I for one know of no better death than to fall in a really good fight."

"All right", Chiao Tai said, "if it comes to an open conflict I shall take care of at least four of those ruffians. Let us now join the others. Don't say a word about this, it is no use alarming the sergeant and Tao Gan."

Ma Joong nodded.

They entered the guard house and fell to their meal with gusto.

When they had eaten their rice Tao Gan wiped his chin and said:

"I have served more than six years under our judge and I thought I had come to understand him fairly well. But now it baffles me how he can be so preoccupied with an old lawsuit and a murder that will probably never take place, at a time when we are confronted with so difficult and urgent a problem as the overthrow of Chien Mow. You, Sergeant, have known His Excellency all your life. What do you say?"

Sergeant Hoong was busy swallowing the last of his soup, lifting his moustache with his left hand. He quietly put the bowl down. Then he said with a smile:

"In all these years I have learned but one thing about understanding our judge. That is, to give up trying to!"

All laughed. They rose and went back to the judge's private office.

As Sergeant Hoong was assisting Judge Dee in changing into his ceremonial robes he said curtly:

"Since I lack all the court personnel, today the four of you must take their places."

So speaking Judge Dee pulled aside the screen that separated his office from the court hall, and ascended the dais.

When he was seated behind the bench the judge ordered Sergeant Hoong and Tao Gan to stand by his side and act as scribes, taking notes of the proceedings. Ma Joong and Chiao Tai were to stand below, in front of the dais, as constables.

As he took up his position Ma Joong shot Chiao Tai a bewildered look. They wondered why the judge insisted on keeping up the semblance of a real session of the tribunal. Looking at the empty court hall Chiao Tai thought to himself that it rather reminded him of a theatrical performance.

Judge Dee hit his gavel on the bench. He said solemnly:

"I, the magistrate, open the first session of this tribunal. Chiao Tai, bring the prisoners before me!"

Soon Chiao Tai came back leading the six robbers and the girl; he had shackled them together on a long chain.

As they approached the dais the prisoners looked amazed at the judge sitting in full ceremonial dress behind the shabby bench in the deserted court hall.

With an impassive face Judge Dee ordered Tao Gan to note down the full name and former profession of each of the prisoners.

Then Judge Dee spoke:

"You men have committed the crime of assault with murderous intent on the public road. The law prescribes for you death by decapitation, confiscation of all your property, and your heads exposed for three days, nailed to the city gate, as a warning to others.

However, in view of the fact that none of your victims was killed and none suffered grievous bodily harm, and because of the special reasons that drove you to this desperate deed, I, the magistrate, decide that in this particular case mercy shall prevail over justice. I shall let you go free on one condition.

This condition is that all of you shall serve for an indefinite time as constables of this tribunal under Fang as your headman, binding yourselves loyally to serve the state and the people until I shall release you."

The prisoners looked dumbfounded.

"Your Honour", Fang spoke up, "these persons are

profoundly grateful for the leniency shown to us. Yet this only means that our death sentence is deferred for a few days. Your Honour does not yet know Chien Mow's vindictive spirit, and . . ."

The judge hit his gavel on the table. He called out in a thunderous voice:

"Look up at your magistrate! Observe carefully these insignia of the power that has been vested in me. Know that on this very day, this very hour all over the Empire thousands of men wearing these same insignia are dispensing justice in the name of the state and the people. Since time immemorial they stand as a symbol of the social order decided upon in the wise counsels of your ancestors, and perpetuated by the mandate of Heaven and the free will of the uncounted millions of our black-haired people.

Have you not seen sometimes people trying to plant a stick in a gushing mountain stream? It will stand for a moment or so, then it is carried away by the mighty stream that flows on for ever. Thus occasionally wicked or ignorant men will rise and endeavour to disrupt the sacred pattern of our society. Is it not crystal clear that such attempts can never end in anything but miserable failure?

Let us never lose faith in these tokens, lest we lose faith in ourselves.

Stand up, and be freed of your chains!"

The prisoners had not followed all the implications of Judge Dee's words. But they were deeply impressed by his utter sincerity and carried away by his supreme confidence. Judge Dee's lieutenants, however, had fully understood and they knew that his words had been meant as much for them as for the prisoners. Ma Joong and Chiao Tai bent their heads and hurriedly loosened the chains.

Judge Dee then addressed the robbers:

"Afterwards each of you will report to Tao Gan and

Sergeant Hoong what wrongs he suffered at the hands of Chien Mow. In due time each single case shall be heard in this tribunal. At present, however, there are more pressing affairs. The six of you will go immediately to the main courtyard and clean the weapons and the old uniforms of the constables. My two lieutenants Ma Joong and Chiao Tai shall instruct you in military drill. Fang's daughter shall report to my house steward for work as a maid in my mansion.

The first session of the tribunal is closed!"

The judge rose and returned to his private office.

He changed into a comfortable informal robe. Just as he was going to sort out some more documents, Headman Fang came in. After he had bowed he said respectfully:

"Your Honour, beyond the valley where the attack took place there live more than thirty other men in an improvised camp. They had to flee the city because of Chien Mow's iniquities. I know them all. Five or six are scoundrels, the rest are honest people whom I'll answer for. It occurred to me that one of these days I might go out there and enlist the best of them for service in the tribunal."

"An excellent idea!", the judge exclaimed. "You will take a horse and go there at once. Select those men you deem suitable. Let them come back to the city at dusk, in groups of two or three and by different routes!"

Headman Fang hurriedly took his leave.

Late that afternoon the main courtyard of the tribunal resembled a military encampment.

Ten men wearing the black lacquered helmets and the leather jackets with red sash that are the regular uniform of constables, were engaged in a drill led by Headman Fang. Ten others clad in light mail coats and decked with shining helmets were practising pike fencing under the supervision of Ma Joong. Chiao Tai was instructing ten more in the secrets of sword fighting.

The gate of the tribunal was closed. Sergeant Hoong and Tao Gan stood on guard.

Later on that night, Judge Dee ordered all the men to assemble in the court hall.

By the light of a single candle the judge issued his instructions. When he had finished he cautioned them all to guard complete silence for a while. Then he snuffed out the candle.

Tao Gan left the court hall. He closed the door carefully behind him and walked through the dark corridors, lighting his way with a small paper lantern.

He went to the jail and unlocked the warden's cell.

Tao Gan loosened the chain with which the warden had been attached to a ring in the wall. He said in a surly voice:

"The judge has decided to dismiss you from his service because of gross negligence. You failed to take proper care of the seals of the tribunal that were entrusted to you. In the coming days our judge shall recruit new personnel of the tribunal, and the first criminal to be kneeling in chains before his dais will be that self-styled tyrant Chien Mow!"

The warden only scowled.

Tao Gan led him through the dark, empty corridors and across the deserted main courtyard. They passed the empty quarters of the guards. Everything was dark and silent.

Tao Gan opened the gate. He gave the warden a push.

"Get out!", he growled. "Never show your ugly face here again!"

The warden looked contemptuously at Tao Gan. He said with a sneer:

"I shall be back sooner than you think, you dogshead!"

Then he disappeared into the dark street.

Fifth Chapter

TWENTY RUFFIANS ATTACK IN THE DEAD OF NIGHT;
JUDGE DEE SETS OUT ON A DANGEROUS EXCURSION

SHORTLY after midnight loud sounds shattered the silence in the dark tribunal.

Hoarse voices shouted orders, weapons clattered. A ram was applied to the main gate; its dull thuds reverberated in the still night air.

But inside the tribunal nothing stirred.

The wood of the gate splintered, heavy wooden boards crashed to the ground. Twenty ruffians swinging clubs and brandishing spears and swords rushed inside. A huge fellow with a lighted torch led the way.

They poured into the first courtyard, shouting:

"Where is that dog-official? Where is that wretched magistrate?"

The big fellow kicked open the gate of the main courtyard and stood aside to let the others pass while he drew his sword.

The ruffians halted inside, for the place was pitch dark.

Suddenly all six doors of the large reception hall swung open. The courtyard was brilliantly lighted by dozens of large candles and lanterns that stood arranged in double rows inside.

The invaders, their eyes blinking from this sudden change from dark to light, vaguely saw soldiers lined up on left and right. The light shone on their helmets and the long points of their pikes, leveled for action. At the bottom of

49

the stairs they saw a row of constables with drawn swords.

On top of the stairs there stood an imposing figure clad in full ceremonial dress of shimmering brocade, the winged judge's cap on his head.

By his side there stood two tall men in the uniform of cavalry captains. Their breast and armplates glittered and coloured pennants fluttered from their pointed helmets. One held a heavy bow ready with an arrow on the string.

The judge called out in a thunderous voice:

"Here is the magistrate of Lan-fang! Surrender your arms!"

The huge ruffian with the naked sword was the first to recover from his surprise.

"Fight your way out!", he yelled to the others.

As he lifted his word he fell backwards with a horrible gasp. Chiao Tai's arrow had pierced his throat.

At the same time a hoarse command rang out from the hall.

"Right about . . . turn!"

Immediately there was a loud clanking of iron and the tramping of heavy feet.

The ruffians looked at each other in consternation. One of them leaped forward. He shouted at the others:

"Brothers, we are done for! The army is here!"

So speaking he threw down his pike in front of the stairs. As he unbuckled his sword belt he said:

"Well, it took me six years to become a corporal. I suppose I shall have to start as private again!"

Ma Joong barked:

"Who calls himself a corporal here?"

The man stood automatically at attention.

"Corporal Ling, sixth detachment foot soldiers, thirty-third army of the Left Wing. At yours orders, Captain!"

"All deserters out in front!", Ma Joong shouted.

CHIEN MOW'S MEN INVADE THE TRIBUNAL

Five men lined themselves up behind the corporal and awkwardly stood at attention.

Ma Joong said curtly:

"You men shall appear before the military tribunal."

In the meantime the other ruffians had handed their arms to the constables. They bound each man's hands behind his back.

The judge spoke:

"Captain, ask how many other deserters there are around in this town."

Ma Joong bellowed the question at the ex-corporal.

"About forty, Sir!"

Judge Dee stroked his beard.

"When you people have gone on to inspect the other border districts", he said to Ma Joong, "I would like to have some soldiers here on guard duty. You will propose to the Commander, Captain, that those deserters are re-enlisted."

Ma Joong barked immediately:

"Corporal Ling and five privates, go back wherever you came from, get rid of those civilian rags, present yourselves here tomorrow at noon sharp, uniform and equipment as per regulation!"

The six men shouted "We obey!" and marched off.

Judge Dee gave a sign. The constables led the prisoners to the jail where Tao Gan was waiting for them.

Tao Gan noted down their names. The fifteenth and last was none other than the dismissed warden. Tao Gan's face lit up in a broad grin.

"You were quite right, you bastard! You are indeed back here earlier than I thought!"

So speaking Tao Gan turned him round and send him back into his former cell with an accurately placed kick.

In the main courtyard, the newly-made soldiers recruited

by Fang had shouldered their pikes, and marched off to the quarters of the guards.

Judge Dee saw that they marched in good order. He said with a smile to Ma Joong:

"That is not bad for one afternoon's drill!"

The judge came down the steps. Two constables closed the doors of the reception hall. Sergeant Hoong emerged loaded with old pans, kettles and rusty chains.

Judge Dee remarked:

"You have a fine commanding voice, Sergeant!"

Early next morning when the sun had just risen, three men left the tribunal on horseback.

Judge Dee rode in the middle clad in hunting dress. Ma Joong and Chiao Tai, resplendent in their uniforms of cavalry captains rode by his side.

As they headed west the judge turned round in his saddle and looked at the large yellow banner that was waving from the roof of the tribunal. It bore an inscription in red letters: "Military Headquarters".

"My ladies worked on that banner till deep in the night!", Judge Dee said with a smile to his companions.

They rode straight to Chien Mow's mansion.

Four stalwart figures armed with halberds stood in front of the gate.

Ma Joong reined in his horse right in front of them. He pointed with his riding whip at the door, and ordered:

"Open up!"

Evidently the deserters who had been sent back the night before had spread the news about the arrival of the soldiers. The guards hesitated but for one moment. Then they threw open the gate and Judge Dee and his leutenants rode through.

In the first courtyard a few dozen men stood about in

groups talking excitedly. They immediately fell silent and cast an apprehensive glance at the three horsemen. Those who carried swords hurriedly tried to conceal these weapons in the folds of their robes.

The three rode on without looking right or left.

Ma Joong forced his horse up the four steps that led to the second courtyard, followed by the judge and Chiao Tai.

Corporal Ling was supervising about thirty men who were busily engaged in polishing swords and spears and oiling leather jackets.

Without stopping Ma Joong called out to the corporal: "Follow with ten privates!"

The third courtyard was deserted but for a few servants who scurried away when they saw the three horsemen.

Ma Joong rode up to the large building at the back, the hoofs of his horse clattering on the flagstones. The beautifully carved, red-lacquered doors indicated that this was the main hall of the mansion.

They dismounted and threw the reins to three of the corporal's men.

Ma Joong kicked open the central door with his iron boot and stepped inside followed by his two companions.

Evidently they interrupted an urgent conference. Three men were sitting close together in the centre of the hall. In the middle, a tall broad-shouldered man sat in a large armchair covered with a tiger skin. He had a heavy-jowled, imperious face, with a thin moustache and a short black beard. He seemed to have just left his bed; he still wore a night robe of white silk, and over it a loose house robe of purple brocade. His head was covered with a small black cap. The two others, both elderly men, were sitting opposite him on footstools of carved ebony. They also apparently had dressed in a hurry.

The hall had a most warlike appearance, it resembled an

MA JOONG AND CHIAO TAI ARREST A CRIMINAL

armoury rather than a reception hall. The walls were decorated with spears, pikes and shields, the floor was covered with the skins of wild animals.

The three men looked up at the intruders in speechless amazement. Judge Dee did not say a word. He walked straight to an empty armchair and sat down. Ma Joong and Chiao Tai planted themselves right in front of Chien Mow and gave him a baleful look.

Chien's two counsellors hastily left their footstools and retreated behind their master's armchair.

The judge addressed Ma Joong in a casual voice:

"Captain, the town is under martial law. So I leave it to you to deal with these rascals!"

Ma Joong turned round.

"Corporal Ling!", he bellowed.

The corporal hurriedly stepped over the threshold, followed by four of his men. Ma Joong asked:

"Which of these criminals is the traitor Chien Mow?"

The corporal pointed to the man in the armchair.

Ma Joong snapped:

"Chien Mow, you are arrested on the charge of sedition!"

Chien jumped up. He stood in front of Ma Joong and shouted in a voice that yielded nothing to Ma Joong's in harshness:

"Who is giving orders in my own house? Guards, cut them down!"

As he spoke Ma Joong struck him with his mailed fist full in the face. Chien fell down upsetting an elegant tea table that crashed to the floor together with a costly porcelain tea set.

Six fierce looking ruffians came rushing from behind the large screen back in the hall. They carried long swords and their leader brandished a double axe.

They suddenly halted when they saw Ma Joong and

56

Chiao Tai in their full armour. Ma Joong folded his arms. He gruffly addressed the body guards:

"Give up your arms! Our commander will decide later whether you underlings are guilty or not."

Chien's nose had been broken, a stream of blood stained his robe. He lifted his head and called out:

"Don't listen to that bastard, men! Have you not eaten my rice for ten years? First kill that dog-official there!"

The leader of the body guard sprang over to the judge raising his axe.

Judge Dee did not move. He slowly caressed his side whiskers staring contemptuously at his attacker.

"Wait, brother Wang!", Corporal Ling shouted, "did I not tell you that the whole town is swarming with soldiers? We have not got a chance, the army has taken over!"

The man with the axe hesitated.

Chiao Tai stamped his foot impatiently on the floor.

"Let us get a move on!", he cried. "We have better things to do than picking up these few rascals!"

He turned round and made to step outside.

Chien Mow had lost consciousness. Ma Joong, completely ignoring the body guards, stooped down and started to bind up Chien.

Judge Dee rose from his chair. As he straightened his robes he said coldly to the man with the axe:

"Put that dangerous instrument down, my man!"

He turned his back on him and looked hard at the two counsellors. They had stood there silently throughout the proceedings. Evidently they did not want to commit themselves either way before the issue was decided.

"Who might you two be?", the judge asked haughtily.

The elder one bowed deeply.

"Your Honour", he replied, "this person has been compelled to serve this man Chien as a counsellor. Allow me to assure Your Honour that . . ."

"You will tell your tale in the tribunal!", Judge Dee interrupted him. To Ma Joong he said: "Let us hurry back to the tribunal. We shall take only this man Chien Mow and his two counsellors. We shall deal later with the rest of them." Ma Joong said promptly:

"As you order, Magistrate!"

He gave a sign to Corporal Ling. The four soldiers bound the two counsellors securely. Chiao Tai unwound a thin chain from his waist. He made a loop at either end and threw the nooses over the heads of the two prisoners. He dragged them outside. As he fastened the chain to his saddle bow Chiao Tai said curtly:

"If you don't want to strangle yourselves you had better walk fast!"

Chiao Tai mounted his horse and Judge Dee followed his example. Ma Joong slung the unconscious Chien Mow over his saddle. He called out to Corporal Ling:

"Divide your soldiers in four groups of twelve. Each group is responsible for ten of Chien's men. Go to the city gates and lock your prisoners in the towers. At noon an officer shall inspect the four gates!"

"I obey!", the corporal shouted.

The three rode across the courtyard, the two counsellors trotting behind Chiao Tai's horse.

In the second courtyard an elderly man with a grey goatee was waiting for them. He fell on his knees and knocked his head on the stoneflags.

Judge Dee halted his horse. He said curtly:

"Rise and state your name!"

The other hastily scrambled up. He replied with a bow:

"This unworthy person is the steward of this mansion."

Judge Dee ordered:

"You will be fully responsible for this mansion and everything in it, including the servants and the womenfolk, till officers from the tribunal come to take over!"

Then the judge rode on.

Ma Joong bent over in his saddle and asked the steward in a conversational tone:

"Have you ever seen how in the army they sometimes flog a criminal slowly to death with a thin rattan? It usually takes about six hours."

The bewildered steward respectfully replied that he had not yet had that advantage.

"That is exactly what will happen to you if you don't execute His Excellency's orders to the letter!", Ma Joong said casually. He spurred on his horse, leaving the steward standing there trembling, his face ashen.

As the three horsemen passed through the main gate of Chien's mansion, the four guards presented arms.

FOUR GUILDMASTERS ARE RECEIVED IN THE MAIN HALL;
MRS. YOO VISITS THE TRIBUNAL WITH AN OLD PICTURE

ONCE returned to the tribunal, Ma Joong and Chiao Tai
delivered the still unconscious Chien Mow and his two
panting counsellors to Headman Fang. Then they went
to Judge Dee's private office. Sergeant Hoong was assisting
the judge to change into his informal dress.

Ma Joong pushed back his iron helmet and wiped the
perspiration from his brow. He looked with admiration at
the judge, exclaiming:

"If that was not the most colossal bluff I have ever seen!"

The judge smiled bleakly.

"It would never have done", he explained, "to fight it
out with Chien. Even if we had really had some two hundred soldiers at our disposal it would have been a sangui-
nary battle. Chien Mow is a rascal but he is by no means a
coward and the men under him would have put up a stiff
fight.

From the beginning I had planned to bluff them, impressing upon Chien and his men that all was over and done
with and our victory a foregone conclusion. My original
plan was to pose as a provincial governor or an Imperial
censor on a border inspection tour.

As soon as Tao Gan informed me that there were many
deserters from the regular army among Chien's men I
changed my plan accordingly."

"Was it not taking a risk to let that corporal and five

men return to Chien's mansion after the attack on the tribunal?", Chiao Tai asked. "They might have started making inquiries and found out that we were bluffing."

"That", Judge Dee replied, "was exactly what decided the issue. No one in his senses would have let six good men march back to their master unless he had overwhelmingly superior numbers behind him. It never occurred to Corporal Ling to check. Chien is a shrewd man but even he did not doubt the presence of the regular army. He decided to die in a last desperate fight but his followers thought better of it, especially when we suggested that we might let them go free."

"Now that we have created this imaginary regiment", Sergeant Hoong asked, "how do we get rid of it again?"

"If I am not greatly mistaken in my estimation of the course a rumour will take", Judge Dee said calmly, "this regiment will first wax in popular imagination till it has become a full-fledged army, and then evaporate again without any effort on our part.

Now about business. First I must organize this tribunal. Then Chien Mow's affairs must be disentangled.

Tao Gan will go out now and summon the wardens of all the quarters of this city to appear before me immediately. He will also invite the masters of the most important guilds to pay me a visit at noon.

Sergeant Hoong, you will go to Chien's mansion with Headman Fang and ten constables. The womenfolk and the servants will remain confined to their quarters until further orders. You will check with the steward all valuables, place them in the strong room and seal the door. Headman Fang will make a search for his son and his eldest daughter, White Orchid.

Ma Joong and Chiao Tai will make the rounds of the four city gates and verify whether Corporal Ling has duly posted his men and whether the forty henchmen of Chien who did not belong to the army have been put under lock and key in the gate towers. If everything is found in order you will inform Ling that he is re-enlisted without loss of rank.

Take your time and find out the antecedents of the ex-soldiers. Those who did not desert in battle or flee because of some major offense can be re-enlisted. This afternoon I shall draw up a report to the Board of Military Affairs to have their position regularized. At the same time I shall apply for hundred soldiers to be sent out here."

Having thus spoken the judge ordered Sergeant Hoong to bring him a large pot of hot tea.

It did not take Tao Gan long to round up the wardens. They did not look very happy when they were shown into Judge Dee's private office.

It was they who, being recruited locally to act as link between the tribunal and the population, were responsible for the reporting of births, deaths and marriages and many other affairs which had been completely neglected under Chien Mow's rule. As members of the district administration, the wardens should have been present in the tribunal to bid welcome to the new magistrate. They expected a severe scolding.

That was exactly what they got, and with a vengeance. They emerged from Judge Dee's office trembling and pale and scurried away as fast as they could.

Judge Dee then walked over to the large reception hall of the tribunal and there received the masters of the guilds of the goldsmiths, the carpenters, the rice dealers and the silk merchants. The judge politely inquired their names, and the steward served refreshments.

The guildmasters congratulated the judge on the speedy arrest of Chien Mow and expressed their joy that now the district would return to normal. They were somewhat disturbed, however, over such a large number of soldiers occupying the city.

Judge Dee raised his eyebrows.

"The only soldiers here", he remarked, "are a few dozen deserters which I have re-enlisted for guard duty."

The master of the goldsmiths' guild gave his colleagues a knowing look. He said with a smile:

"We fully understand, Your Honour, that your lips are sealed. But the guards of the northern gate told that when Your Honour entered the city they were nearly trampled down by an escadron of cavalry. Last night a goldsmith saw a column of two hundred soldiers march through the main street with straw wrapped round their boots."

The master of the guild of silk merchants added:

"My own cousin saw a row of ten horsecarts pass by, loaded with army supplies. However, Your Honour can fully trust us. We realize that a military inspection tour of the border districts must be kept secret lest the barbarian hordes over the river hear about it. The news shall not spread outside the city. Would it not be better, however, if the Commander did not display his flag over the tribunal? If the spies of the barbarian tribes see this flag, they will know that the army is here."

"That flag", Judge Dee answered, "I put up myself. It only means that I, the magistrate, have temporarily placed this district under martial law, as I am entitled to do in a state of emergency."

The guildmasters smiled and bowed deeply.

"We perfectly understand Your Honour's discretion!", the eldest said gravely.

Judge Dee did not comment further on this but broached quite a different subject. He requested the masters to send him that very afternoon three elderly men qualified and willing to serve in the tribunal respectively as senior scribe, head of the archives, and warden of the jail; and a dozen dependable youngsters to serve as clerks. The judge further requested them to lend the tribunal two thousand silver pieces to pay for elementary repairs of the court hall and for the salaries of the personnel; this sum would be paid back as soon as the case against Chien Mow had been concluded and his property confiscated.

The guildmasters readily agreed.

Finally Judge Dee informed them that the next morning he would open the case against Chien Mow, and asked them to make this fact known throughout the district.

When the guildmasters had taken their leave the judge went back to his private office. There he found Headman Fang waiting for him together with a good-looking young man.

Both knelt before the judge. The young man knocked his head on the floor three times in succession.

"Your Honour", Fang said, "allow me to present my son. He was kidnapped by Chien's henchmen and compelled to work as a servant in his mansion."

"He shall serve under you as a constable", Judge Dee said. "Did you find your eldest daughter?"

"Alas", Fang replied with a sigh, "my son has never seen her and the most diligent search did not produce any trace of her. I closely questioned the steward of Chien's mansion. He remembers that at one time Chien Mow expressed the desire to acquire White Orchid for his harem but maintains that his master dropped the matter when I refused to sell my daughter. I do not know what to think."

Judge Dee said pensively:

"It is your assumption that Chien Mow kidnapped her, and you may yet be proved right. It is not unusual for a man like Chien to keep a secret love nest outside his mansion. On the other hand we must also reckon with the possibility that he had really nothing to do with her disappearance. I shall question Chien on this subject and institute a thorough investigation. Do not give up hope too soon!"

As the judge was speaking, Ma Joong and Chiao Tai came in.

They reported that Corporal Ling had executed his orders to the letter. Ten soldiers were stationed at each of the four city gates and a dozen of Chien's men were locked in each gate tower. The number of prisoners had been increased by five ex-soldiers who had deserted to escape punishment for real crimes. Corporal Ling had demoted to water carriers the loafers who had been guarding the gates before.

Ma Joong added that Ling had all the qualities of a good military man; he had deserted because of a quarrel with a dishonest captain and was overjoyed at being once more in the regular army.

Judge Dee nodded and said:

"I shall propose that Ling is made a sergeant. For the time being we shall leave the forty men stationed at the gates. If their morale remains good I propose to quarter them all together in Chien's mansion. In course of time I shall designate that as garrison headquarters. You, Chiao Tai, will remain commanding officer of those forty men and the twenty we trained here in the tribunal, till the soldiers I shall send for have arrived."

Having thus spoken the judge dismissed his lieutenants. He took up his brush and drafted an urgent letter to the far-away prefect describing the events of the past two days. The judge added a list of the men he wanted re-enlisted and a proposal that Corporal Ling be promoted to sergeant. Finally he requested that one hundred soldiers be send to Lan-fang as permanent garrison.

As he was sealing this letter the headman came in. He reported that a Mrs. Yoo had come to see the judge. She was waiting at the gate of the tribunal.

Judge Dee looked pleased.

"Bring her in!", he ordered.

As the headman was showing the lady into Judge Dee's office he gave her an appraising look. She was about thirty years old and still a remarkable beautiful woman. She was not made up and very simply dressed.

Kneeling before the desk she said timidly:

"Mrs. Yoo *née* Mei respectfully greets Your Honour."

"We are not in the tribunal, Madam", Judge Dee said kindly, "so there is no need for formality. Please rise and be seated!"

Mrs. Yoo rose slowly and sat down on one of the footstools in front of the desk. She hesitated to speak.

"I have always", Judge Dee said, "greatly admired your late husband Governor Yoo. I consider him as one of the greatest statesmen of our age."

Mrs. Yoo bowed. She said in a low voice:

"He was a great and a good man, Your Honour. I would not have dared to intrude upon Your Honour's valuable time were it not that it is my duty to execute my late husband's instructions."

Judge Dee leaned forward.

"Pray proceed, Madam!", he said intently.

Mrs. Yoo put her hand in her sleeve and took out an oblong package. She rose and placed it on the desk.

"On his deathbed", she began, "the Governor handed me this scroll picture which he had painted himself. He said that this was the inheritance he bequeathed to me and my son. The rest was to go to my stepson Yoo Kee.

Upon that the Governor started coughing and Yoo Kee left the room to order a new bowl with medicine. As soon as he had gone the Governor suddenly said to me: 'Should you ever be in difficulties you will take this picture to the tribunal and show it to the magistrate. If he does not understand its meaning you will show it to his successor, until in due time a wise judge shall uncover its secret.' Then Yoo Kee came in. The Governor looked at the three of us. He laid his emaciated hand on the head of my small son, smiled and passed away without saying another word."

Mrs. Yoo broke down sobbing.

Judge Dee waited until she was calmer. Then he said:

"Every detail of that last day is important, Madam. Tell me what happened thereafter."

"My stepson Yoo Kee", Mrs. Yoo continued, "took the picture from my hands saying that he would keep it for me. He was not unkind then. It was only after the funeral that he changed. He told me harshly to leave the house immediately with my son. He accused me of having deceived his father and forbade me and my son ever to set a foot in his house again. Then he threw this scroll picture on the table and said with a sneer that I was welcome to my inheritance."

Judge Dee stroked his beard.

"Since the Governor was a man of great wisdom, Madam, there must be some deep meaning in this picture. I shall study it carefully. It is my duty to warn you, however, that I keep an open mind as to the portent of its secret message. It may either be in your favour or prove that you have been guilty of the crime of adultery. In either case I shall take appropriate steps and justice shall take its course. I leave it to you, Madam, to decide whether you will want me to keep this scroll or whether you prefer to take it back with you and withdraw your claim."

Mrs. Yoo rose. She said with quiet dignity:

"I beg Your Honour to keep this scroll for study. I pray

to Merciful Heaven that it will grant you to solve its riddle."

Then she bowed deeply and took her leave.

Sergeant Hoong and Tao Gan had been waiting outside in the corridor. Now they came in and greeted the judge. Tao Gan was carrying an armful of document rolls.

The sergeant reported that they had inventoried Chien Mow's property. They had found several hundred gold bars and a large amount of silver. This money they had locked in the strongroom together with a number of utensils of solid gold. The women and the house servants had been confined to the third courtyard. Six constables of the tribunal and ten soldiers had been quartered in the second courtyard under supervision of Chiao Tai, to guard the mansion.

Tao Gan placed with a contented smile his load of documents on the desk. He said:

"These, Your Honour, are the inventories we made, and all the deeds and accounts that we found in Chien Mow's strongroom."

Judge Dee leaned back in his chair and looked at the pile with undisguised distaste.

"The disentangling of Chien Mow's affairs", he said, "will be a long and tedious task. I shall entrust this work to you, Sergeant, and Tao Gan. I don't expect that this material will contain anything more important than evidence of unlawful appropriation of land and houses and petty extortion. The guildmasters have promised to send me this afternoon suitable persons to take up the duties of the clerical personnel, including a head of our archives. They should be useful in working out these problems."

"They are waiting in the main courtyard, Your Honour", Sergeant Hoong remarked.

"Well", the judge said, "you and Tao Gan will instruct them in their duties. Tonight the head of the archives will

GOVERNOR YOO'S PICTURE

assist you in sorting out these documents. I leave it to you to draft for me an extensive report with suggestions as to how Chien Mow's affairs should be dealt with. You will keep apart, however, any document that has a bearing on the murder of my late colleague, Magistrate Pan.

I myself wish to concentrate on this problem here."

As he spoke the judge took up the package that Mrs. Yoo had left with him. He unwrapped it and unrolled the scroll picture on his desk.

Sergeant Hoong and Tao Gan stepped forward and together with the judge they looked intently at the picture.

It was a medium-sized picture painted on silk, representing an imaginary mountain landscape done in full colours. White clouds drifted amoung the cliffs. Here and there houses appeared amidst clusters of trees, and on the right a mountain river flowed down. There was not a single human figure.

On top of the picture the Governor had written the title in archaic characters. It read:

BOWERS OF EMPTY ILLUSION

The Governor had not signed this inscription, there was only an impression of his seal in vermilion.

The picture was mounted on all four sides with borders of heavy brocade. Below there had been added a wooden roller and on top a thin stave with a suspension loop. This is the usual mounting of scroll pictures meant to be hung on the wall.

Sergeant Hoong pensively pulled his beard.

"The title would seem to suggest", he remarked, "that this picture represents some Taoist paradise or an abode of immortals."

Judge Dee nodded.

"This picture", he said, "requires careful study. Hang

it on the wall opposite my desk so that I can look at it whenever I like!"

When Tao Gan had suspended the picture on the wall between the door and the window, the judge rose and walked over to the main courtyard.

He saw that the prospective members of his clerical staff were decent looking men. The judge addressed them briefly, and concluded:

"My two lieutenants will now instruct you. Listen carefully, for tomorrow you will have to start your duties when I hold the morning session of this tribunal."

THREE ROGUISH MONKS RECEIVE THEIR JUST PUNISHMENT;
A CANDIDATE OF LITERATURE REPORTS A CRUEL MURDER

THE next morning, before the break of dawn, the citizens of Lan-fang began trooping to the tribunal. When the hour of the morning session approached a dense crowd filled the street in front of the main gate.

The large bronze gong was sounded three times. The constables threw the double gate open and the crowd poured inside and into the court hall. Soon there was not a single standing place left.

The constables ranged themselves in two rows to right and left in front of the dais.

Then the screen at the back was pulled aside. Judge Dee ascended the dais clad in full ceremonial dress. As he seated himself behind the bench his four lieutenants took up their position by his side. The senior scribe and his assistants stood next to the bench, now covered with a new cloth of scarlet silk.

A deep silence reigned as the judge took up his vermilion brush and filled out a slip for the warden of the jail.

Headman Fang took it respectfully with two hands and left the court hall with two constables.

They came back with the elder of Chien's two counsellors. He knelt in front of the dais.

Judge Dee ordered:

"State your name and profession!"

"This insignificant person", the man spoke humbly, "is

called Liu Wan-fang. Until ten years ago I was the house steward of Chien Mow's late father. After the latter's death Chien kept me as his adviser. I assure Your Honour that I have always on every possible occasion urged Chien to mend his ways!"

The judge observed with a cold smile:

"I can say only that your attempts had a remarkably small result! The tribunal is collecting and sifting the evidence of your master's crimes; doubtless this material will prove your complicity in many of Chien's misdeeds. However, at present I am not concerned with the minor crimes you and your master committed. For the present I wish to confine myself to the major issues. Speak up, what murders did Chien Mow commit?"

Liu answered:

"Your Honour, it is true that my master appropriated unlawfully people's land and houses and he often had persons severely beaten up. But to the best of my knowledge Chien never did wilfully kill anyone."

"Liar!", Judge Dee shouted. "What about Magistrate Pan who was dastardly murdered here?"

"That murder", Liu replied, "baffled my master as much as myself!"

The judge shot him an incredulous stare.

"Of course we knew", Liu continued hurriedly "that His Excellency Pan was evolving plans to oust my master from his position. Since Judge Pan had no one with him but one assistant, my master did not act for a few days. He wished to wait and see what course of action Judge Pan would take. Then one morning two of our men came running to our mansion. They reported that Judge Pan's body had been found on the river bank.

My master was greatly vexed because he knew that people would say that he was responsible for this murder.

He hurriedly drew up a false report to the prefect stating that Judge Pan and six militia had ventured over the river to apprehend a rebel Uigur chieftain, and that the judge was slain in the ensuing fight. Six of Chien's men signed as witnesses, and . . ."

Judge Dee hit his gavel on the bench.

"I have never", he exclaimed angrily, "heard such a string of outrageous lies! Give that dogshead twentyfive lashes with the whip!"

Liu started to protest but the headman promptly hit him in his face. The constables tore Liu's robe from his back, threw him on the floor, and the whip swished through the air.

The thin thong cut deeply in the flesh. Liu screamed desperately that he was telling the truth.

After the fifteenth blow the judge raised his hand. He knew that there was no reason for Liu to shield his fallen master and that Liu would realize that the testimony of the other prisoners would soon expose him if he tried to lie. Judge Dee wished to confuse him so that he would tell all he knew, reflecting that fifteen lashes with the whip was probably but a fraction of the punishment that this scoundrel deserved.

The headman gave Liu a cup of bitter tea. Then Judge Dee continued the interrogation.

"If what you say is true, why then did Chien Mow not try to discover the real murderer?"

"That", Liu replied, "was unnecessary since my master knew who had committed that foul deed."

Judge Dee raised his eyebrows.

"Your tale", he remarked dryly, "becomes increasingly absurd. If your master knew the murderer's identity, why did he not arrest him and forward him to the prefect? That would have gained Chien the confidence of the authorities."

Liu shook his head dejectedly.

"That question, Your Honour, can only be answered by Chien himself. Although my master consulted us in minor matters he never told us one word about things of real importance. I know that in all major issues my master let himself be directed by a man whose identity we have never been able to guess."

"I thought", Judge Dee observed, "that Chien was perfectly capable to conduct his affairs himself. Why should he need to employ some mysterious adviser?"

"My master", Liu replied, "is a clever and brave man, expert in all martial arts. But after all, he was born and brought up in this small border town. What do we of Lan-fang know about the handling of a prefect and how to deal with the central authorities? It was always after a visit of the stranger that my master made one of the many clever moves that prevented the prefect from intervening in affairs here."

Judge Dee leaned forward in his chair. He asked curtly: "Who was that secret adviser?"

"For the last four years", Liu said, "my master used to receive regularly secret visits from that man. Late at night my master would send me to the side gate of our mansion and inform the guards that he expected a guest who was to be conveyed immediately to his library. This visitor always came on foot clad in a monk's cloak with a black scarf wrapped round his head. None of us ever saw his face. My master used to be closeted with him for hours on end. Then he would depart as silently as he had come. My master never gave us any explanation of these visits. But they were always the prelude to some major undertaking.

I am convinced that this man had Judge Pan murdered without my master's previous knowledge. He came that same night. He must have had a violent quarrel with my master; outside in the corridor we heard them shout at each other although we could not distinguish any words. After that interview my master was in a bad temper for several days."

The judge said impatiently:

"I have heard enough of this mysterious tale. What about Chien's kidnapping the son and the eldest daughter of the blacksmith Fang?"

"It is about affairs such as these", Liu said, "that I and my colleagues can give Your Honour full particulars. Fang's son was indeed taken by Chien's men. The mansion was short of coolies and Chien sent out his henchmen to collect a few strong young men in the street. They brought in four. Three were later returned when their parents paid ransom. The blacksmith made trouble with the guards so Chien decided to keep his son to teach the blacksmith a lesson.

As to the girl, I know that my master happened to see her when he passed her father's shop in his palanquin. He took a fancy to her and made an offer to buy her. When the blacksmith refused my master soon forgot all about it. Then the blacksmith came to our mansion and accused us of having kidnapped her. My master was angry and sent his men to burn the blacksmith's house."

Judge Dee leaned back in his chair and slowly stroked his long beard. He reflected that Liu was evidently speaking the truth. His master had had nothing to do with the disappearance of Fang's eldest daughter. Quick measures should be taken to arrest Chien's secret adviser. If at least it was not too late for that already.

Then he ordered:

"Tell me what happened after my arrival here two days ago!"

"One week ago", Liu replied, "Magistrate Kwang reported to my master Your Honour's scheduled arrival. He asked leave to depart early in the morning since he thought it awkward to meet Your Honour. My master agreed. He ordered that no one should take the slightest notice of Your Honour's arrival in order 'to show the new magistrate his place', as he put it.

My master then waited for the old jail warden to report. He failed to show up on the first day. He came the next evening and told my master that Your Honour was determined to attack him. He added that there were only three or four men in the tribunal but he described them as exceedingly fierce and rough men."

Here Tao Gan smiled proudly. It was not often that he heard such a flattering description of himself.

"My master", Liu continued, "ordered twenty of his men to enter the tribunal that very night, capture the magistrate and give all others a thorough beating. When Ling and five men came back with the alarming news that a regiment of the regular army had quietly occupied the city, my master was asleep and nobody dared to disturb him. Early yesterday morning I myself brought Ling to my master's bedroom. He ordered a small black flag to be hoisted immediately over the main gate and then rushed to the main hall. When we were consulting about what to do, Your Honour came with the officers and arrested us."

"What was the meaning of that black flag?", the judge inquired.

"We understand that that was the summons for the mysterious visitor. Every time the flag was hoisted, he used to come that same night."

Judge Dee gave a sign to the headman. Liu Wan-fang was led away.

Then the judge filled out another slip for the warden of the jail and handed it to the headman.

77

After a while Chien Mow was brought in and led before the dais.

A murmur rose from the crowd as they saw the man who had ruled them with an iron hand for the past eight years.

Chien certainly was an imposing figure. He was well over six feet tall. His broad shoulders and his thick neck showed his great strength.

He made no move to kneel. First Chien looked haughtily at the judge, then turned round and surveyed with a sneer the gaping crowd.

"Kneel before your magistrate, you insolent dog!", the headman barked.

Chien Mow grew purple with rage. Thick veins stood out like whipcords on his forehead. He opened his mouth to speak. Then suddenly a stream of blood gushed from his broken nose. He tottered on his feet for a moment, then collapsed on the floor in a heap.

On a sign of the judge the headman stooped down and wiped the blood of Chien's face. He was unconscious.

The headman sent a constable for a bucket of cold water. They loosened Chien's robe and bathed his forehead and breast. But all was in vain. Chien did not regain consciousness.

Judge Dee was greatly annoyed. He ordered the headman to recall Liu Wan-fang.

As soon as he was kneeling before the bench the judge asked:

"Was your master suffering from any disease?"

Liu looked in consternation at the prone figure of Chien. The constables were still trying to revive him.

Liu shook his head.

"Although my master has an extraordinarily strong body", he said, "he suffers from a chronic disease of the brain. He has been consulting doctors for years but no medicine was of any avail. When he flew in a rage he would often collapse like this and remain unconscious for several hours. The doctors said that the only means to cure him was to open his skull and let out the poisonous air inside. But no doctor in Lan-fang possessed that particular skill."

Liu Wan-fang was led away. Four constables carried the limp form of Chien Mow back to the jail.

"Let the wardèn report to me as soon as this man recovers!", Judge Dee ordered the headman.

The judge reflected that this collapse of Chien Mow was extremely unfortunate. It was of urgent importance to learn from Chien the identity of his mysterious visitor. Every hour delay gave that shadowy figure in the background a better chance to make good his escape. The judge regretted deeply that he had failed to question Chien directly after his arrest. But who could have foreseen that he had this unknown accomplice?

With a sigh Judge Dee straightened himself in his chair. He hit his gavel on the bench. In a clear voice he spoke:

"During eight years the criminal Chien Mow has been usurping the privilege of our Imperial Government. From now on law and order are re-established in Lan-fang. The good will be protected, the wicked relentlessly persecuted and punished according to the laws of the land.

The criminal Chien Mow has been guilty of sedition and shall receive his just punishment. In addition to the crime of sedition he has committed a number of other criminal acts. Everyone who has a complaint against Chien Mow shall file this with the tribunal. Every case shall be investigated and compensation given wherever possible. It is my duty to warn you that the settling of all those cases will take time. You can rest assured, however, that in due time your wrongs will be righted and justice done."

The crowd of spectators burst out in loud cheers. It took the constables some time before order was restored in the court hall.

In a corner three Buddhist monks had not taken part in the general excitement. They stood huddled together in a whispered consultation.

Now they pressed forward through the crowd, shouting at the top of their voices that they were suffering under a terrible wrong.

As they approached the dais Judge Dee noticed that none of the three looked very prepossessing. They had coarse, sensuous faces and shifty eyes.

When they were kneeling in front of the dais Judge Dee ordered:

"Let the eldest of you state his name and his complaint!"

"Your Honour", the monk in the middle spoke, "this ignorant monk is called Pillar of the Doctrine. I live with my two colleagues here in a small temple in the southern quarter of this town. We pass our days in devout prayer and self-examination.

Our poor temple has but one valuable possession, to wit a golden statue of our Gracious Lady Kwan Yin, Amen! Two months ago that villain Chien Mow came to our temple and took the holy statue away. In the Nether World he will be boiled in oil for this awful sacrilege. In the mean time, however, we humbly pray Your Honour to have the holy treasure returned to us or, should that scoundrel have had it melted, to grant us compensation in gold or silver!"

Having thus spoken the monk knocked his head three times on the floor.

Judge Dee slowly caressed his side whiskers. After a while he asked in a conversational tone:

"Since this statue is the only treasure your temple possesses, I suppose that you looked after it with due care and devotion?"

THREE MONKS REPORT A THEFT TO THE TRIBUNAL

"Indeed, Your Honour", the monk answered hurriedly, "every morning I personally dusted it with a silk whisk, reciting prayers all the while!"

"I trust", the judge continued, "that your two colleagues were equally diligent in serving the goddess?"

"This insignificant person", the monk on right said, "has for several years every morning and night burned incense in front of our Gracious Lady, and reverently contemplated her merciful features, Amen!"

"This ignorant monk", the third added, "every day spent enraptured hours in front of our Gracious Lady, Amen!"

Judge Dee nodded with a satisfied smile. Turning to the senior scribe he said curtly:

"Give each of the complainants a piece of charcoal and a sheet of white paper!"

As these implements were handed to the astonished monks the judge ordered:

"You there on left walk to the left side of the dais. The monk on right goes to stand on right. You, Pillar of the Doctrine, turn round and face the audience!"

The monks shuffled to the positions indicated.

Then Judge Dee said peremptorily:

"Kneel and draw me a sketch of that golden statue!"

A murmur rose from the crowd.

"Silence!" shouted the constables.

The three monks were quite some time over their work. From time to time they scratched their bald heads. They perspired freely.

At last Judge Dee ordered Headman Fang:

"Show me those sketches!"

When the judge had seen the three sheets he pushed them disdainfully over the edge of the bench.

As they fluttered to the floor everyone could see that

they were completely different. One showed the goddess with four arms and three faces, the second with eight arms, and the third was an attempt to depict her in the familiar two-armed form with a small child by her side.

Judge Dee called out in a thunderous voice:

"These scoundrels filed a false accusation! Give them twenty blows with the bamboo!"

The constables threw the three monks with their faces on the floor. They turned up their robes and pulled down their loincloths. The bamboo sticks swished through the air.

The monks screamed and cursed as the bamboo tore their flesh. But the constables did not release them until they had had the full number of strokes.

They could not walk. A few helpful spectators dragged them away.

The judge announced:

"Before these crooked monks came forward I was just going to issue a warning that no one should try to gain illegal profit by filing trumped-up claims against Chien Mow. Let the fate of these three monks be a warning example!

I wish to add that since this morning this district is no longer under martial law."

Having thus spoken Judge Dee turned to Sergeant Hoong and whispered something. The sergeant hurriedly left the hall.

As he came back he shook his head.

"Order the warden of the jail", the judge said in a low voice, "to call me immediately Chien Mow regains consciousness, even if it should be in the middle of the night!"

Then Judge Dee lifted his gavel. He was about to close the session when he noticed a commotion at the entrance of the court hall.

A young man was making frantic efforts to push through the packed crowd.

The judge ordered two constables to lead the newcomer before him.

As he sank panting to his knees before the dais, Judge Dee recognized Candidate Ding, the young man with whom he had drunk tea two days before.

"Your Honour!", Candidate Ding cried out, "that fiend Woo has foully murdered my old father!"

Eighth Chapter

AN OLD GENERAL IS MURDERED IN HIS OWN LIBRARY;
JUDGE DEE GOES TO VISIT THE SCENE OF THE CRIME

JUDGE DEE leaned back in his chair.

He slowly folded his hands in his wide sleeves and said:
"State when and how the murder was discovered!"

"Last night", Candidate Ding began, "we celebrated my
father's sixtieth birthday. The entire family had gathered
round the festive dish in the main hall of our mansion and
everyone was in high spirits. It was near midnight when
my father rose and left the table. He said he would retire
to his library and on this auspicious day write the preface
to his history of the border wars. I myself conducted him to
the door of the library. I knelt and wished him good night.
My father closed the door and I heard him push the crossbar in its place.

Alas, that was the last time I saw my revered father
alive. This morning our steward knocked on the library
door to apprise my father that breakfast was ready. When
he received no answer despite repeated knocking, the steward called me. Fearing that my father had fallen ill
during the night, we forced the door by beating in a panel
with an axe.

My father was lying slumped over his desk. I thought
he was asleep and lightly touched his shoulder. Then I
knew he was dead. I saw the hilt of a small dagger protrude
from his throat.

I rushed to this tribunal to report that Woo has dastardly done to death my defenseless old father. I beseech Your Honour to avenge this terrible wrong!"

Candidate Ding burst out sobbing and knocked his head on the floor several times.

Judge Dee remained silent for a while, his thick eyebrows knitted in a deep frown. Then he spoke:

"Compose yourself, Candidate Ding! This tribunal shall open the investigation without delay. As soon as my suite is ready I shall proceed to the scene of the crime. Rest assured that justice shall be done!"

The judge hit his gavel on the bench and announced the session closed. He rose and disappeared behind the screen of his private office.

The constables had some difficulty in clearing the court hall. The spectators were eagerly discussing the exciting events. Everyone was full of praise for the new magistrate and admired his shrewdness in exposing the fraud of the three greedy monks.

Corporal Ling had followed the proceedings accompanied by two young soldiers. As he tightened his belt to go he remarked:

"That judge is an imposing magistrate, although he lacks of course that fine bearing of our two captains Ma and Chiao. That can be acquired only by long years of military service."

One of the soldiers, a shrewd young fellow, asked:

"The judge announced that the martial law has been ended. That means that the army units that were here left during the night. But I have not seen one single soldier except our own!"

The corporal gave him a condescending look. He said sternly:

"Privates should not concern themselves with high strategy. Since, however, you are a keen youngster, I shall go so far as to disclose to you that the regiment passed through here on an inspection tour of the entire border. This is an important military secret. One word about it and I'll have your head chopped off!"

The soldier asked:

"But how could they leave without anybody seeing them, Corporal?"

"Soldier", the corporal replied proudly, "nothing is impossible for our Imperial army! Did I never tell you about the crossing of the Yellow River? There was no bridge or ferry, and our General wished to cross. So two thousand of us jumped in the water holding each other's hands so as to form two rows. One thousand soldiers stood themselves in between holding their shields over their heads. The General galloped on his horse over this iron bridge!"

The young soldier thought to himself that this was the most incredible story he had ever heard. But knowing the Corporal's short temper he said respectfully "Yes, Sir!" They left the court hall together with the last spectators.

In the main courtyard the official palanquin of the judge had been put in readiness. Six constables were standing in front and six behind. Two soldiers were holding the horses of Sergeant Hoong and Tao Gan by the reins.

Judge Dee emerged from his office, still clad in his ceremonial dress. Sergeant Hoong assisted him while ascending the palanquin.

Then the sergeant and Tao Gan mounted their horses. The cortège moved out into the street. Two constables ran in front carrying long poles with placards bearing the inscription "The Tribunal of Lan-fang" in large letters. Two others beating copper hand-gongs headed the procession. They shouted: "Make way! Make way! His Excellency the Magistrate is approaching!"

The crowd stood respectfully aside. When they saw

Judge Dee's palanquin they broke out in loud cheers, shouting "Long live our Magistrate!"

Sergeant Hoong who was riding by the side of the judge's palanquin bent over to the window and remarked happily:

"That is quite different from three days ago, Your Honour!"

Judge Dee smiled bleakly.

The Ding mansion proved to be an imposing building.

Young Ding came out into the first courtyard to welcome the judge. As Judge Dee descended from his palanquin an old man with a shaggy grey beard came forward and presented himself as the coroner. In daily life he was the proprietor of a well known medicine shop.

Judge Dee announced that he would proceed directly to the scene of the murder. Headman Fang and six constables would go to the main hall and there set up a temporary tribunal and make the necessary preparations for the autopsy.

Candidate Ding invited the judge and his assistants to follow him.

He led them along a winding corridor to the back courtyard. They saw a charming landscape garden with artificial rocks and a large goldfish pond in the middle. The doors of the main hall stood wide open. The servants were busy clearing away the furniture.

Candidate Ding opened a small door on left and led them through a dark, covered corridor to a small yard of eight feet square, enclosed on three sides by a high wall. The wall opposite showed a narrow door of solid wood. One panel had been battered in. Young Ding pushed this door open and stood aside to let the judge pass.

A smell of stale candles hung in the air.

Judge Dee stepped over the threshold and looked around.

It was a fairly large room of octagonal shape. High up

on the wall there were four small windows with panes of coloured glass that filled the room with a soft, diffused light. Above the windows there were two grated openings of about two feet square. This was the only ventilation; except for the door through which they had entered, there were no other openings in the wall.

A spare figure clad in a house robe of dark green brocade was slumped over the huge writing desk of carved ebony standing in the centre of the room, facing the door. The head leaned on the crooked left arm, the right hand was stretched out on the desk still holding a writing brush of red lacquer. A small skull cap of black silk had dropped to the floor exposing the victim's long grey hair.

The desk showed the usual array of writing implements. A blue porcelain vase with wilted flowers stood on a corner. On either side of the dead man there stood a copper candle stick; the candles had burned down entirely.

Judge Dee looked at the walls covered with bookshelves as high as a man can reach. He said to Tao Gan:

"Examine those walls for a secret panel. Inspect the windows and those openings there!"

As Tao Gan took off his outer robe preparatory to climbing on the bookshelves, the judge ordered the coroner to inspect the body.

The coroner felt the shoulders and arms. Then he tried to lift the head. The body had grown stiff. He had to turn it over backwards in the armchair in order to expose the dead man's face.

The unseeing eyes of the old general stared at the ceiling. He had a lean, wrinkled face, frozen in an expression of surprise. From his scraggy throat there emerged an inch of a thin blade, not thicker than half a finger. It had a curious hilt made of plain wood, not much thicker than the blade and only half an inch long.

Judge Dee folded his arms and looked down on the body. After a while he said to the coroner:

"Pull that knife out!"

The coroner had difficulty in getting a hold on the diminutive hilt. When he had it between his thumb and forefinger, however, it came out easily. It had not penetrated deeper than about a quarter of an inch.

As the coroner carefully wrapped up the short weapon in a sheet of oil paper he observed:

"The blood has thickened and the body is entirely stiff. Death must have ensued late last night."

The judge nodded. He mused:

"When the victim had barred the door he took off his ceremonial robe and cap that are hanging there next to the door, and changed into his house dress. Then he sat down behind the desk, rubbed ink and moistened his brush. The murderer must have struck shortly after, for the general had written only two lines when he was interrupted.

The curious fact is that there cannot have been more than a few moments between his seeing the murderer and the dagger being stuck in his throat. He did not even lay down his brush."

"Your Honour", Tao Gan interrupted, "there is one fact which is still more curious. I cannot see how the murderer entered this room, let alone how he left it!"

Judge Dee raised his eyebrows.

"The only way by which a person can enter this room", Tao Gan continued, "is by that door. I have examined the walls, the small windows above the bookshelves and the grated openings. Finally I examined the door itself for a secret panel. But there are no hidden entrances of any description!"

Tugging at his moustache Judge Dee asked Candidate Ding:

"Could the murderer not have slipped in shortly before or after your father entered here?"

Candidate Ding who had been standing with a glazed stare by the door now took a hold of himself and replied:

"Impossible, Your Honour! When my father came here he unlocked the door. He stood for a moment in the entrance while I knelt. Our steward stood behind me. Then I rose and my father closed the door. No one could have entered then or before. My father keeps that door always locked and he has the only key."

Sergeant Hoong bent over to the judge and whispered in his ear:

"We shall have to hear that steward, Your Honour. Yet even if we assume that the murderer somehow or other slipped in here unobserved, I cannot see how he went out again. This door was found barred on the inside!"

Judge Dee nodded. To Candidate Ding he said:

"You assume that this murder was committed by Woo. Can you point out anything that proves that he was in this room?"

Ding slowly looked round. He sadly shook his head and said:

"That Woo is a clever man, Your Honour, he would not leave any traces. But I am convinced that a further investigation will bring to light clear proof of his guilt!"

"We shall have the body removed to the main hall", Judge Dee said. "You will now go there, Candidate Ding, and see that everything is ready for the autopsy!"

Ninth Chapter

JUDGE DEE PONDERS ALONE IN A DEAD MAN'S ROOM;
THE AUTOPSY BRINGS TO LIGHT THE CAUSE OF DEATH

As soon as Candidate Ding had left Judge Dee ordered Sergeant Hoong:

"Search the victim's clothes!"

The sergeant felt through the sleeves of the robe. He took from the right sleeve a handkerchief and a small set consisting of toothpick and earcleaner in a brocade cover. He found in the left sleeve a large key of intricate design and a cardboard box. Then he felt in the dead man's girdle but found only another handkerchief.

Judge Dee opened the cardboard box. It contained nine crystallised plums, neatly arranged in three rows of three. These sweet plums are a delicacy for which Lan-fang is famous. The cover of the box bore a strip of red paper with an inscription: "With respectful congratulations".

The judge sighed and put the box down on the desk. The coroner removed the writing brush from the stiff fingers of the body. Two constables entered, and the dead General was carried away on a stretcher of bamboo poles.

Judge Dee sat down in the victim's armchair.

"You will all go to the main hall", he ordered. "I shall stay here for a while."

When the others had gone the judge leaned back in the chair and looked pensively at the bookshelves loaded with books and documents. The only empty wall space was on both sides of the door. It was flanked by scroll paintings,

JUDGE DEE IN GENERAL DING'S LIBRARY

and above it there hung a horizontal board with the engraved inscription: "Studio of Self-examination". This evidently was the name that old General Ding had bestowed on his library.

Then Judge Dee looked at the set of writing materials neatly arranged on the desk. The stone slab for rubbing the ink was a beautiful specimen, and the bamboo brush holder by its side was ·delicately carved. Next to the ink slab stood a red porcelain water container for moistening it. It was marked in blue letters "Studio of Self-examination"; evidently it had been made specially for General Ding. A cake of ink was lying on a dimunitive stand of carved jade.

On the left the judge saw two bronze paper weights. They too bore an engraved inscription: "The willow trees borrow their shape from the spring breeze; the rippling waves derive their grace from the autumn moon". This poetical couplet was signed: "The Recluse of the Bamboo Grove". Judge Dee assumed that this was the pen name of one of the General's friends who had had these paper weights made for him.

He took up the brush that the dead man had been using. It was a very elaborate one with a long tip of wolf's hair. The shaft was of carved red lacquer and bore the inscription: "Reward of the Evening of Life". Alongside there was engraved in very small, elegant characters: "With respectful congratulations on the completion of six cycles. The Abode of Tranquillity". Thus this brush was an anniversary gift from another friend.

The judge laid the brush down and had a closer look at the sheet of paper the dead man had been writing on. There were only two lines, written in a bold hand:

"Preface. Historical records go back till the distant past. Many are the illustrious men who have preserved the events of former dynasties for posterity."

Judge Dee reflected that this was a complete sentence. Thus the General had not been interrupted in the midst of his writing. Probably he had been pondering over the next sentence when the murderer struck.

The judge took up once more the red lacquer brush and idly looked at its intricate carved design of clouds and dragons. It struck him how quiet this secluded library was. Not a sound from outside penetrated here.

He suddenly felt a vague fear assail him. He was sitting in the dead man's chair, in exactly the same position as the General had been when he died.

The judge quickly looked up. He noticed with a shock that the scroll painting by the door was hanging askew. He felt a sudden panic. Was it from a secret panel behind that scroll that the murderer had stepped into the room and thrust his dagger into the General's throat? It flashed through his mind that if that were so he himself was now at the murderer's mercy. He stared fixedly at the scroll, expecting it to move aside and reveal the menacing shape.

With an effort the judge mastered his emotion. He reasoned that Tao Gan would never have overlooked so obvious a place for a secret door. Tao Gan must have left the scroll hanging askew when he had examined the wall behind.

Judge Dee wiped the cold perspiration from his forehead. His fright had passed but he still could not rid himself of the uncanny feeling that he was very close to the murderer.

He moistened the brush in the water jar and bent forward over the desk to try how it wrote. He noticed that the candlestick on his right was in the way. The judge was just going to push it aside when he suddenly arrested his movement.

He leaned back in the armchair and looked pensively at the candle. After he had written down the first two lines the murdered man had apparently paused a moment to draw that candle nearer. Not for seeing better what he was writing, for then he would have pushed the candle to the left. His eye must have fallen on something he wished to observe closely under the light. At that very moment the murderer had struck.

Judge Dee frowned. He put the writing brush down and took the candlestick in his hand. He scrutinized it carefully but could not discover anything extraordinary about it. He put it back where it had stood before.

The judge shook his head in doubt. Then he rose abruptly and left the library.

As he passed the two constables standing on guard in the corridor he ordered them to watch the library closely and let no one come near it until the broken panel would have been repaired and the door sealed.

In the main hall everything had been put in readiness.

Judge Dee seated himself behind the temporary bench. On the floor in front, the General's body was lying stretched out on reed mats.

When Candidate Ding had duly testified that that was the body of his father, Judge Dee ordered the coroner to proceed with the autopsy.

The coroner carefully took off all the dead man's garments. The poor emaciated body now was lying there fully exposed.

Candidate Ding had covered his face with the sleeve of his robe. The scribes and the other court personnel looked on in silence.

The coroner squatted by its side and examined the body inch by inch. He paid special attention to all the vital spots and felt the skull. He broke open the mouth with a silver lamella and inspected the tongue and the throat.

Finally the coroner stood up and reported: "The victim was apparently in good health and without physical defects.

On the arms and the legs there appear discoloured spots of the size of a copper cash. The tongue is covered by a thick grey film. The wound in the throat was not lethal. Death was caused by a virulent poison administered by means of the thin blade stuck in the victim's throat."

The audience gasped. Candidate Ding lowered his arm and looked at the body with a horrified expression.

The coroner unwrapped the dagger and placed it on the bench.

"Your Honour will please notice", he said, "that next to the dried blood the point shows some alien substance. That is the poison."

Judge Dee took the small dagger up by its hilt. He scrutinized the dark brown stains on the point.

"Do you know", he asked the coroner, "what poison this is?"

The coroner shook his head. He said with a smile:

"We have no means, Your Honour, to determine the nature of a poison that is administered externally. Those used internally are well known to us and we are familiar with the symptoms they produce, but those used to poison daggers are very rare. I will only go as far as saying that the colour and shape of the spots on the body suggest that it consisted of the venom of some poisonous reptile."

The judge made no further comment. He entered the coroner's statement on an official form and ordered him to read it and affix his thumbmark to it.

Then Judge Dee spoke:

"The body can now be dressed and encoffined. Bring the house steward before me!"

As the constables covered the body with a shroud and placed it on the stretcher, the house steward entered the hall and knelt before the bench.

Judge Dee addressed him:

"You are responsible for the routine of this household. Tell me exactly what happened last night. Begin with the dinner party."

"The anniversary dinner for His Excellency", the steward began, "was held in this very hall. The General presided over the table here in the middle.

Gathered round it were the General's Second, Third and Fourth Ladies, young master Ding and his wife, and two young cousins of the General's First Lady who died ten years ago. A hired band of musicians played on the terrace outside. They left two hours before the General retired.

When the hour of midnight was approaching the young master proposed a final toast. Then the General rose saying that he would retire to his library. The young master accompanied the General. I followed behind with a lighted candle.

The General unlocked the door. I stepped inside and lighted the two candles on the desk with the one I had in my hand. I can testify that the room was completely empty. When I stepped out again the young master was kneeling before the General and bidding him good night. He rose. The General put the key in his left sleeve, went inside and closed the door. Both the young master and I heard him push the crossbar in its place. This is the complete truth!"

The judge gave a sign to the senior scribe. He read out his notes of the steward's statement. The latter agreed that that was what he had said, and affixed his thumbmark.

Judge Dee dismissed the steward. He asked Candidate Ding:

"What did you do thereafter?"

Candidate Ding looked uncomfortable and hesitated to speak.

"Answer my question!", the judge barked.

"As a matter of fact", Ding said reluctantly, "I got involved into a violent quarrel with my wife. I went straight to my own quarters and my wife accused me of not having shown her proper respect during dinner. She averred that I had made her lose face to the other ladies. I felt tired after the feast and did not say much in return. Sitting on the bed I drank a cup of tea while two maids helped my wife to undress. Then my wife complained of a headache and made one of the maids massage her shoulders for half an hour or so. Then we went to bed."

Judge Dee rolled up the paper where he had jotted down his own notes. He said in a casual voice:

"I have found no evidence linking this crime with Woo."

"I beseech Your Honour", Candidate Ding cried, "to put the question to that murderer under torture! Then he will confess how he committed this foul crime!"

The judge rose and announced that the preliminary investigation was closed.

He walked back to the front courtyard without saying a word. As he ascended his palanquin Candidate Ding bowed deeply.

Once returned to the tribunal Judge Dee went straight to the jail. The warden informed him that Chien Mow was still unconscious.

The judge ordered him to have a physician called. He was to do all he could to revive Chien Mow. Then Judge Dee took Tao Gan and Sergeant Hoong to his private office.

As he sat down behind his desk the judge took from his sleeve the murderer's dagger. He told the clerk to bring a pot of hot tea.

When they had drunk a cup the judge leaned back in his chair. Slowly stroking his beard he said:

"This is a most extraordinary murder. Apart from the motive and the murderer's identity we are faced with two practical problems. First, how did the murderer enter and leave that sealed room? Second, how did he manage to thrust this queer weapon in his victim's throat?"

Sergeant Hoong shook his head in perplexity. Tao Gan looked intently at the small dagger. Letting the three long hairs sprouting from his left cheek glide through his fingers he said slowly:

"For a moment, Your Honour, I thought that I had solved the problem. When I was roaming through the southern provinces I heard people tell stories about the savages that live in the mountains; they hunt with long blow pipes. I thought that this small blade with its weird tubular handle might have been shot from such a blow pipe, and reasoned that the murderer could have aimed it from outside through the grates in the wall.

Then, however, I found that the angle at which this weapon entered the victim's throat is wholly irreconcilable with this theory, unless the murderer had been sitting under the table! Moreover I found that right opposite the back-wall of the library there is another high, blind wall. Nobody could have placed a ladder there."

Judge Dee slowly sipped his tea.

"I agree", he said after a while, "that the blow-pipe theory is untenable. Yet I also agree with your point that this dagger was not stuck directly in the victim's throat. The hilt is so small that even a child could not hold it.

I further draw your attention to the unusual shape of the blade. It is concave and resembles a gouge rather than a dagger. In the present stage of our investigation I would not like to make even a guess at how it was used. You, Tao Gan, will fashion for me an exact replica of this dagger in wood, so that I can safely experiment with it. But be careful while handling this thing, Heaven knows what deadly poison was smeared on its tip!"

"It is clear, Your Honour", Sergeant Hoong observed, "that we must also investigate further the background of this murder. Should not we summon Woo for an interrogation here?"

The judge nodded.

"I was just going to propose", he said, "that we go to visit Woo now. I always prefer to see a suspect in his own surroundings. I shall go there incognito and you, Sergeant, shall accompany me."

Judge Dee rose.

Suddenly the warden of the jail came bursting into the office.

"Your Honour!", he cried, "Chien Mow has regained consciousness. But I fear that he is dying!"

The judge hurriedly ran after him, followed by Sergeant Hoong and Tao Gan.

They found Chien Mow stretched out on the wooden couch in his cell. The warden had placed a piece of cloth dipped in cold water on his forehead. His eyes were closed and his breath came in gasps.

Judge Dee bent over him.

Chien opened his eyes and looked up at the judge.

"Chien Mow", Judge Dee asked intently, "who killed Magistrate Pan?"

Chien stared at the judge with burning eyes. He moved his lips but no sound came from his mouth. With a tremendous effort he finally brought out one indistinct sound. Then his voice trailed away.

Suddenly his large frame shook in a convulsive shudder. He closed his eyes and stretched his body as if to find a more comfortable position. Then he lay quite still.

Chien Mow was dead.

Sergeant Hoong exclaimed excitedly:

"He started to say 'You . . .' but could not continue the sentence!"

Judge Dee straightened himself. He nodded slowly and said:

"Chien Mow died before he could give us the information we need so badly!"

Looking down on the still body he added in a forlorn voice:

"Now we shall never know who murdered Magistrate Pan!"

Putting his hands in his wide sleeves the judge walked back to his private office.

Tenth Chapter

JUDGE DEE PAYS A VISIT TO AN ECCENTRIC YOUNG MAN;
HE PRESIDES AN ARTISTIC MEETING IN THE TRIBUNAL

JUDGE DEE and Sergeant Hoong had some difficulty in locating Woo's dwelling place. They asked several shops behind the Temple of the War God, but no one had heard of a man called Woo Feng.

Then the judge remembered that he lived over a wine shop called "Eternal Spring". This proved to be a well known establishment, famous for the superior quality of its wines. A street urchin took them into a side alley where they saw a red cloth banner marked "Eternal Spring" fluttering in the wind.

The shop was open in front, a high counter separated it from the street. Along the walls inside a number of large earthenware wine jars were standing on wooden shelves. Red labels pasted on their side proclaimed the excellent quality of the contents.

The proprietor, a pleasant looking round-faced man stood behind the counter idly looking out in the street while picking his teeth.

The judge and Sergeant Hoong walked round the counter and sat down at the square table inside. Judge Dee ordered a small jar of good wine. As the proprietor was wiping the table Judge Dee inquired how his business was doing.

The proprietor shrugged his shoulders.

"Nothing to boast of", he replied, "but fairly steady. And, as I always say, just enough is better than too little!"

"Have you no one to help you in the shop?", the judge asked.

The proprietor turned round to ladle some pickled vegetables from a jar in the corner. He put them in the platter on the table and said:

"I could do with some help, but unfortunately there always goes a hungry mouth with two helping hands. No, I prefer to look after things myself. And what might you two gentlemen be doing in this town?"

"We are just passing through", the judge replied. "We are silk merchants from the capital."

"Well, well!", the other exclaimed, "then you must meet my lodger, a Mr. Woo Feng, who is also from the capital."

"Is this Mr. Woo a silk merchant too?", asked the sergeant.

"No", the proprietor answered, "he is a kind of painter. I don't claim to be a judge in these matters but I have heard people say that he is quite good. And I would say that he is bound to be, for he is at it from morning till night!" Walking over to the stairway he called up: "Master Woo, here are two gentlemen with the latest news from the capital!"

A voice shouted from upstairs:

"I can't leave my work just now. Let them come up!"

The wine merchant was visibly disappointed. The judge consoled him by leaving a generous tip on the table.

They climbed the wooden stairs.

The second floor consisted of one large room lighted by a row of broad lattice windows in front and at the back, pasted over with fine white paper.

A young man clad in outlandish garb was working on a picture representing the Black Judge of the Nether World. He wore a gaudy jacket and his head was covered by a high turban of coloured silk such as is worn by some barbarian tribes over the border.

JUDGE DEE IN WOO FENG'S STUDIO

The painter had spread the silk canvas out on the huge table that stood in the middle of the room. The wall space between the windows was covered entirely by a great number of finished pictures, provisionally mounted on paper scrolls. A bamboo couch stood against the back wall.

"Sit for a while on that couch, gentlemen!", the young man said without looking up from his work, "I am putting in some blue paint here and if I stop the colour will not dry evenly."

Sergeant Hoong sat down on the couch. Judge Dee remained standing and looked with interest at the young man as he was deftly handling his brush. He noticed that the picture, though expertly drawn, showed a number of unfamiliar features, especially in the treatment of the folds in the dresses and of the faces of the persons represented. Looking round at the pictures hanging on the wall the judge found that all of them showed these same foreign features.

The young man added a last stroke, then straightened himself and started washing his brush in a porcelain bowl. As he did so he gave the judge a penetrating look. Slowly moving the brush round in the bowl he said:

"So Your Honour is the new magistrate. Since evidently you are here incognito, I shall not embarrass you with the usual formalities!"

Judge Dee was quite taken back by this sudden statement.

"What makes you think that I am a magistrate?", he asked.

The young man smiled condescendingly. He left the brush in the jar. Folding his arms he leaned back against the table so that he faced Judge Dee and remarked:

"I fancy myself as a portrait painter. Now you, Sir, are the very prototype of a judge. Pray observe this Infernal Judge on this picture here! You could have sat as model for it, though I admit it is by no means a flattering portrait!"

The judge could not forbear smiling. He realized that it was no use to try to fool this clever young man. So he said:

"You are not mistaken, I am indeed Dee Jen-djieh, the new magistrate of Lan-fang, and this is my lieutenant."

Woo nodded slowly. Looking straight at the judge he said:

"Your name is well known in the capital, Sir. Now to what am I indebted for the honour of this visit? I don't think you have come to arrest me. That job you would have left to your constables."

"What", Judge Dee inquired, "makes you think that you might be arrested?"

Woo pushed his turban back.

"Sir, please forgive me for skipping all the usual polite preliminaries. Let me save your time and mine. This morning the news spread that the old General Ding had been murdered. That, by the way, is just what the hypocritical scoundrel deserved. Now that sneaking son of his has been passing the word around that I, the son of Commander Woo who is known to be the General's arch-enemy, intended to kill him. Young Ding has been snooping in this neighbourhood for more than a month, trying to worm information about me out of the proprietor of the shop here, at the same time telling all kinds of slanderous tales.

Doubtless young Ding has now accused me of having killed his father. An ordinary magistrate would have sent out his constables to arrest me immediately. But you, Sir, are known as a man of unusual perspicacity. So you thought you would first come round here yourself and see what I looked like."

Sergeant Hoong had been listening with mounting anger tot his nonchalant statement. Now he jumped up exclaiming:

"Your Honour, the insolence of this dogshead is unbearable!"

Judge Dee raised his hand. He said with a thin smile:
"Mr. Woo and I understand each other perfectly, Sergeant! I for one find him rather refreshing!"

As the sergeant sat down again the judge continued:
"You are right, my friend. Now I shall be as direct as yourself: why did you, the son of a well known military commander in the Board of Military Affairs, settle down all alone in this out-of-the-way place?"

Woo looked round at his pictures on the wall.

"Five years ago", he replied, "I passed the examination for Junior Candidate. To the disappointment of my father I then resolved to break off my studies and devote myself to painting. I worked under two famous masters in the capital but was not satisfied with their style.

Two years ago I happened to meet a monk who had come all the way from Khotan, the tributary kingdom in the far west. That man showed me his style of painting, full of life and exciting colours. I realized that our Chinese artists ought to study that style in order to renew our national art. I thought that I might become the pioneer and resolved to travel to Khotan myself."

"Personally", the judge remarked dryly, "I find our national art perfectly satisfactory and I fail to see what a barbarian foreign nation could ever teach us. But I don't pretend to be a connoisseur. Pray proceed!"

"So I wangled travelling funds from my good father", Woo went on. "He let me go in the hope that this was youthful extravagance, and that some day I would return as a sedate young official. Until two years ago the route to the western kingdoms led via Lan-fang, thus I came here. Then I found that this route had been abandoned for the northern one. Now the plains to the west of this town are inhabited only by roaming Uigur hordes, people without art or culture."

"That being so", Judge Dee interrupted him, "why did you not leave this district at once and travel north to continue your journey?"

The young man smiled.

"That, Sir, is not so easy to make you understand. You must know that I am a lazy man and much given to moods. Somehow or other I felt comfortable here and thought that I might as well stay on for a while and practise. Moreover I took a liking to this house. I am mighty fond of wine and it suits me to have my dealer right under the same roof. That man has an uncanny intuition for a good wine and his stock can compare with the best shops in the capital. So I just stayed on here."

The judge did not comment on this statement. He said:

"Now I come to my second question. Where were you last night, say from the first to the third night-watch?"

"Here!", the young man replied immediately.

"Have you witnesses who can testify to that?"

Woo sadly shook his head.

"No", he replied, "it so happened that I did not know that the General was going to be murdered last night!"

Judge Dee went to the stairway and shouted for the proprietor.

When his round face appeared at the bottom of the stairs the judge called out:

"Just to settle a friendly argument. Did you notice whether Master Woo went out last night?"

The man scratched his head, then said with a grin:

"I am sorry I can't oblige, Sir! Last night there was much coming and going here, I really could not say whether Master Woo went out or not!"

Judge Dee nodded. He stroked his beard for some time, then said:

"Candidate Ding reported that you have hired men to spy on his mansion!"

Woo burst out laughing.

"What a ridiculous lie!", he exclaimed. "I studiously ignore that faked General. I would not spend one copper for knowing what he is doing!"

"What", the judge asked, "did your father accuse General Ding of?"

Woo's face grew serious.

"That old scoundrel", he said bitterly, "sacrificed the lives of one battalion of the Imperial army, eight hundred good men in all, to extricate himself from a difficult position. Every single man was hacked to pieces by the barbarians. General Ding would have been beheaded were it not for the fact that at that time there was widespread discontent among the troops. Therefore the authorities did not want the General's foul deed to become common knowledge. He was ordered to tender his resignation."

Judge Dee said nothing.

He walked along the walls and examined Woo's work. It were all pictures of Buddhist saints and deities. The goddess Kwan Yin was very well represented, sometimes single, sometimes with a group of attendant deities.

The judge turned round.

"If I may end a frank conversation with a frank statement", he remarked, "allow me to observe that I don't think that your so-called new style is an improvement. Maybe one must get accustomed to it. You might give me one of those pictures so that I can study your work at leisure."

Woo gave the judge a doubtful look. After a moment of hesitation he took down a medium-size picture showing the goddess Kwan Yin accompanied by four other deities. He spread it out on the table and picked up his seal, an intricately carved small block of white jade. It stood on a diminutive blackwood stand. Woo pressed the seal on a vermilion seal pad and then stamped it in a corner of the picture. The impression showed a quaint, archaic form of the character Feng, his personal name. Then he rolled the picture up and presented it to the judge.

"Am I under arrest?", he asked.

"A feeling of guilt seems to weigh heavily on your mind", the judge remarked dryly. "No, you are not under arrest. But you will not leave this house until further notice. Good day, and thanks for the picture!"

Judge Dee gave a sign to Sergeant Hoong. They went down the stairway. Woo bowed his farewell. He did not bother to conduct them to the door.

As they were walking down the main street Sergeant Hoong burst out:

"That insolent yokel would talk quite differently if he was lying in the screws before Your Honour's dais!"

The judge smiled.

"Woo is an extremely clever young man", he commented, "but he has already made his first bad mistake!"

Tao Gan and Chiao Tai were waiting in the judge's private office.

They had spent the afternoon in Chien's mansion and collected evidence relating to a few cases of extortion. Tao Gan confirmed Liu Wan-fang's statement in court that Chien Mow had personally directed most affairs; his two counsellors seemed to be just hangers-on who said "Yes!" to their master whenever required.

Judge Dee drank the cup of tea that Sergeant Hoong offered him.

Then he unrolled Woo's picture and said:

"Let us now start our artistic studies! Tao Gan, hang

this picture on the wall, next to Governor Yoo's landscape!"

The judge settled back in his armchair and looked for some time at the two paintings.

"These two pictures", he said at last, "contain the key to the Governor's last will, and to the murder of General Ding!"

Sergeant Hoong, Tao Gan and Chiao Tai turned their footstools round so that they faced the paintings.

Ma Joong came in. He looked astonished at this unusual scene.

"Sit down, Ma Joong!", the judge ordered, "and join this gathering of connoisseurs!"

Tao Gan rose and stood himself with his hands on his back in front of the Governor's landscape. After a while he turned round and shook his head.

"For a moment", he said, "I thought that some inscription in very small letters might be hidden among the leaves of the trees or in the outlines of the rocks. But I cannot discover as much as one single character!"

Judge Dee pensively tugged at his whiskers.

"Last night", he spoke, "I have pondered over that landscape for several hours and early this morning I again scrutinized it inch by inch. I must confess that this painting baffles me."

Tao Gan stroked his ragged moustache. He asked:

"Could not it be, Your Honour, that a sheet of paper has been concealed at the back of the picture, between the lining?"

"I had thought of that possibility too", the judge answered, "and therefore I examined the picture against a strong light. If a sheet of paper had been pasted between the lining it should have shown."

"When I was living in Canton", Tao Gan said, "I learned the art of mounting pictures. Shall I remove the lining

entirely and investigate also the space covered by the brocade frame? At the same time I could verify whether the
wooden rollers at top and bottom of the scroll are solid; it
is not unthinkable that the old Governor concealed a tightly
rolled piece of paper inside."

"If thereafter you can restore the scroll again to its
original form", the judge answered, "by all means try. Although I must confess that such a hiding place seems rather
crude to me and unworthy of the Governor's brilliant mind.
But we can not afford to pass over the slightest chance for
solving this riddle.

This Buddhist picture by our friend Woo is quite
another proposition. It contains a definite clue."

Sergeant Hoong asked astonished:

"How can that be, Your Honour? Woo selected that
picture for you himself!"

Judge Dee smiled his thin smile.

"That is because Woo did not realize how he had betrayed himself", he answered. "Woo may have no high
opinion of my artistic sense, but I saw something in his
picture that he himself had overlooked."

Judge Dee sipped his tea. Then he ordered Ma Joong to
call Headman Fang.

When Fang was standing in front of the desk Judge Dee
looked at him gravely for a while. Then he said kindly:

"Your daughter Dark Orchid is doing well, my First
Lady informs me that she is an industrious and intelligent
worker."

The headman bowed deeply.

"I am rather reluctant", the judge continued, "to take
your daughter from her present safe surroundings, all the
more so since there is as yet no news about the fate of your
eldest daughter White Orchid. On the other hand Dark
Orchid is the most suitable person to gather information

for me in the Ding household. With the impending funeral of the General the house will be in great confusion and they will need extra-servants. If Dark Orchid could get herself a position there as temporary maid, she could find out much inside information from the other servants. I do not wish to do anything, however, without the consent of you, her father."

"Your Honour", the headman answered quietly, "I and my family consider ourselves your slaves. Moreover my youngest daughter is an independent and enterprising girl, she would enjoy executing such an order."

Ma Joong had been shifting uneasily on his chair. Now he interrupted:

"Is that not rather a job for Tao Gan, Your Honour?"

The judge shot a shrewd glance at Ma Joong. He replied:

"There is no better source of information on what is going on in a household than the tittle-tattle of the maids. Instruct your daughter, Headman, to go to the Ding mansion straight away!

As to our friend Woo, I want a double watch on him. You, Ma Joong, will go there tonight as the open watcher. You should make it appear as if you try to remain unobserved but in such a way that Woo realizes that you are a man from the tribunal sent to watch him. You will give him every opportunity to leave the house unobserved. Put all your skill and experience in this job, Ma Joong. This Woo is an extraordinarily clever young fellow!

Tao Gan will be the real watcher, he should take good care to remain hidden. As soon as Woo has eluded Ma Joong, Tao Gan will follow Woo secretly and find out where he goes and what he does. If he tries to leave the city you can come out in the open and arrest him."

Tao Gan looked pleased. He said:

"Ma Joong and I have practised this trick of the double

watch before, Your Honour! I shall now first take the Governor's painting and moisten it so that the lining can soak loose during the night. Then I shall start out with Ma Joong."

When Tao Gan and Ma Joong had taken their leave, the judge consulted with Chiao Tai and Headman Fang about the affairs of the Chien mansion.

He decided that Chien Mow's wives and concubines could be sent back to their respective families. The house servants should be released with one month salary advanced by the tribunal. Only the steward was to be detained for further questioning.

Chiao Tai reported that he was very satisfied with the discipline of the soldiers. Every morning and afternoon he took them through a strenuous military drill. He added that they stood in deadly fear of Corporal Ling.

When the headman and Chiao Tai had left, Judge Dee leaned back in his armchair.

He reflected that after all these years of working together he really knew very little about Chiao Tai. He had been Ma Joong's companion in "the green woods", but about his earlier life the judge knew nothing. Judge Dee had heard Ma Joong's entire story, and several episodes of it even twice. But Chiao Tai had always been very reticent. He seemed to take so much pleasure in his military duties in Lan-fang that Judge Dee wondered whether Chiao Tai had not been originally a career officer. He promised himself that he would try to find out in the near future.

But there were many other more pressing affairs. With a sigh the judge started to study the documents relating to Chien Mow's misdeeds that Tao Gan had placed on his desk.

Eleventh Chapter

TAO GAN HAS AN ADVENTURE IN AN OLD TEMPLE;
MA JOONG MEETS HIS MATCH IN A DRINKING BOUT

MA JOONG thought it unnecessary to disguise himself. He
only changed the black cap that marked him as an officer
of the tribunal for a pointed bonnet such as is worn by
people of the working class. Tao Gan replaced his cap by
a collapsible one of black, thin gauze.

Before leaving, the two held a brief consultation in the
quarters of the guards.

"It is easy enough", Ma Joong remarked, "to make
myself conspicuous and give Woo to understand that I am
stationed there to watch that he does not leave his quarters. But we don't know how that bastard will react. What
if he goes out and tries to shake me off on the way?"

Tao Gan shook his head.

"He won't do that", he replied. "The point is that Woo
does not know what your instructions are. He won't dare
to go out and risk your arresting him on the spot, for that
would be construed by the tribunal as a suspicious move.
No, my only worry is that Woo won't try to elude you at
all and decides to stay at home as ordered. But if he slips
out, you can be sure that I'll pick him up!"

Then they left the tribunal. Ma Joong walked ahead and
Tao Gan followed him at some distance.

Sergeant Hoong had explained to Ma Joong the location.
He found the Eternal Spring wine shop without difficulty.

Its interior looked most inviting. The light of two coloured

116

paper lanterns shone on the red labels of the wine jars. The proprietor was measuring a pint of wine. Two loafers were leaning on the counter in front, leisurely picking pieces of salted fish from a platter.

Ma Joong saw that opposite the shop stood a middle-class dwelling house. He went to stand on the raised porch with his back against the black-lacquered door.

On the second floor of the wine shop several candles had been lighted. Ma Joong saw a shadow move across the paper of the lattice windows. Apparently Woo was hard at work.

Ma Joong bent forward and looked up and down the dark street. There was no sign of Tao Gan. He folded his arms and prepared himself for a long wait.

When the two happy drinkers had finished their pint of wine, the door behind Ma Joong suddenly swung open. An elderly gentleman was shown out by the gatekeeper. As he saw Ma Joong he asked:

"Did you wish to see me?"

"Not me!" said Ma Joong curtly. He turned round and leaned against the doorpost.

"Now listen!", the gentleman said angrily, "this happens to be my house. Since you admit that you have no business here, I would thank you for walking on!"

"This street", Ma Joong growled, "is public property. No one can prohibit me from standing here!"

"You make yourself scarce quickly, my man!", the gentleman called out, "or I shall call the nightwatch!"

"If you don't like me to stand here, you bastard", Ma Joong shouted, "you just try and push me!"

The two loafers had turned round to follow the altercation. Leaning their backs against the counter they contentedly folded their arms to watch the fight.

A window on the second floor was pushed open. Woo

looked out and shouted encouragingly to no one in particular: "Hit him over his head!"

"Shall I call the other servants, Master?" the gatekeeper asked.

"Call all the bastards together!", Ma Joong barked, "I am ready for them!"

The gentleman seeing his bellicose attitude thought better of it.

"I won't have fisticuffs in front of my door", he snapped. "Let that yokel stand there till his bones rot!"

Then he walked away, muttering angrily.

The gate keeper slammed the door shut. Ma Joong heard a crossbar being pushed in its position.

Woo, disappointed, closed his window.

Ma Joong sauntered over to the wine shop. The two loafers hurriedly made room for him along the counter.

Ma Joong gave them a baleful look and said sourly:

"I hope that you two don't belong to that pleasant household over there."

"No, we are from the next street", replied one. "That fellow who lives opposite is a schoolmaster, and always grumpy."

"We don't come here to recite our lessons", the other loafer added, "but for a snack and a drink at this hospitable counter!"

Ma Joong guffawed. He put a handful of coppers on the counter and called out to the proprietor:

"One pint of the best!"

The proprietor came forward hurriedly. He filled the cups to the brim and placed a new platter with dried fish and salted vegetables in front of them. He asked cheerfully:

"Where might you be coming from, stranger?"

Ma Joong drained his cup in one gulp and waited till the proprietor had refilled it. Then he said:

"I am the coachman of Mr. Wang, the big tea dealer from the capital. We arrived here this afternoon with three carts of tea cakes to be sold over the border. The master gave me three good silver pieces and told me to go and amuse myself. I meant to find myself a handsome wench. But I must have come to the wrong quarter!"

"Yes, in that case you are surely a long way from your destination", the proprietor answered. "The barbarian beauties from over the border are located in the Northern Row, nearly an hour's walk from here. The Chinese ladies live in the Southern Row, beyond the lotus lake in the southeastern corner of the city." Then he added ingratiatingly: "But the women here won't seem any good to a refined gentleman from the capital like you. Now yours must be a very lively profession. Why don't you come in and tell us a few of your adventures on the road?"

As he spoke he pushed the coppers back to Ma Joong and said:

"That first round was on the house!"

The two loafers, looking forward to a gratis drinking bout were immediately full enthusiasm.

"A hefty fellow like you", one said to Ma Joong, "certainly has knocked out many a dangerous robber in his day!"

Ma Joong let himself be persuaded. They entered the shop and sat down at the square table. Ma Joong chose the seat facing the stairs.

The proprietor joined them and soon the cups were passing round with amazing swiftness.

When Ma Joong had told some hair-raising stories he saw Woo coming down the stairs.

He stopped halfway and shot Ma Joong a penetrating look.

"Won't you join us, Master Woo?", the proprietor called out. "This gentleman tells the most remarkable stories!"

"I am busy just now", Woo replied, "but I shall come down later in the evening. See that there is something left for me!"

So speaking he went up again.

"That is my lodger, a jovial fellow", the proprietor remarked. "You will enjoy talking with him. Don't leave before he comes down!"

And he poured out another round.

In the mean time Tao Gan had been busy.

As soon as he had seen Ma Joong take up his position opposite the wine shop, Tao Gan had entered a dark alley. He quickly took off his robe, and put it on again inside out.

Now this robe was specially made. Its outside was good brown silk and looked very dignified. But the lining consisted of rough hemp-cloth with dirty spots and several clumsy patches. Tao Gan gave a pat on his cap; it flattened out and became a bonnet as is often worn by beggars.

In this disreputable attire he entered the narrow space that divided the row of houses in Woo's street from the backwalls of those in the next.

Between the walls it was very dark, the ground was covered with refuse. Tao Gan had to pick his way carefully. He halted when he thought that he would be at the back of the wine shop. Tao Gan stood on his toes and found that he could just reach the top of the wall. He pulled himself up and looked over the wall.

The back of the shop itself was dark. On the floor above, however, all windows were lighted. The backyard was full of empty winejars neatly stacked in double rows. There was no doubt that this was the rear of Woo's house.

Tao Gan let himself down again. He rummaged about till he had found a broken wine jar. He rolled it to the foot of the wall. Standing on top of it he could place his elbows on the wall. He laid his chin on his arms and leisurely surveyed the situation.

A narrow balcony ran all along the rear of Woo's atelier. The painter had placed there a row of potted plants. Below there was the plastered backwall of the wine shop. A narrow door stood ajar. Next to it Tao Gan saw a small outhouse that he took to be the kitchen. He reflected that it would be easy for Woo to leave his room by climbing down from the balcony.

He waited patiently.

After about half an hour one of Woo's windows was slowly pushed open. Woo looked out.

Tao Gan did not move. He knew that he was invisible against the darkness behind him.

Woo stepped over the window sill. He walked as surefooted as a cat along the narrow balcony till he was above the outhouse. Then he climbed over the balustrade and let himself down on the sloping roof. For a moment he crouched on the tiles, apparently looking for an empty space among the winejars below. Then he jumped down neatly between two stacks and quickly made for the narrow passage that separated the wine shop from the house next door.

Tao Gan left his observation post. He ran out of the alley as fast as he could. He nearly broke a leg when he stumbled over an old wooden box. When he turned the corner of the alley he collided with Woo.

Tao Gan uttered a low-class oath. But Woo hurried on without looking back, making for the main street.

Tao Gan followed him at some distance.

There was a large crowd about in the street and Tao Gan needed not be careful to keep in the shadows. Woo was easy to follow because of his outlandish turban that bobbed over the black caps of the crowd.

Woo kept walking on in southerly direction. Suddenly he turned into a side street.

Here there were fewer people about. Without stopping in his brisk walk, Tao Gan pulled up the button in the middle of his cap till it had become the pointed bonnet of a commoner. He took from his sleeve a bamboo tube of about one foot long. This was one of Tao Gan's many clever devices. It was a trick tube that contained six others of decreasing size. He pulled it out and it became a bamboo staff. Tao Gan changed his gait into the more sedate walk of an elderly householder.

He walked on till he was quite near Woo.

The painter turned into another alley and Tao Gan walked on behind him. They were now in a quiet area, Tao Gan reflected that they could not be far from the eastern city wall. Woo seemed to be quite familiar with this neighbourhood. He entered a narrow side street that seemed completely deserted.

Tao Gan looked round the corner before he followed Woo. He saw that it was a blind street that ended in the archway of a small Buddhist temple. It had apparently been abandoned for the wooden gate had been demolished and no light showed within. There was no one about.

Woo walked straight on and climbed the crumbling stone steps leading up to the archway. There he stood still and turned round. Tao Gan hastily drew his head back.

When he looked again, Woo had disappeared into the temple.

Tao Gan waited a while, then emerged in the open and calmly sauntered to the temple. Over the archway he could faintly see three characters of weather-beaten colour-ed tiles inlaid among the bricks. They read: "Hermitage of the Three Treasures".

Tao Gan went up the steps and entered.

The temple seemed to have been deserted many years ago. All the furniture was gone and the place where the altar had stood was empty. He saw nothing but bare stone walls. Here and there the roof had caved in and he could see stars in the evening sky.

Tao Gan explored its interior, walking on tiptoe. But there was no trace of Woo.

Finally he looked out of the back door. He hastily withdrew behind the doorpost.

There was a small walled-in garden with a fishpond in the middle. On its bank stood an old stone bench. Woo was sitting there alone.

He had cupped his chin in his hands and seemed to find the old pond of absorbing interest.

"This must be a secret trysting place!", Tao Gan said to himself.

He found a window niche where he could sit down and keep an eye on Woo, while at the same time he remained hidden for any newcomers.

Having established himself there Tao Gan folded his arms and closed his eyes, straining his ears for any sound. He did not dare to look at Woo too often for he knew that many people are sensitive to a hidden stare.

He sat there for quite some time. Nothing happened.

Woo occasionally would change his posture. Once or twice he picked up a few pebbles and amused himself by throwing them into the pond. Finally he rose and started pacing up and down the yard, apparently lost in deep thought.

Another half hour passed.

Then suddenly Woo made to leave.

Tao Gan shrank back in his niche, flattening himself against the damp stone wall.

Woo walked back home at a brisk pace, looking neither left nor right.

Returned to his own alley he stood still on the corner and

looked out. Evidently he wanted to see whether Ma Joong was out in the street. Then he swiftly walked on and disappeared into the narrow passage between the wine shop and its neighbour.

Tao Gan sighed resignedly and strolled back to the tribunal.

In the wine shop all were in high spirits.

After Ma Joong's fund of stories had become exhausted, the proprietor had told quite a number of his own. The two loafers were a grateful audience. They vigorously clapped their hands after every story and were fully prepared to keep this up for hours on end.

Finally Woo came downstairs and joined the party.

Ma Joong had drunk more rounds of wine than he cared to remember. But he had a tremendous capacity and his head was still clear. He thought that if he could make Woo drunk he might elicit some useful information from him.

Thus he hailed Woo boisterously as a fellow-citizen of the capital, and offered him a toast.

That was the beginning of a drinking bout that was talked about in that quarter for many months afterwards.

Woo complained that he was far behind the others. He emptied half a jar of strong white liquor in a rice bowl, and drank it down in one gulp. The wine had as little effect on him as if it had been water.

Then he shared a pint with Ma Joong, and told a long but very amusing story.

Ma Joong began to notice the influence of the wine. He racked his brain and told a rowdy tale. With some difficulty he reached the end of his narration.

Woo shouted his approval. He emptied three cups in rapid succession. Then he pushed his turban back from his forehead, placed his elbows on the table and started to tell a string of queer stories about events in the capital, pausing only to drink some more.

THE DRINKING BOUT IN THE ETERNAL SPRING WINE SHOP

This he did with great relish, emptying his cup always in one draught.

Ma Joong kept him faithful company. He thought vaguely that Woo was a very companiable man. He remembered that he wanted to ask him something but could not think what it was. Ma Joong proposed another round.

The two loafers were the first to pass out. The proprietor had them carried home by some friends of the neighbourhood. Ma Joong concluded that he was getting very drunk. He started to tell a spicy story but somehow or other he got mixed up when he approached the end. Woo emptied another cup and told a ribald joke that made the proprietor howl with mirth. The point of the tale had escaped Ma Joong but he still thought it a remarkably funny one and laughed loudly. He drank another toast to Woo.

Woo's face had turned red and perspiration trickled down his brow. He took off his turban and threw it in a corner.

From that moment on the conversation was very confused. Ma Joong and Woo talked both at the same time. They paused only for clapping their hands and drinking more.

It was past midnight when Woo announced that he wanted to go to bed. He rose with difficulty from his chair and succeeded in reaching the bottom of the stairs, all the time haranguing Ma Joong about their eternal friendship.

As the proprietor helped Woo to climb up Ma Joong reflected that the wine shop was a very pleasant and hospitable place. He quietly slid to the floor and immediately started to snore uproariously.

Twelfth Chapter

JUDGE DEE DISCUSSES THE SECRETS OF TWO PICTURES;
A YOUNG GIRL DISCOVERS PASSIONATE LOVE LETTERS

THE next morning when Tao Gan was crossing the main courtyard on his way to the judge's private office, he saw Ma Joong sitting hunched on a stone seat, his head in his hands.

Tao Gan stood still and looked for a moment at this silent figure. Then he asked:

"What is wrong with you, my friend?"

Ma Joong made a vague gesture with his right hand. Without looking up he said in a hoarse voice:

"Go away, brother, I am resting. Last night I had a few drinks with Woo. Since it had grown late I decided to stay overnight in that wine shop, hoping that I would learn more about Woo's activities. I walked back here half an hour ago."

Tao Gan gave him a doubtful look. Then he said impatiently:

"Come along! You must hear my report to His Excellency and see what I have brought here!"

As he spoke he showed Ma Joong a small package wrapped up in oil paper.

Ma Joong reluctantly rose from his seat. They left the courtyard and entered Judge Dee's private office.

The judge was sitting behind his desk absorbed in a document. Sergeant Hoong was sitting in a corner sipping his morning tea. Judge Dee looked up from his papers.

"Well, my friends", he said, "did our painter go out last night?"

Ma Joong rubbed his big hand over his forehead.

"Your Honour", he said unhappily, "my head feels as if it were full of stones. Tao Gan will be able to present our report!"

Judge Dee shot a searching look at Ma Joong's gaunt features. Then he turned to listen to Tao Gan.

Tao Gan related in detail how he had followed Woo to the "Hermitage of the Three Treasures", and about his curious behaviour there.

When he had finished, Judge Dee remained silent for a while, a deep frown furrowing his brow. Then he exclaimed:

"So the girl did not turn up!"

Sergeant Hoong and Tao Gan looked astonished and even Ma Joong evinced some interest.

The judge took the picture that Woo had given him. He rose and unrolled it on the desk, placing a paper weight on either end.

Then Judge Dee took a few sheets of writing paper and covered the picture up in such a way that only the face of the goddess Kwan Yin was visible.

"Look carefully at this face!", he ordered.

Tao Gan and the sergeant rose. They bent their heads over the picture. Ma Joong was going to leave his footstool also but he sat down again quickly with a look of pain.

Tao Gan said slowly:

"This certainly is an unusual face for a goddess, Your Honour! Buddhist female deities are always depicted with a serene, quite impersonal face. This, however, rather seems a portrait of a living young girl!"

Judge Dee looked pleased.

"That is exactly what it is!", he exclaimed. "Yesterday when I looked over Woo's pictures it struck me that all his paintings of Kwan Yin show the same, very human face.

I concluded that Woo must be deeply in love with a certain girl. Her image is continually in his mind. Thus whenever he paints a female deity he gives it the features of this girl, probably without realizing it himself. Since Woo undoubtedly is a great artist, this picture must be a good portrait of that mysterious girl. It shows a definite personality.

I am convinced that this girl is the explanation why Woo did not leave Lan-fang. She may provide the clue that links him with the murder of General Ding!"

"It should not be too difficult to trace this girl", Sergeant Hoong observed. "We might have a look around in the neighbourhood of that Buddhist temple."

"That", Judge Dee said, "is a very good idea. All three of you will imprint this picture on your memory!"

Ma Joong rose with a groan and had a look at the picture too.

He pressed his hands against his temples and closed his eyes.

"What ails our wine bibber?", Tao Gan inquired nastily.

Ma Joong opened his eyes.

"I am sure", he said slowly, "that I have met that girl once. Somehow or other her face is familiar to me. But try as I may I cannot remember when and where I saw her!"

Judge Dee rolled the scroll up again.

"Well", he said, "when your head is clear it may come to your mind. Now what have you brought there, Tao Gan?"

Tao Gan opened the package with great care. It contained a wooden board with a small square sheet of paper pasted on its surface.

He put it in front of the judge saying:

"Your Honour please be careful! The thin paper is still moist and will easily tear. Early this morning as I was peeling off the lining of the Governor's painting, I discovered this sheet pasted behind the lining of the brocade mounting. This is the testament of Governor Yoo!"

The judge bent forward over the small writing.

Then his face fell. He leaned back in his chair and angrily tugged at his whiskers.

Tao Gan shrugged his shoulders.

"Yes, Your Honour, appearances often prove deceptive. That Mrs. Yoo has been trying to fool us."

The judge pushed the board over to Tao Gan.

"Read it aloud!" he ordered curtly.

Tao Gan read:

> "I, Yoo Shou-chien, feeling the end of my days draw near, hereunder state my last will and testament.
>
> Since my second wife Mei has been guilty of adultery and the son she gave birth to is not my flesh and blood, all my possessions shall go to my eldest son Yoo Kee who shall continue the tradition of our ancient house."
>
> Signed and sealed: Yoo Shou-chien

After a slight pause Tao Gan remarked:

"Of course I compared the seal impressed on this document with the Governor's seal on the painting itself. They are perfectly identical."

A deep silence reigned.

Then Judge Dee leaned forward and crashed his fist on the table.

"Everything is completely wrong!", he exclaimed.

Tao Gan gave Sergeant Hoong a doubtful look. The sergeant imperceptibly shook his head. Ma Joong goggled at the judge.

Judge Dee said with a sigh:

"I shall explain to you why I am certain that there is something fundamentally wrong here.

I depart from the premise that Yoo Shou-chien was a wise and farsighted man. He fully realized that his eldest son Yoo Kee had a wicked character and that he was violently jealous of his young half-brother; until Yoo Shan was born Yoo Kee had for years considered himself as the only heir. When the Governor's end drew near his last thoughts were how to protect his young widow and his infant son against the wiles of Yoo Kee.

The Governor knew that if he divided his property equally between his two sons, not to speak of disinheriting Yoo Kee, the latter would certainly harm his infant half-brother and perhaps even kill him to appropriate his part of the inheritance. Therefore the Governor made it appear as if he disinherited Yoo Shan."

Sergeant Hoong nodded and gave Tao Gan a significant look.

"At the same time", the judge went on, "he concealed in this picture the proof that half or the greater part of his property should go to Yoo Shan. This is evident from the curious formula which the old Governor employed when he expressed his last will. He said clearly that the scroll should go to Yoo Shan, and 'the rest' to Yoo Kee; he carefully refrained from defining this 'rest'.

The Governor's idea was through this hidden testament to protect his infant son until he would have grown into a young man and could take possession of his inheritance. He hoped that after ten years or so a wise magistrate would discover the hidden message of the scroll and restore to Yoo Shan his rightful inheritance. It is therefore that he instructed his widow to show the scroll to every new magistrate that would be appointed to this district."

"That instruction, Your Honour", Tao Gan interrupted, "may never have been given. We have only Mrs. Yoo's word for it. In my opinion this document proves clearly that Yoo Shan is an illegitimate child. The Governor was a kind and forbearing man, he wished to prevent Yoo Kee from avenging the wrong done to his father. At the same time he wished to make sure that in due time the truth could be established beyond doubt. This is why he concealed the document in this scroll. When a clever magistrate would have discovered it he would be able to dismiss any claim that Mrs. Yoo might try to file against Yoo Kee."

The judge had listened carefully to this argument. He asked:

"How then do you explain that Mrs. Yoo is so eager that the riddle of this scroll is solved?"

"Women", Tao Gan replied, "are liable to overrate the influence they have on the man who loves them. I am convinced that Mrs. Yoo hopes that the old Governor in his benevolence has concealed in the scroll some money draft or a direction how to find a hidden sum of money, to compensate her for losing part of the property."

The judge shook his head.

"What you say", he remarked, "is quite logical, but it does not accord with the old Governor's character. I am convinced that this document here is a forgery produced by Yoo Kee. It is my theory that the Governor hid some unimportant document in this scroll in order to lead Yoo Kee on to a false trail. As I said before, this is too crude a device for Governor Yoo to have used for concealing something of real importance. Next to this false clue, the picture must contain a real message concealed in a much more ingenious manner.

Since the Governor feared that Yoo Kee would suspect that this scroll contained something valuable and would have it destroyed, he inserted some document in the lining for Yoo Kee to find. Thus he made sure that Yoo Kee, having found that, would not search further for the real clue.

Mrs. Yoo told me that Yoo Kee kept the scroll for over a week. That would have given him sufficient time for discovering the document. Whatever it was, he replaced it by this spurious testament, so that he would be safe no matter what Mrs. Yoo would do with the scroll."

Tao Gan nodded. He said:

"I admit, Your Honour, that that is also a very attractive theory. But I still think that mine is the simpler one."

"It should not be too difficult", Sergeant Hoong remarked, "to find a specimen of Governor Yoo's handwriting. Unfortunately he used archaic script for his inscription on this landscape painting."

Judge Dee said pensively:

"I had planned to visit Yoo Kee in any case. I shall go there this afternoon and try to secure a good specimen of the Governor's regular handwriting and of his signature. You will go there now with my namecard, Sergeant, and announce my visit."

The sergeant and his colleagues rose and took their leave.

As they were crossing the courtyard the sergeant said:

"Ma Joong, what you need is a large pot of hot, bitter tea. Let us sit down in the guard house for a while. I would not like to leave the tribunal before we had cheered you up a bit!"

Ma Joong agreed.

In the guard house they found Headman Fang sitting at the square table talking earnestly with his son. The latter rose hastily when he saw the three men enter and offered them seats.

They all sat down and the sergeant ordered the constable on duty to bring a pot of bitter tea.

After some desultory talk Headman Fang said:

"When you people came in I was just discussing with my son where we should search for my eldest daughter."

Sergeant Hoong sipped his tea. Then he said slowly:
"I don't wish to mention a subject that must be painful
to you, Headman. Yet I feel that we should not ignore the
possibility that White Orchid had a secret lover and eloped
with him."

Fang shook his head emphatically.

"That girl", he said, "is quite different from my youngest
daughter. Dark Orchid is headstrong, she has a very
independent character. She knew exactly what she wanted
ever since she was but as high as my knee, and usually
knew how to get it too. Dark Orchid should have been
born a boy. My eldest, on the contrary, was always quiet
and obedient. She has a soft, pliable character. I can assure
you that she never even thought of having a lover, let alone
eloping with one!"

"That being so", Tao Gan remarked, "I fear that we
must be prepared for the worst. Could not some low ruffian
have kidnapped her and sold her to a brothel?"

Fang sadly nodded his head.

"Yes", he said with a sigh, "you are quite right. I too
think that we should check the licensed quarters. You know
that there are two of that kind in this town. One, called the
Northern Row, is located in the northwest corner of the
city wall. The girls there are mostly from over the border,
that quarter prospered greatly during the time when the
route to the west still led through Lan-fang. Now that
Northern Row has fallen on bad times, it is a favourite
haunt for the scum of this city.

"The other one, known as Southern Row, consists of
high-class establishments only. The girls there are all
Chinese, and some are quite educated. They are not unlike
the courtesans and singing girls of the larger cities."

Tao Gan pulled at the three hairs on his left cheek.

"I would say", he observed, "that we should start with

the Northern Row. I gather from what you say that the houses of the Southern Row would not dare to kidnap girls. High class establishments like those are always careful not to offend against the law; they buy their girls in the regular way."

Ma Joong laid his big hand on the headman's shoulder:

"As soon as our judge has cleared up the murder of General Ding", he said, "I shall request that the job of locating your eldest daughter is entrusted to Tao Gan and me. If there is any man who can find her, it is this wily old trickster, especially when I am at hand to do the rough work for him!"

Fang thanked Ma Joong with tears in his eyes.

At that moment Dark Orchid entered the gate, demurely dressed as a housemaid.

"How do you like the work, my girl?", Ma Joong called out.

Dark Orchid ignored him completely. She bowed deeply to her father and said:

"I would like to report to His Excellency, father. Would you kindly take me there?"

Fang rose and excused himself. Sergeant Hoong went out to transmit Judge Dee's message to Yoo Kee, and the headman crossed the courtyard followed by his daughter.

They found Judge Dee sitting alone in his office, his chin cupped in his hands. He was deep in thought.

As he looked up and saw Fang and his daughter his face brightened. He acknowledged their bows with a friendly nod and then said eagerly:

"Take your time, my child, and tell me all about your experiences in the Ding household!"

"There can be no doubt, Your Honour", Dark Orchid began, "that the old General was in great fear for his life. The maids in the Ding mansion told me that all the food had first to be fed to a dog in order to prove that it had not been poisoned. The front and side gates had to be kept locked day and night, which is a great nuisance for the servants as they have to unlock the door for every visitor or tradesman who comes to the house. The servants don't like working there, everyone in his turn is the object of the old General's suspicion, and closely questioned by the young master. They don't stay longer there than a few months on end."

"Describe the members of the household!", the judge ordered.

"The General's First Lady died some years ago and now the Second Lady directs the household. She is in continual fear lest the others shouldn't treat her with sufficient respect and she is not an easy mistress to work for. The Third Lady is quite an uneducated person, fat and lazy, but not hard to please. The Fourth Lady is very young; the General acquired her here in Lan-fang. I suppose that she is of the kind that men find attractive. But while she was dressing this morning I noticed that she has an ugly mole on her left breast. She spends the greater part of the day in front of her mirror, if she is not trying to wangle some money from the Second Lady.

Young Master Ding lives with his wife in a small, separate courtyard. They have no children. She is not very good-looking and a few years older than her husband. But they say that she is quite accomplished and has read many books. The young master has occasionally brought up the question of taking a second wife, but she would never allow it. He now tries to make up to the young maidservants but without much success. Nobody likes to work in that household and the maids don't care whether they offend the young master or not.

This morning when I was cleaning young Master

Ding's room, I rummaged a bit in his private papers."

"That was not what I ordered you", the judge remarked dryly.

Fang gave his daughter an angry look.

Dark Orchid blushed and went on quickly:

"I found in the back of a drawer a package of poems and letters written by young Master Ding. The literary style was too difficult for me, but I gathered from the few sentences I was able to understand that the contents are very peculiar. I brought the package with me to show to Your Honour."

As she spoke she put her slender hand in her sleeve and took out a bundle of papers. She handed them to the judge with a respectful bow.

Judge Dee shot a quizzical look at the indignant Fang, then rapidly glanced through the papers.

He put them down and said:

"These poems speak of a forbidden love affair, and in such a passionate language that it is all to the good that you could not understand them. The letters are of similar content, and all signed 'Your slave Ding'. Apparently young Ding wrote them to give vent to his passion, for they were apparently never sent to their destination."

"The young master would hardly have written such things for the blue-stocking that his wife is!", Dark Orchid remarked.

Her father soundly boxed her ears, shouting:

"Don't you dare to speak if you are not asked to, you forward hussy!" Turning to the judge he added apologetically: "It is all because my good wife is not there to educate her, Your Honour!"

Judge Dee smiled.

"When we are through with this murder case, Headman" he said, "I shall arrange a suitable marriage for your daughter. There is nothing better for a wayward young girl than to settle down to the regular household routine."

Fang respectfully thanked the judge. Dark Orchid looked furious but she did not dare to speak.

Tapping the package with his forefinger, Judge Dee said:

"I shall have these copied out immediately. This afternoon you will put back the originals where you found them. You did not do badly, young woman! Keep your ears and eyes open, but be careful not to pry into closed drawers and cupboards. Report again to me tomorrow."

As Fang and his daughter took their leave, the judge had Tao Gan called in.

"I have here a collection of letters and poems", he said. "You will copy them out carefully and try to deduce from all these passionate effusions some clue as to the identity of the lady to whom they are addressed."

Tao Gan glanced the poems through. His eyebrows shot up.

YOO KEE WELCOMES JUDGE DEE TO HIS MANSION

Thirteenth Chapter

THE judge went to Yoo Kee's mansion accompanied only by Sergeant Hoong and four constables.

As his palanquin was being carried over the ornamental marble bridge he looked with appreciation at the nine-storied pagoda that rose up from the lotus lake on left.

Then they turned west and followed the river till they came to the deserted southwest corner of the city.

Yoo Kee's mansion stood apart on a stretch of waste-land. The judge noted that it was surrounded by quite a formidable wall. He reflected that this property was near the Watergate; people would like to have solid houses here in case of raids on the city by the barbarians from over the river.

As soon as the sergeant had knocked on the main gate the double doors swung open. Two doorkeepers bowed deeply while Judge Dee's palanquin was carried into the main courtyard.

When the judge descended a plump man of medium height hurriedly came down the steps of the reception hall. He had a large, round face with a short, pointed moustache. His small eyes darted to and fro under thin eyebrows, matching his quick movements and his hurried speech.

Bowing respectfully he said:

"This person is the landowner Yoo Kee. Your Excellency's visit is a signal honour for my poor hovel. Please deign to enter!"

Yoo Kee led the judge up the stairs and through the high door of the reception hall. He offered his guest the seat of honour in front of the large, altar-like table against the back wall.

Judge Dee saw at a glance that the hall was furnished in a quiet, refined style. He assumed that the solid antique chairs and tables, and the fine paintings on the walls came from the collection of old Governor Yoo.

While a servant was pouring out the tea in a set of choice antique porcelain, the judge began:

"I have made it a habit always to visit the prominent citizens of the district where I am appointed magistrate. In your case this is all the more pleasant since I had been looking forward to meeting the son of so distinguished a statesman as the late Governor Yoo Shou-chien."

Yoo Kee jumped from his chair. He bowed quickly three times in succession before the judge. As he sat down again he rattled on:

"Ten thousand thanks for Your Honour's kind words! Yes, my late father was a most remarkable man, most remarkable indeed! How unfortunate that this person is so unworthy a son of so great a father! Alas, real talent is bestowed by Heaven. It can be further cultivated through assiduous study. If, however, as in my own case, Your Honour, the foundation is not there, study from morning till night will be of no avail. But I hope I can claim at least that I realize my own limitations. I am not a gifted man, Your Honour, therefore I never dared to aspire to any high office. I merely pass my days quietly, supervising my houses and my land!"

He smiled ingratiatingly, rubbing his plump hands. Judge Dee opened his mouth to speak but Yoo Kee went on:

"I am ashamed that I am so unworthy of conversing with a man of Your Honours' learning. Most vexing, for I feel immensely honoured that so famous a magistrate condescends to visit my poor house. I humbly congratulate Your Honour on the quick arrest of that scoundrel Chien Mow. What a brilliant achievement! Former magistrates here just submitted to Chien. Most regrettable! I well remember that my revered father often commented unfavourably on the low moral standard of the younger officials. Ahem, Your Honour is of course an exception. I mean to say, as is well known . . ."

Yoo Kee hesitated a moment. Judge Dee quickly interrupted:

"The late Governor must have left you quite some property."

"Yes indeed!", the other replied, "and what a misfortune that I am so stupid! It takes practically all my time to look after the administration of the land. And the tenants, Your Honour, the tenants! Quite honest people of course, of the best, I dare say, but always those arrears in the rent! And the local servants here, what a difference to the people in the capital! I always say . . ."

"I gather", Judge Dee said firmly, "that you have a beautiful country estate outside the cast gate."

"Oh yes", Yoo Kee replied, "yes, that is a fine piece of land."

Then, for once, he stopped of his own account.

"Some day", Judge Dee said, "I should like to see the famous maze out there."

"An honour! An honour!", Yoo Kee exclaimed excitedly. "Unfortunately the place is in a bad state. I would have liked to rebuild the mansion but my revered father was so fond of it and even gave special instructions that nothing should be touched. Yes, Your Honour, I am a stupid man, yet not deficient in filial piety, I fondly hope. My father left an old couple in charge, faithful old retainers, but quite incapable of keeping the estate. But you know how it is with those old servants, it is more or less understood that they should not be bothered. I have never gone out there, as a matter of fact, Your Honour will understand, the old couple might think . . ."

"I am particularly interested in that maze", Judge Dee said patiently. "I hear that it is a most ingenious one. Have you ever been inside?"

Yoo Kee's small eyes flashed with an uneasy glint.

"No, that is to say . . . No, I have never ventured inside. To tell Your Honour the truth, my father was very particular about that maze. He alone knew the secret . . ."

"I suppose", Judge Dee remarked casually, "that the late Governor's widow knew the secret of that maze?"

"A sad thing!", Yoo Kee cried, "Your Honour must know that my mother died when I was still very young. What a misfortune that was! And after a long, painful illness too!"

"As a matter of fact", Judge Dee observed, "I rather referred to the Governor's second wife, your stepmother."

Yoo Kee again jumped from his chair with amazing agility. As he walked up and down in front of the judge he exclaimed:

"That distressing affair! How unfortunate that we must speak about that! Your Honour will realize how painful it is for a devoted son to be compelled to admit that his revered father ever made a mistake. A most human mistake, I should add, and one inspired only by his lofty, generous nature.

Alas, Your Honour, my father let himself be deceived by a clever, wicked woman. She succeeded in exciting his pity, and he married her. Ah, these women! Instead of being grateful, she deceived him with Heaven knows what young rascal. Adultery, Your Honour, a black, abominable crime! My father knew, but he suffered in silence. Not even to me, his own son, did he communicate his sorrow. It was only on his deathbed, in his last words, that at last he revealed this awful wrong!"

Judge Dee tried to say something but Yoo Kee went on:

"I know what Your Honour is going to say: I should have accused that woman in the tribunal. But I could not bear the thought that my old father's private affairs would be dragged out in the tribunal before the vulgar crowd. I could not bear it!"

Yoo Kee covered his face with his hands.

"To my great regret", the judge said dryly, "this affair will have to be discussed in the tribunal. Your stepmother filed a complaint against you, contesting the oral will and claiming half of the property."

"The ingrate!", Yoo Kee cried, "the unspeakable woman! She must be an evil fox-spirit, Your Honour! No human being could sink so low!"

He burst out in sobs.

Judge Dee slowly emptied his teacup. He waited till Yoo Kee had sat down and composed himself. Then he said in a conversational tone:

"I always regret that it has never been given to me to meet your late father. But a man leaves his spirit behind in his handwriting. Would it be importunate to ask you whether I might see some specimens of his calligraphy? The late Governor was famous for his original hand."

"Ah!", Yoo Kee exclaimed, "another misfortune! How embarrassing that I am unable to obey Your Honour's orders! This was another of my father's unexpected traits. No, let me put it correctly, another proof of his great modesty. When he felt his end approaching he gave me strict orders to burn all his writings. He observed that there was no specimen of his brushwork that deserved being preserved for posterity. What a sublime character!"

Judge Dee murmured a suitable comment. Then he asked:

"Since the Governor was such a famous man, I suppose that many people here in Lan-fang cultivated his friendship?"

Yoo Kee smiled disdainfully.

"This border place", he replied, "has not one single man with whom my late father cared to converse. Barring, of course, Your Honour! How my revered father would have enjoyed talking with Your Honour! He always was so interested in administrative affairs . . . No, my father was greatly occupied by his own literary studies and spent all his spare time supervising the work of the peasants on his land. That is why that woman was able to make up to him . . . Well, well, how I am chattering away!"

Yoo Kee clapped his hands and ordered more tea.

Judge Dee silently stroked his beard. He reflected that his host was an extremely astute man. He said so much that he said practically nothing.

While Yoo Kee prattled on and on about the inclement climate of Lan-fang, Judge Dee slowly sipped his tea.

Suddenly he asked:

"Where did your father paint his pictures?"

Yoo Kee gave his guest a bewildered look. He did not reply for a few moments. He scratched his chin. Then he answered:

"Wel, not being much of an artist myself . . .Let me see now. Yes, my father did his painting in a pavilion behind the country mansion. Lovely place, right at the back of the garden, neàr the entrance of the maze. I believe that the large table my father used to work on is still there. At least if the old doorkeeper has taken proper care of it. Your Honour knows, those old servants . . ."

Judge Dee rose.

Yoo Kee insisted that he should stay a little longer. He set out on another, confused story.

It was not without difficulty that the judge at last succeeded in taking leave of his host.

Sergeant Hoong was waiting for his master in the gate-keeper's lodge. They returned to the tribunal.

As Judge Dee sat down behind his desk he heaved a deep sigh.

"What a tiring man is that Yoo Kee!", he remarked to Sergeant Hoong.

"Did Your Honour discover new data?", the sergeant asked eagerly.

"No", the judge replied, "but Yoo Kee said one or two things that may perhaps prove to be important. I did not succeed in securing a specimen of the Governor's handwriting to compare with the testament Tao Gan found inside the scroll. Yoo Kee claims that his father ordered him to destroy all his writings after his death. I thought that perhaps the Governor's friends here in Lan-fang might possess some, but Yoo Kee avers that his father had not one single friend. What is your impression of that mansion, Sergeant?"

"While I was waiting in the gatekeeper's lodge", Sergeant Hoong replied, "I had a long talk with the two door-men. They think that their master is a bit queer in the head. He is as eccentric as his father but he lacks the Governor's brilliant mind.

Although Yoo Kee himself is far from an athlete, he has a great love of boxing, wrestling and swordfighting. Most of the servants in that mansion have been selected for their physical prowess. Yoo Kee likes nothing better than to see them practise. He has made the second courtyard into a kind of arena and he will sit there for hours, shouting encouragement to the fighters and giving prizes to the winners."

Judge Dee slowly nodded his head.

"Weak men", he observed, "will often have an exaggerated veneration for physical strength."

"The servants say", the sergeant continued, "that Yoo Kee once lured the best fencing master of Chien Mow's mansion away by offering him a huge bribe. Chien was very angry. Yoo Kee is not a brave man, he expects every day that the barbarians will come and raid the city. That is the reason why he insists that his servants must be good fighters. He has even hired two Uigur warriors from over the river to instruct his servants in Uigur fighting methods!"

"Did the servants say anything about the old Governor's attitude to Yoo Kee?", inquired Judge Dee.

"Yoo Kee must have stood in deadly fear of his father", Sergeant Hoong replied. "Even the old Governor's death did not alter this. After his burial Yoo Kee sent all the old servants away because they reminded him too much of the awful presence of the old Governor. Yoo Kee has executed all his father's last instructions to the letter, including that everything on the country estate had to be left exactly as it was. Yoo Kee has never gone there since his father's death. The servants say that he changes colour if one as much as mentions that place!"

Judge Dee stroked his beard.

"One of these days", he said pensively, "I shall visit that country mansion and have a look at the famous maze. In the meantime you will inquire where Mrs. Yoo and her son are living and invite them to come and see me. Perhaps Mrs. Yoo has kept some specimens of the old Governor's handwriting. Then I can also verify Yoo Kee's statement that his father had no friends here in Lan-fang.

As to the murder of Magistrate Pan, I have not yet given up hope entirely of obtaining a clue to that mysterious visitor of Chien Mow's. I instructed Chiao Tai to question all the former guards of Chien's mansion, and Headman Fang would interrogate Chien's second counsellor in jail. I am also considering whether to send Ma Joong to investigate the haunts where the low-class criminals of this city gather. If it was that mysterious man in the background who murdered Magistrate Pan, he must have had accomplices."

"And at the same time, Your Honour", the sergeant remarked, "Ma Joong might make inquiries there about the headman's eldest daughter, White Orchid. We talked it over with Fang this morning and he admits that very likely she was kidnapped and sold to a brothel."

The judge said with a sigh:

"Yes, I fear that that is indeed what happened to that poor girl."

After a while Judge Dee continued:

"As yet we have made very little progress with General Ding's murder. I shall order Tao Gan to go tonight to the Temple of the Three Treasures and see whether Woo or that unknown woman he is so fond of depicting shows up there."

The judge took a document from the pile that Tao Gan had brought during his absence. Sergeant Hoong, however, seemed reluctant to go. After some hesitation he said:

"Your Honour, I cannot get it off my mind that we overlooked something in General Ding's library. The more I think about it the more I am convinced that the clue to that riddle is to be found there!"

Judge Dee put the document down and looked intently at the sergeant.

He opened a small lacquer box and took out the replica of the small dagger that Tao Gan had made for him. While he let it rest on his palm he said slowly:

"Sergeant, you know that I have no secrets from you.

Although I am considering various vague theories about the background of General Ding's murder, I must state frankly that I have not the faintest idea how this dagger was used, or how the murderer entered and escaped!"

Both were silent for some time.

Suddenly the judge made a decision.

"Tomorrow morning, Sergeant, we shall again go to the Ding mansion and search that library. Perhaps you are right and it is there that we must look for the solution of this crime!"

Fourteenth Chapter

A STRANGE CLUE IS FOUND IN A DEAD MAN'S ROOM;
JUDGE DEE SENDS HIS MEN TO ARREST A CRIMINAL

THE next morning the weather was fine. It promised to be
a clear and sunny day.

After he had had his breakfast Judge Dee informed
Sergeant Hoong that he planned to go the Ding mansion
on foot.

"I shall also take Tao Gan", the judge added. "A little
exercise will do him good!"

They left the tribunal by the western gate.

The judge had not informed Candidate Ding in advance
of his intended visit. They found the mansion in the midst
of preparations for the burial.

The steward led the judge and his two companions to a
side room. The main hall had been converted into a mor-
tuary, and there the body of the General was lying in state
in an enormous coffin of lacquered wood before which
twelve Buddhist priests were reading sutra's aloud. Their
monotonous chanting and the beating of wooden gongs
resounded through the mansion, and the smell of incense
hung heavily in the air.

Judge Dee noticed in the corridor a side table loaded
with piles of anniversary gifts, all wrapped in red paper
with congratulary messages attached.

The steward saw the judge's astonished look and hastened
to apologize. He said that these presents which now seemed
so macabre would have been cleared away long since, were

it not that all the servants were wholly occupied in making the preparations for the General's burial.

Young Ding came rushing into the room clad in a mourning robe of white hemp cloth. He started to apologize profusely for the disorder in his house.

Judge Dee cut short his explanations.

"Today or tomorrow", he said, "I shall hear your case in the tribunal. Since there are two or three points I wished to verify, I resolved to pay you this quite informal visit.

I shall now proceed once more to your late father's library. You need not bother to accompany us."

They found two constables on guard in the dark corridor that led to the library. They reported that no one had even approached that place.

Judge Dee broke the seal and opened the door.

He hastily stepped backward covering his face with his long sleeve.

A nauseating smell assailed their nostrils.

"There is something dead in there", the judge said. "Go to the main hall, Tao Gan, and ask those priests for a few sticks of Indian incense!"

Tao Gan hurried away.

He came back with three lighted incense sticks in each hand. They made a dense smoke with a penetrating smell.

The judge took them and once more entered the library waving the sticks so that he was enveloped in a cloud of blue smoke.

The sergeant and Tao Gan waited outside.

After a while Judge Dee emerged. He was carrying a thin forked stick that is used for suspending scroll pictures on the wall. On its end rested the half decayed body of a mouse.

He handed the stick to Tao Gan and ordered: "Have the constables put this dead animal in a sealed box!"

Judge Dee remained standing in front of the open door. He had placed the sticks of incense in the brush holder on the desk inside. Clouds of smoke wafted out of the door.

As they were waiting for the stench to disappear Sergeant Hoong remarked with a smile:

"That little animal gave me quite a fright, Your Honour!"

Judge Dee's face was impassive.

"You will not laugh, Sergeant, after you have entered that room. It is full of the spirit of violent death!"

When Tao Gan had come back all three of them entered the library.

Judge Dee pointed to a small cardboard box that was lying on the floor.

"The other day", he said, "I left that box on the desk, next to the ink slab. It is the box with the sweet plums that we found in the General's sleeve. A mouse smelled them. See, its little feet are clearly visible in the dust that gathered on the desk."

The judge stooped and picked up the box carefully with two fingers. He laid it on the desk.

They saw that a corner of the cover had been gnawed away.

The judge opened the box. One plum of the nine was missing.

"This was the murderer's second weapon", Judge Dee said gravely. "These plums are poisoned!"

He ordered Tao Gan:

"Search the floor for that plum. Don't touch it!"

Tao Gan went down on his knees. He found the plum, half eaten, under one of the bookshelves.

Judge Dee took a toothpick from the seam of his robe and stuck it in the plum. He put it back in the box and replaced the cover.

"Wrap this box up in a sheet of oilpaper", he said to

Sergeant Hoong. "We shall take it to the tribunal for further investigation."

The judge looked around. Then he shook his head.

"Let us return to the tribunal", he said. "Tao Gan will seal this door again, and the two constables shall remain on guard outside."

They walked back in silence.

As he entered his private office the judge called out to the clerks to bring a pot of hot tea.

He sat down behind his desk. Tao Gan and the sergeant sat down on their customary footstools.

Silently they drank a cup of tea.

Then Judge Dee spoke:

"Sergeant, let one of the runners go out and call that old coroner here!"

When the sergeant had gone the judge said to Tao Gan:

"This murder becomes more and more complicated. Before we have even determined how the murderer struck we find that he kept a second weapon in reserve. As soon as we find out that the accused Woo has a mysterious girl friend, we learn that also the complainant Ding has a secret lover!"

"Could not it be, Your Honour", Tao Gan said slyly, "that it is one and the same girl? If Woo and Ding are rivals in love, that would throw an entirely new light on the latter's accusation!"

Judge Dee looked pleased.

"That", he said, "is a very interesting suggestion!"

After a pause Tao Gan resumed:

"I still can't understand how the murderer succeeded in making General Ding accept that box with poisoned plums! The murderer must have handed it to him personally. We saw the pile of anniversary gifts on the table in the corridor. He would not have put it there, for how could he be sure that the General would pick up that particular box? It might have as well been taken by Candidate Ding or another member of the household."

"And then", the sergeant remarked, "we have also this problem: why did the murderer not remove this box from the General's sleeve after he had killed him? Why leave this piece of evidence on the scene of the crime?"

Tao Gan shook his head perplexedly. After a while he said:

"Seldom have we been confronted with so many difficult problems at the same time. Apart from this murder we have the hidden message in that landscape painting there on the wall, and all the while Chien Mow's mysterious visitor is still roaming about freely and planning Heaven knows what new mischief. Is there no clue to his identity at all?"

Judge Dee smiled bleakly.

"Nothing at all", he replied. "Last night Chiao Tai told me that he had interrogated Chien's former guards and his counsellors. None of them could supply any information. The mysterious stranger always came late at night and his long cloak concealed his build. He never spoke a word. The ower part of his face was covered by his neckcloth, the upper lpart concealed by the shadow of his hood. He even didnot show his hands, he always kept them inside his sleeves!"

They drank another cup of tea.

Then a clerk announced that the coroner had arrived.

Judge Dee gave the old drug dealer a sharp look.

"The other day when you performed the autopsy on the General's body", he said to him, "you stated that most poisons used internally can be identified. Now I have here a box with sweet plums. A mouse ate one and died on the spot. You will examine these plums in my presence and try to determine what poison they contain. If necessary you can also examine the dead mouse."

Judge Dee handed the cardboard box to the coroner.

The old man opened the small bundle he had brought and took out a leather folder. It contained a set of thin knives with short blades and long handles. He selected one that had a fine, hair-sharp blade.

Then he took a square pad of white paper from his sleeve and put it on the corner of the desk. He picked up with a pair of pincers the plum the mouse had eaten from and laid it on the pad. With remarkable dexterity he cut from its flesh a slice as thin as the thinnest tissue paper.

The judge and his two lieutenants eagerly followed his every movement.

The coroner smoothed out the slice on the pad using the blade of the knife. He peered intently at it. Then he looked up and asked for a cup of boiled water, an unused writing brush, and a candle.

When a clerk had brought the required materials, the coroner moistened the brush and soaked the thin slice in water. Then he took a small square piece of very white, glazed paper, spread it out over the slice and pressed it with the palm of his hand.

The coroner lighted the candle. He took up the glazed paper and showed it to the judge; it bore the wet imprint of the slice. The coroner held it over the flame till it had dried.

He took the paper over to the window and scrutinized it for some time, softly running his forefinger over it. Tao Gan left his chair and looked over the coroner's shoulder.

The coroner turned round and handed the paper to the judge. He said:

"I beg to report that this plum contains a large dose of a poisonous dye called gamboge. It was introduced by means of a hollow needle."

Judge Dee slowly caressed his whiskers. After a glance at the paper he asked: "How do you prove that?"

"This method", the coroner said with a smile, "has been used in our trade for many centuries. The alien matter in the juice of the plum is recognized by its colour and granulation. If Your Honour observes this imprint, a yellow tinge will be clearly recognisable. The difference in granulation can be noticed only by the sensitive fingers of an experienced drug dealer. Since the slice shows a number of small round spots I conclude that the gamboge was introduced by means of a hollow needle."

"Excellent work!", the judge said approvingly. "You will now examine the other plums."

As the coroner set to work Judge Dee idly played with the empty cardboard box. He pried loose the folded white paper that covered its bottom. Suddenly he bent over it and peered intently at a faint red mark on the edge of the paper.

"Well, well", he remarked, "what a careless thing to do!"

Sergeant Hoong and Tao Gan rose and eagerly bent their heads over the paper. Judge Dee pointed with his forefinger at the red mark.

"That is half of Woo's seal!", the sergeant exclaimed. "The same seal as the one he impressed on the picture the other day!"

The judge leaned back in his armchair.

"Thus two clues point straight to our painter", he said. "First, the poison used. Gamboge is used by all painters as a yellow pigment and they are familiar with the fact that it is dangerous poison. Second, this sheet of paper employed as filling of the box. I suppose that Woo once used it as support for impressing his seal on a picture; inadvertently half of the seal impression was transferred on this paper underneath."

"This is the sort of thing we have been waiting for!", Tao Gan exclaimed excitedly.

The judge did not comment. He waited silently till the coroner had completed his examination of the other plums.

Finally the old man reported:

"Everyone of these contains a lethal dose of gamboge, Your Honour!"

The judge selected a sheet of the official writing paper on his desk and pushed it over to the coroner.

"Please record your testimony on this paper!", he ordered, "and affix your thumbmark to it!"

The old coroner moistened his brush and filled out the document. After he had affixed his thumbmark to it the judge dismissed him with a few kind words. Then he ordered, a clerk to call Headman Fang.

When the headman came in Judge Dee ordered curtly:

"Take four constables and arrest the painter Woo Feng!"

Fifteenth Chapter

PAINTER WOO REVEALS HIS SECRET IN THE TRIBUNAL;
JUDGE DEE ORDERS A SEARCH OF THE EASTERN CITY

THREE beats of the large bronze gong resounded through the tribunal announcing the opening of the afternoon session.

A fair crowd of spectators had assembled in the court hall. The old General Ding had been a well-known resident of Lan-fang.

Judge Dee ascended the dais. He ordered Candidate Ding to come forward.

As he was kneeling in front of the bench Judge Dee spoke:

"The other day you appeared before this tribunal and accused Woo Feng of having murdered your father. I have made a painstaking investigation and assembled evidence that warranted Woo's arrest. Yet there are not a few points that need clarification.

I shall now hear the accused and you will listen carefully. If there should come up any point concerning which you can supply additional information, you shall not fail to speak!"

Judge Dee filled out a slip for the warden of the jail. Soon two constables led Woo into the court hall. As he approached the dais Judge Dee noticed that he looked quite unperturbed.

Woo knelt and waited respectfully till the judge addressed him.

"State your name and profession!", the judge said curtly.

"This insignificant person", Woo replied, "is called Woo Feng. I am a Junior Candidate by profession and a painter by preference."

"You", said the judge sternly, "are accused of having murdered General Ding Hoo-gwo. Speak the truth!"

"Your Honour", Woo said calmly, "I emphatically deny the accusation. I am familiar with the victim's name and the crime for which he was dismissed from military service because I often heard my father speak about that disgraceful affair. But I beg to state that I have never met the General. I did not even know that he was living in Lan-fang until his son started to spread malignant rumours about me. Those rumours I totally ignored since they were so ridiculous as to make refutation quite unnecessary."

„If that is so", Judge Dee said coldly, "why then did the General stand in constant fear of you? Why did he keep the gates of his mansion closed day and night and confine himself to his locked library? And if you did not plan some foul scheme against the General, why did you hire ruffians to spy on his mansion?"

"As to Your Honour's first two questions", Woo replied, "they concern the internal affairs of the Ding mansion. Since I am completely ignorant of such things, I am in no position to express any opinion. As regards the last query, I deny ever having hired any people to spy on the Ding family. I challenge my accuser to produce one of those men I allegedly hired and confront him with me!"

"Don't be too sure, young man!", the judge said sternly. "As a matter of fact I have already apprehended one of those ruffians. You will be confronted with him in due time!"

Woo shouted angrily:

"That scoundrel Ding bribed him to give false testimony!"

When he saw that at last Woo had lost his temper, Judge Dee thought to himself that this was the right moment to spring another surprise on the accused.

He leaned forward in his chair and said sharply:

"I, the magistrate, shall tell you why you hated the Ding family! Not because of the feud between your father and General Ding. No, you had a quite personal and despicable motive. Look at this woman here!"

While he was saying this the judge had taken from his sleeve a section cut out of Woo's painting showing only the face of the goddess Kwan Yin.

As he handed it to Headman Fang to pass it on to Woo, Judge Dee kept his eye on both the accused and Candidate Ding. He noticed that as soon as he had referred to a woman in the case both young men had turned pale. Ding's eyes widened in sudden fear.

Judge Dee heard a stifled cry by his side.

Headman Fang stood there with the picture still in his hand. His face had turned ashen, he looked as if he had seen a ghost.

"Your Honour!", he cried out, "this is my eldest daughter, White Orchid!"

A murmur rose from the crowd at this unexpected revelation.

"Silence!" the judge shouted in a thunderous voice.

He did not betray his own utter amazement but said quietly:

"Headman, give that picture to the accused!"

Judge Dee had not failed to observe that while Woo was greatly perturbed by the headman's identification, Candidate Ding looked relieved. That young man heaved a deep sigh and the colour came back to his cheeks.

Woo looked at the picture with a fixed stare.

"Speak up!", the judge barked, "what are your relations with this girl?"

Woo was deadly pale. But his voice was steady as he replied: "I refuse to answer!"

The judge leaned back in his chair. He said coldly:
"The accused seems to forget that he is in the tribunal. I order you to answer my question!"

"You can torture me to death", Woo replied in a clear voice, "but you will never succeed in making me answer that question!"

Judge Dee sighed. He said:

"You are guilty of contempt of court!"

At a sign from the judge, two constables tore down Woo's robe. Two others grabbed his arms and pressed him forward till his face touched the floor. Then they looked expectantly at Headman Fang who was standing there with the heavy whip in his hand.

The headman looked up at the judge with a tortured expression on his face.

Judge Dee understood. Fang was a just man, he feared that in his anger he would flog Woo to death. The judge pointed at a sturdy constable.

He took over the whip from the headman. He raised his muscular arm and the thin thong descended on Woo's bare back.

Woo groaned as welt after welt rose on his flesh. After the tenth blow the blood streamed from his torn back. But he gave no sign that he would speak.

After the twentieth blow his body grew limp.

The constable reported that he had fainted. Judge Dee gave a sign and two constables jerked Woo to his knees. They burned vinegar under his nose till he had regained consciousness.

"Look at your magistrate!", Judge Dee ordered.

A constable gripped Woo by his hair and pulled his head back.

The Judge leaned forward and looked intently at his contorted face.

Woo's lips moved convulsively. Then he said in a toneless voice: "I shall not speak!"

The constable with the whip was going to strike Woo in his face with the heavy handle. But Judge Dee raised his hand. He addressed Woo in a conversational tone:

"Woo, you are an intelligent youngster. You must realize how utterly foolish your attitude is. Let me tell you that I know more about your relations with that poor misguided girl than you think!"

Woo only shook his head.

"I know", the judge continued calmly, "all about your meeting White Orchid in the Hermitage of the Three Treasures, near the east gate, and . . . "

Suddenly Woo jumped up. He tottered on his feet and a constable had to grip his arm to steady him. Woo did not notice it. He lifted his bare right arm, streaked with blood. Shaking his fist at the judge he cried in a strident voice:

"Now she is lost! It is you, you dog-official, who have murdered her!"

Loud exclamations rose from the crowd. Headman Fang stepped forward and stammered incoherent questions. The constables did not know what to do.

Judge Dee hammered his gavel on the bench. He shouted in a stentorious voice:

"Silence and order!"

The murmur died out.

"If I have to issue one more warning", Judge Dee said sternly, "I shall have the hall cleared! Everyone stand in his appointed place!"

Woo had collapsed on the floor. His body shook with sobs. Headman Fang stood stiffly at attention. He bit his lips till the blood trickled from his chin.

Judge Dee slowly stroked his beard.

Then his deep voice broke the uneasy silence.

"Junior Candidate Woo, you will realize that there is nothing left but to tell the entire story. If, as I gather from your last remark, I have endangered White Orchid's life by mentioning your meeting her in that deserted temple, it is you who are responsible for her plight. You had ample opportunity to warn me."

The judge gave a sign to the constables. They offered Woo a cup of strong tea. He gulped it down. Then he said in a forlorn voice:

"Her secret is now known to the entire town! She cannot be saved!"

Judge Dee observed dryly:

"Leave it to this tribunal to decide whether she can be saved or not! I repeat, tell the entire story!"

Woo mastered himself. He began in a low voice:

"Near the East Gate there stands a small Buddhist temple, called Hermitage of the Three Treasures. Many years ago, when the route to the west still led over this city, monks from Khotan built that hermitage. Later they left. The temple fell into decay, people of the neighbourhood took away the doors and other woodwork for firewood. But the magnificent wall paintings by the monks remained.

I discovered those murals by accident when I was roaming over the city in search of Buddhist works of art. I often went there and made copies of the murals. I took a liking to the small secluded garden behind the temple. I used to stroll out there at night to enjoy the moon.

One evening, about three weeks ago, I had been drinking heavily. I resolved to walk to the temple to let my head cool in the garden there.

When I was sitting on the stone bench, I suddenly saw a girl enter the garden."

Woo bent his head further down. Deep silence reigned in the court hall.

Woo looked up with unseeing eyes. He went on:

"She seemed to me our Lady Kwan Yin descended upon earth. She was clad in a single thin robe of white silk. A white silk shawl covered her head. Her lovely face bore an expression of deep, unutterable sadness, tears glistened on her pale cheeks. Those heavenly features are engraved on my mind. I shall remember them as long as I live!"

He covered his face with his hands. Then he let his arms drop listlessly.

"I rushed to her, stammering I know not what confused words. She shrank back in fright and whispered: 'Don't speak, go away! I am afraid!' I sank to my knees in front of her and implored her to trust me.

She drew her robe closer round her and said in a low voice: 'I have orders never to leave the house, but tonight I slipped away. I must go back now, else I shall be killed! Tell no one. I shall come again!'

Then a cloud obscured the moon. In the darkness I faintly heard her quick footsteps.

That night I searched the temple and its neighbourhood for hours. But I could find no trace of her."

Woo paused. Judge Dee gave a sign to offer him another cup of tea. Woo impatiently shook his head and continued:

"Since that unforgettable evening I have gone to that temple nearly every night. But she never came. It is clear that she is kept a prisoner. Now that her secret visit to the temple is known, the fiend that keeps her will kill her!"

Woo broke out in sobs.

After a short pause Judge Dee spoke:

"Now you see for yourself how dangerous it is not to tell the complete truth. The tribunal shall do all that is possible to locate that girl. You, meanwhile, had now better confess how you murdered General Ding!"

Woo cried:

WOO FENG'S STRANGE ENCOUNTER IN THE TEMPLEGARDEN

"I shall confess anything you like! But not now. I beseech Your Honour to send out your men now to save that girl! It may yet not be too late!"

Judge Dee shrugged his shoulders. He nodded to the constables. They dragged Woo up and led him back to the jail.

"Candidate Ding", the judge spoke, "this is quite an unexpected development. Evidently it has nothing to do with Woo's murdering your father. It is clear, however, that the accused is in no condition to be interrogated further.

I here break off the hearing of your case. It will be continued in due time."

The judge let his gavel descend on the bench. Then he rose and left the dais.

The crowd of spectators slowly filed out of the court hall, busily discussing amongst each other the exciting new developments.

While Judge Dee changed in his informal robe he ordered Sergeant Hoong to call Headman Fang.

Ma Joong and Tao Gan sat down on footstools by the side of the judge's desk.

When the headman had entered Judge Dee said:

"Headman, this is a great shock for you. It is unfortunate that I did not show you that picture earlier, but I could not have surmised that it was in any way connected with your eldest daughter. However, this is the first definite indication of her whereabouts."

While speaking the judge had taken up his vermilion brush and filled out three official forms.

"You will now", he continued, "collect twenty armed constables and go immediately to that Hermitage of the Three Treasures. Ma Joong and Tao Gan shall direct you. They are the two best men I have, with great experience in such work. These warrants will authorize you to enter and search every house in that quarter!"

The judge impressed the large seal of the tribunal on the documents and handed them to Ma Joong.

Ma Joong hastily stuffed them in his sleeve. Then all three rushed away.

Judge Dee ordered the clerk to bring a pot of hot tea. When he had drunk a cup he said to Sergeant Hoong:

"I am glad that the headman has at least some information about his missing daughter. Now it has come out that it was she who is depicted on Woo's paintings, I realize that there is some resemblance to Fang's youngest daughter, Dark Orchid. I ought to have noticed that immediately!"

"The only one who did see some resemblance, Your Honour", the sergeant said slyly, "was our brave fighter Ma Joong!"

The judge smiled thinly.

"It would seem", he said, "that Ma Joong observed Dark Orchid with more attention than you or I!"

Then the judge's face set again in its usual stern mien. He said slowly:

"Heavens knows in what condition they will find that poor girl, if at all. If one translates the poetic description of our excitable artistic friend into everyday language, it is clear that on her visit to the temple White Orchid wore a common night robe. That means that she was kept imprisoned in a house quite near that temple, probably by some degenerate lecher. When he discovered that she had secretly left the house he may well have become afraid and killed her. Some day her body will be discovered in a dry well..."

"In the meantime", Sergeant Hoong observed, "this does not bring us much nearer to the solution of the General's murder. I fear that we shall have to put the question to Woo under torture."

The judge did not react on the sergeant's second remark. He said:

"I noticed one interesting fact. When during the session I mentioned a woman in the case both Woo and Ding turned pale; the latter was definitely afraid. As soon as Ding heard that it was the headman's daughter, he was visibly relieved. This means that there is also a woman connected with the General's murder. Evidently the same person as the one Ding wrote his passionate poetry to."

A soft knock sounded on the door.

Sergeant Hoong rose and opened. Dark Orchid came in. She bowed deeply before the judge and said:

"I could not find my father, Your Honour, so I made bold to come here alone to present my report."

"You are most welcome, young woman!", Judge Dee said eagerly. "We were just discussing the Ding mansion. Tell me, do you know whether young master Ding spends much of his time outside?"

Dark Orchid emphatically shook her small head.

"No, Your Honour", she replied, "the servants wish he would go out more. He hangs about in the house practically the entire day, snooping round and trying to catch them out in some mistake or omission. Once one of the maids even saw him late at night walking stealthily down a corridor. Probably he was checking up on whether the servants were gambling!"

"What was the reaction to my unexpected visit this morning?" the judge asked.

"I was in the young master's room when a servant reported Your Honour's arrival. He was sitting there drawing up an estimate of the costs of the funeral with his wife. The young master was very pleased that Your Honour had come again. He said to his wife: 'Did I not tell you that that first investigation of father's library was very superficial?

DARK ORCHID REPORTS TO JUDGE DEE

I am glad that the judge has come back, I feel certain that they overlooked many clues!' His wife remarked sourly that he should not think that he was more clever than a magistrate and he hastily went out to welcome Your Honour."

The judge silently sipped his tea. Then he said:

"Well, I am grateful to you for the work you have done. You have sharp ears and eyes! It is not necessary that you return to the Ding mansion. This afternoon we obtained some information about your elder sister, and your father has gone to search for her. Go to your quarters now; I hope sincerely that when your father comes back he will have good news!"

Dark Orchid hastily took her leave.

"It is curious", Sergeant Hoong remarked, "that Candidate Ding did not often go out at night. One would expect that he had some secret love-nest where he met that unknown woman!"

Judge Dee nodded.

"On the other hand", he said, "it may be an old affair that is long over and done with. Sentimental people have an unfortunate habit of keeping souvenirs of past affairs. Yet the originals that Dark Orchid showed me seemed written very recently. Did Tao Gan find any clue to the woman's identity in those papers he copied out?"

"No", Sergeant Hoong replied, "but Tao Gan certainly enjoyed that work! He copied the texts out in his best calligraphy, chuckling all the time."

Judge Dee smiled indulgently. He rummaged among the piles of documents on his desk till he found Tao Gan's copies, neatly written out on ornamental letter paper.

Leaning back in his armchair the judge started reading. After a while he said:

"Well, it is all about the same subject, expressed in different ways. Candidate Ding was deeply enamoured. As if poetry could serve no better purpose! Listen:

The studded door is locked, the bed curtains drawn close,
Embroidered coverlets are a soft home of love;
Who thinks of Rites and Proper Conduct in this trance?
Empassioned lovers care not what the Codes impose.
Her feet like lotus buds, her lips like pomegranate,
Her rounded thighs, her breasts like fresh-fallen snow —
Who ever deems the full moon marred by its spots?
It's the blemish that completes the beauty of agate.
Who praises perfumes rare of the far-distant West?
The fragrance of her limbs bemuses the enraptured mind
He is a fool who with such beauty right before his eyes,
Still travels far and wide, a useless quest . . .

The judge threw the paper disdainfully on his desk.

"It rhymes", he remarked dryly, "that is about all that can be said for it!" He slowly smoothed his long beard.

Suddenly the judge stiffened. He picked up the sheet which he had been reading aloud and eagerly scanned it.

Sergeant Hoong knew that Judge Dee had made a discovery. He rose and looked over the judge's shoulder.

Judge Dee crashed his fist on the table.

"Get me the testimony of the house steward, delivered during the preliminary hearing in the Ding mansion!", he ordered.

Sergeant Hoong fetched the leather box that contained the file of General Ding's murder. He extricated a sealed document.

Judge Dee read it through from beginning to end.

Then he put it back in the box. He left his armchair and started pacing the floor.

"What incredible fools people in love are!" the judge suddenly exclaimed. "I have now found the solution of half the General's murder. What a foul, despicable crime!"

MA JOONG INVESTIGATES THE LICENSED QUARTER;
HE IS MADE A PARTNER IN A NEFARIOUS SCHEME

THE first nightwatch had sounded when Ma Joong, Tao Gan and Headman Fang gathered in the house of the warden of the eastern quarter. Their faces were tired and drawn in the light of the candles. They sat down silently at the square table.

They had combed out the entire quarter, in vain.

Ma Joong had divided the constables into three groups of seven. One group was headed by Tao Gan, one by Headman Fang, and the third by Ma Joong himself. They had entered the quarter in inconspicuous groups of two or three and by different ways. Under various pretexts these groups had made inquiries in shops and other public places, then they had entered private houses and conducted a thorough search.

The headman's group broke up a secret meeting of thieves, Ma Joong dispersed a gambling party, and Tao Gan disturbed two frightened couples in a clandestine house of assignment. But not one trace of White Orchid was discovered.

Tao Gan closely questioned the woman who kept the house of assignment. He knew that if a girl is kidnapped and kept captive somewhere, such a woman will sooner or later come to know about it. However, half an hour of skilful questioning convinced Toa Gan that she knew nothing about White Orchid; he only learned one or three queer facts about certain leading citizens.

Finally they had to come out in the open and made a systematic search of every household, checking the inhabitants with the census register kept by the warden. But now they had to admit that the search had been a failure.

After a while Tao Gan said:

"There is but one possibility left, namely that the girl was held for a few days only in a house near here. When her captor discovered that she had made a secret trip to the temple, he became alarmed and moved her either to a secret assignment house elsewhere in the city, or placed her in a brothel."

Headman Fang shook his head dejectedly.

"I don't believe", he said, "that they would have sold her to a brothel. We have lived here all our lives and they would run the risk that some visitor to the establishment would recognize her and inform me.

A clandestine assignment house is the most likely place. But to check all those would take many days!"

"Did I not hear", Ma Joong remarked, "that the so-called Northern Row, the licensed quarter in the northwest corner of the town, is rarely visited by Chinese?"

The headman nodded.

"That is a low-class place", he replied, "used only by Uigurs, Turks and other barbarians from over the border. The girls are a motley crowd, left over from the prosperous days when this town was full of wealthy barbarian chieftains and traders from the western tributary kingdoms."

Ma Joong rose and tightened his belt.

"I shall go there now", he said curtly. "To avoid rousing suspicion, I shall go alone. I'll meet you later tonight in the tribunal!"

Tao Gan had been tugging at the three hairs on his left cheek.

"That is a good idea", he said pensively, "we had better

act quickly, for by tomorrow the news of this raid will be all over the town. I shall go now to the Southern Row and have a talk with the owners of the houses there. I am not very hopeful but we cannot afford to neglect even that possibility!"

The headman insisted that he should accompany Ma Joong.

"The scum of the city gathers in that Northern Row", he said. "To go out there alone is asking to be murdered on the spot!"

"Don't worry!", Ma Joong said, "I know how to handle those rascals!"

He threw his cap to Tao Gan and bound up his hair with a dirty strip of cloth. Then he tucked the slips of his robe in his girdle and rolled up his sleeves.

Cutting short the headman's protestations Ma Joong walked out into the street.

In the main street there were still many people about. But Ma Joong made quick progress, all passers-by hastily made way when they saw this huge ruffian approaching.

When he had crossed the market of the Drum Tower he found himself in the quarter of the poor. Rows of low, tumble-down houses lined the narrow streets. Here and there a street vender had lighted his oil lamp. The wares on sale were cheap flour cakes and dregs of wine.

As he approached the Northern Row the scene became more lively. People in queer foreign attire were loitering about the wine shops, talking loudly in raucous, strange languages. They gave Ma Joong but a casual look. Here his disreputable figure was a common sight.

Turning a corner he saw a row of houses garishly lighted by coloured lanterns of oil paper. He heard barbarian guitars being strummed and farther on the strident tones of a flute tore the air.

Suddenly a thin man clad in a ragged gown detached himself from the shadows. He said in broken Chinese:

"Would the master like an Uigur princess?"

Ma Joong stood still and looked the fellow up and down. The man smirked ingratiatingly, showing his broken teeth.

"If I should beat your face to pulp", Ma Joong said sourly, "I could not possible make you uglier! Run ahead and lead me to a good place. But cheap, mind you!"

As he spoke he jerked the man round and gave him a well-aimed kick.

"Yah, yah!", the other cried. He quickly led Ma Joong into a sidestreet.

On both sides stood one-storied houses. Once their façades had been gaily decorated with reliefs in plaster work. But wind and rain had washed off the colours and nobody had bothered to repair them.

Greasy, patched curtains screened the door openings. As they approached heavily made-up girls clad in garish rags pulled aside the screens and invited them in in a mixture of Chinese and foreign languages.

The guide took Ma Joong to a house that looked slightly better than the others. Two large paper lanterns hung over the door.

"Here you are, master!", the guide said. "All Uigur princesses of the blood!" He added an obscene remark, then held out his dirty palm.

Ma Joong gripped him by the throat and bumped his head against the ramshackle door.

"That will serve to announce my arrival!", he said. "Your commission you will get from the house. Don't try to earn a double fee, you bastard!"

The door swung open and a tall fellow with naked torso appeared. His bare head was closely shaved. He looked at Ma Joong with one baleful eye. The place of the other eye was taken by an ugly red scar.

"This dogshead", Ma Joong said gruffly, "wants to extract an extra tip from me!"

The other turned savagely on the guide.

"Get away!", he barked. "You can come back later for your commission!" And to Ma Joong, sullenly:

"Come in, stranger!"

A nauseating smell of burned lambsgrease hung in the room. It was stifling hot. In the middle of the stamped-earth floor stood a large iron brazier with glowing coals. Half a dozen people were sitting round it on low wooden benches. They were roasting pieces of lambfat stuck on copper pins. There were three men. They had stripped to their baggy trousers, the light of a coloured paper lantern shone on their perspiring faces. The women that accompanied them wore wide pleated red and green muslin skirts and sleeveless short jackets. Their hair was done up in thick rolls mixed with red woollen cords. Their jackets hung open displaying their naked breasts.

The doorkeeper gave Ma Joong a suspicious look.

"Fifty cash for a meal and a woman, to be paid in advance!" he said.

Ma Joong muttered something and started fumbling in his sleeve. He produced a string of money, and loosened the knot laboriously. Then he slowly counted out fifty coppers on the dirty counter.

The other stretched out his hand. But Ma Joong quickly gripped his wrist and pressed his hand down on the counter before he could scoop up the money.

"Don't you serve a drink with the meal?", he growled.

The man grimaced as Ma Joong tightened his grip.

"No!" he snarled.

Ma Joong let go and roughly pushed him back. He started to gather up the money saying:

"Nothing doing! There are other places besides yours!"

The other looked greedily at the disappearing heap of coppers.

"All right!", he said, "you can have one jug of wine!"

"That is better!", Ma Joong said.

He turned round and prepared to join the company round the brazier. Adapting himself to the style of the establishment he first slipped his right then his left arm out of his robe, and knotted the empty sleeves round his waist. He let himself down on the empty bench.

The others looked thoughtfully at his heavy torso, covered with scars.

Ma Joong pulled a stick with lambsfat from the fire. He was something of a gourmet and the rancid smell made his stomach turn. But he ripped off a piece with his teeth and ate it.

One of the three Uigurs was very drunk. He had put his arm round the waist of the girl next to him and rocked to and fro softly humming a queer little tune. Perspiration streamed down his head and shoulders.

The two others were sober. They were spare men but Ma Joong knew that their flat, wiry muscles were not to be despised. They spoke rapidly together in their own tongue.

The owner placed a small earthenware jug on the floor by Ma Joong's side.

One of the girls rose and walked over to the counter. She took a three-stringed guitar from one of the shelves. Leaning against the wall she started to sing accompanying herself on the guitar. Her voice was hoarse but the chant had a lilt that was not unpleasing. Ma Joong noticed that the wide muslin skirts of those girls were so thin that one could see right through.

From the door opening in the back emerged a fourth girl, not unattractive in a vulgar way. She was barefoot and dressed only in a loose pleated skirt of faded silk. Her naked torso was shapely but her breasts and arms were smeared with soot. Apparently she had been helping in the kitchen.

A faint smile appeared on her round face as she sat down next to Ma Joong.

He put the jug to his lips and swallowed a draught of the fiery liquor. Then he spat in the fire and asked:

"What is your name, beauty?"

The girl smiled and shook her head. She did not understand Chinese.

"Fortunately my business with this wench does not include conversation!", Ma Joong remarked to the two men opposite.

The taller of the two men guffawed. He asked in atrocious Chinese:

"What is your name, stranger?"

"My name is Yoong Bao", Ma Joong replied. "What is yours?"

"I am called The Hunter", the other answered. "Your girl's nickname is Tulbee. What brought you here?"

Ma Joong gave him a meaningful look. He laid his hand on the thigh of the girl by his side.

"You need not come all the way out here for that!", The Hunter said with a sneer.

Ma Joong scowled angrily. He rose. The girl tried to pull him down but he roughly pushed her back. He walked round the brazier and jerked The Hunter up by his arm. Swinging him round he barked:

"What do you mean by interrogating me, you dirty dogshead?"

The Hunter looked at the others. The second Uigur concentrated on a piece of roasted fat. The owner stood leaning on the counter picking his teeth. They made no

MA JOONG MEETS TULBEE

sign to come to his assistance. The Hunter said sullenly:

"Don't take offence, Yoong Bao! I just asked because Chinese rarely come here."

Ma Joong let him go and returned to his seat. The girl put her arm round him and he fondled her for a while. Then he emptied his jug in one gulp.

Wiping his mouth with the back of his hand he said:

"Well, since we are gathered here as old friends, I don't mind after all to answer your question. A few weeks ago I had a friendly argument with a fellow in the military post three days from here. I patted him on the head and the fellow's skull broke. Since the authorities often misunderstand such incidents, I thought I had better do some travelling. Now I am here, and my funds have dwindled to practically nothing. If there is any job to be done with money in it, I am your man!"

The Hunter rapidly translated for the other man, a squat fellow with a bullet-shaped head. They gave Ma Joong an appraising look.

"There is not much going on just now, brother!", The Hunter said cautiously.

"Well", Ma Joong said, "what about kidnapping a girl? That is a commodity that is always in demand!"

"Not in this town, brother!", the other answered. "All the houses have enough and to spare. A few years ago, when all the traffic went through this town, yes, then one could get good silver for a girl. But not now!"

"Is there no Chinese girl in this quarter?", Ma Joong inquired.

The Hunter shook his head.

"Not one", he replied. "But what is wrong with that wench by your side?"

Ma Joong pulled the girl's skirt loose.

"Nothing", he replied, "and anyway I am not particular!"

"It would just be like you haughty Chinese to despise an Uigur girl!", the other said nastily.

Ma Joong thought it better not to make a quarrel. So he said:

"Not me! I like your girls the way they are!" And as the girl made no attempt to cover herself up again, he added: "They are not prudish either!"

"Yes", The Hunter said, "we are a fine race. Much more virile than you Chinese. Some day we shall swoop down on you from north and west and conquer your entire country!"

"Not in my life time!", Ma Joong said cheerfully.

The Hunter gave Ma Joong another sharp look. Then he started on a long story to the other Uigur. The latter first shook his head emphatically. Then he seemed to agree.

The Hunter rose and came over to Ma Joong. He pushed the girl away unceremoniously and sat down by Ma Joong's side.

"Listen, brother", he said confidentially, "we might let you in on a nice job! Are you familiar with the weapons used in your regular army?"

Ma Joong thought that this was a curious question. He replied eagerly:

"I have been a soldier for a couple of years, my friend! I know all about it!"

The Hunter nodded.

"There is a bit of fighting coming on", he said, "and there is a lot in it for a good man!"

Ma Joong held out his open hand.

"No", The Hunter said, "not in cash. But when we start in a couple of days, as much in loot as you can grab!"

"I am ready!", Ma Joong exclaimed enthusiastically. "Where shall I join you?"

The Hunter again talked rapidly to the other man. Then he rose and said:

"Come along, brother, I shall take you to our headman!"

Ma Joong jumped up and drew his robe over his shoulders. He gave the girl a friendly pat and said:

"I'll be back, Tulbee!"

They left the house, The Hunter walking in front.

He led Ma Joong through two dark alleys, then entered what seemed to be a ruined compound. They halted in front of a small hovel.

He knocked on the door. There was no answer.

The Hunter shrugged his shoulders and pushed the door open, beckoning Ma Joong to follow him.

They sat down on low footstools covered with sheepskin. The room was bare but for a low wooden couch.

"The boss will be back soon", The Hunter said.

Ma Joong nodded and prepared himself for a long wait.

Suddenly the door burst open and a broad-shouldered man came running in. He shouted excitedly at The Hunter.

"What is he jabbering about?", asked Ma Joong.

The Hunter looked frightened.

"He says that the constables have just raided the east quarter!"

Ma Joong jumped up.

"This is the time for me to leave!" he exclaimed. "If they come here I am lost! I'll be back tomorrow. How can I find this wretched place?"

"Just ask for Orolakchee!", the other replied.

"I am off now. That wench will keep!"

And Ma Joong rushed out.

He found Judge Dee sitting alone in his private office, apparently deep in thought.

When Judge Dee saw Ma Joong he said with a frown:

"Tao Gan and Headman Fang came in a few moments ago. They reported that the search had been a failure. Tao Gan went to the Southern Row, but they have bought no new girls there since the last half year. Did you find any clue to White Orchid's whereabouts in that northern licensed quarter?"

"Nothing that pointed to the kidnapped girl", Ma Joong answered, "but I heard a queer story."

Then he told the judge all about his adventure with The Hunter and Tulbee.

Judge Dee listened absent-mindedly. He said:

"Those rascals probably want you to join them in a raid on another tribe. I would not venture out with them into the plain over the river if I were you!"

Ma Joong shook his head doubtfully but the judge continued:

"Tomorrow morning I want you to accompany me and Sergeant Hoong on a visit to the country estate of Governor Yoo. But tomorrow night you can go out to the Northern Row again and try to learn more about the headman of those barbarian rascals."

MRS. YOO PAYS A SECOND VISIT TO THE TRIBUNAL;
A QUEER DISCOVERY IS MADE IN AN OLD MANSION

JUDGE DEE had planned to set out for the Governor's country
estate early in the morning. But just as he was finishing his
morning tea, Sergeant Hoong announced that Mrs. Yoo
and her son Yoo Shan had come to see the judge as requested.

Judge Dee had them brought in.

Yoo Shan was tall for his age. He had an open, intelligent
face and an air of self-assurance that pleased the judge.

He made Mrs. Yoo and her son sit down in front of his desk.
After the exchange of the usual courtesies the judge said:

"I regret, Madam, that pressure of other business has
prevented me from devoting as much time to your case as
I would have liked. I have not yet succeeded in solving the
riddle of the Governor's scroll picture. However, I have a
feeling that if I knew more about the general situation in
your household when your late husband was still alive, I
would be in a better position to solve the problem. Hence
I would like to ask you a few questions, for my own
guidance."

Mrs. Yoo bowed.

"In the first place", Judge Dee continued, "I wondered
about the old Governor's attitude to his eldest son, Yoo
Kee. According to your testimony, Yoo Kee is a heartless
man. Did the Governor realize that his son had a wicked
character?"

"It is my duty to stress", Mrs. Yoo replied, "that until

his father's death, Yoo Kee behaved most correctly. I would never have dreamed that he was capable of such cruelty as he showed later. My husband always spoke to me kindly about Yoo Kee, he used to say that Yoo Kee was a diligent man and a great help to him in the administration of the family property. And Yoo Kee struck me as an exemplary son who tried to anticipate his father's every wish."

"Then, Madam", Judge Dee went on, "I would like you to give me a few names of the Governor's friends here in Lan-fang."

Mrs. Yoo hesitated. Then she answered:

"The Governor did not like company, Your Honour. He used to spend every morning out in the fields. In the afternoon he would enter the maze alone and stay there for an hour or so."

"Did you ever go inside?", the judge interrupted.

Mrs. Yoo shook her head.

"No", she said, "the Governor always said that it was too damp there. Afterwards he used to drink tea in the garden pavilion behind the mansion. He either read a book or worked on his paintings. I knew a Mrs. Lee, who is quite a gifted amateur painter. The Governor would often invite Mrs. Lee and myself to join him in the pavilion and discuss his pictures."

"Is Mrs. Lee still alive?" inquired the judge.

"Yes, I think so. Formerly she lived not far from our town mansion. She would often come to see me. She is a very kind lady who had the misfortune to lose her husband shortly after their marriage. I once met her when she was walking through the rice fields near our farm and she seemed to take a liking to me. After the Governor married me, she kept up our friendship, and my husband encouraged it.

He was so considerate, Your Honour! He understood

that I, as the mistress of such a large mansion full of people I had not known before, would sometimes feel lonely. I know that it was for this reason that he encouraged Mrs. Lee to come often, although as a rule he did not like visitors."

"Did Mrs. Lee break off the relationship when the Governor died?", Judge Dee asked.

Mrs. Yoo blushed.

"No", she said, "it is entirely my fault that I did not see her again. After Yoo Kee had expelled me from the mansion I felt so humiliated and ashamed that I just went back to my father's farm. I have never been to see Mrs. Lee."

The judge saw that she was deeply moved. He asked hastily:

"Thus the Governor had no friends at all here in Lan-fang?"

Mrs. Yoo mastered herself. She nodded and said:

"My husband preferred to be alone. Once, however, he told me that somewhere in the mountains near this town there lived a very old and intimate friend of his."

Judge Dee leaned forward eagerly.

"Who was that, Madam?"

"The Governor never mentioned his name, but I received the impression that he had the greatest regard and affection for him."

Judge Dee's face fell.

"This is very important, Madam. Try to think back whether you cannot remember something more about that friend!"

Mrs. Yoo slowly drank her tea. Then she said:

"I remember now that he must have visited the Governor once, because that was rather a peculiar occurrence. My husband used to receive his tenant farmers once every month; everyone who had a complaint or who wanted advice could come to see him that day.

Once there was an old peasant waiting in the courtyard. As soon as the Governor had seen him he rushed to him and bowed deeply. He took that peasant straight to his library and remained closeted with him for several hours. I thought that that might have been the Governor's friend, probably a recluse. But I never asked."

Judge Dee stroked his beard.

"I suppose", he said after a pause, "that you kept some scrolls written by your husband?"

Mrs. Yoo shook her head.

"When the Governor married me", she said simply, "I could neither read nor write. He himself taught me a little, but of course I never made such progress as to enable me to appreciate calligraphy. There must be some specimens of the Governor's calligraphy in Yoo Kee's mansion. Your Honour might refer to him."

Judge Dee rose.

"I appreciate that you took all the trouble to come, Madam. Rest assured that I shall do my utmost to discover the hidden message of the Governor's picture. Let me congratulate you on your son. He seems a most intelligent youngster!"

Mrs. Yoo and Yoo Shan rose and bowed deeply. Then Sergeant Hoong saw them out.

As he came back he said:

"Nothing, Your Honour, seems more difficult than to obtain a specimen of the Governor's handwriting! Perhaps we could apply to the capital for one. The Grand Secretary must have many original memoranda to the Throne drawn up by the Governor."

"That would take several weeks", the judge replied. "Perhaps that Mrs. Lee has a picture inscribed by the Governor. Try to find out whether she is still alive, and where she lives, Sergeant. The information about that hermit who was a friend of Governor Yoo is so vague that I have little hope of locating him. Probably he is dead."

"Does Your Honour intend to hear the case of Candidate Ding this afternoon?", the sergeant inquired.

The night before Judge Dee had vouchsafed no further explanation of the discovery he had made in Candidate Ding's poem, and the sergeant was curious to know.

Judge Dee did not answer for a while. Then he rose and said:

"To tell you the truth, Sergeant, I have not yet made up my mind. Let us see when we have come back from our expedition to the country house. Please go out and see whether my palanquin is ready, and have Ma Joong called!"

Sergeant Hoong knew that it was no use insisting. He went out and had Judge Dee's private palanquin made ready, with six bearers.

The judge ascended his palanquin. Ma Joong and Sergeant Hoong mounted their horses.

They left the city by the east gate and moved along the narrow road through the rice fields.

When they were approaching elevated terrain, Ma Joong asked a peasant about the way. It appeared that they should take the first road to the right.

This side road proved to be very neglected. It was so overgrown with wild weeds and shrubs that only a footpath in the middle remained.

The bearers put the palanquin down. Judge Dee descended.

"We had better proceed on foot, Your Honour!", Ma Joong observed. "The palanquin cannot pass through here."

So speaking, he fastened the reins of his horse to a tree. Sergeant Hoong followed his example.

They went on in single file, the judge in front.

After many turns they came unexpectedly upon a large gate house. The double doors had once been covered with gold and red lacquer but now there was nothing left but the cracked boards. One panel hung loose.

"Anyone can walk in here!", said the judge in amazement.

"Yet there is no safer place in Lan-fang!", Sergeant Hoong remarked. "Even the most audacious robber would not dare to cross this threshold. This is haunted ground!"

The judge pushed the creaking door open and entered what had once been a beautiful park.

Now it was a wilderness. The roots of towering cedar trees had broken through the flagstones and thick undergrowth obstructed the way. Deep silence reigned. Even the birds did not sing.

The path seemed to disappear into a cluster of shrubs. Ma Joong parted the thick foliage to let the judge pass through. They saw a dilapidated mansion surrounded by a broad elevated terrace.

It was a one-storied, quite extensive building that must once have been an impressive sight. Now the roof had caved in at several places, and wind and rain had played havoc with the carved woodwork of doors and pillars.

Ma Joong went up the crumbling steps of the terrace and looked around. There was no one about.

"Visitors have arrived!" he shouted in a stentorian voice.

The echo was the only answer.

They entered the main hall.

Here the plaster hung down in strips from the walls. A few pieces of broken, bare furniture stood in a corner.

Ma Joong shouted again. But there was stilll no answer. Judge Dee lowered himself carefully into an old chair. He said:

"You two had better have a look round. You will probably find the old couple working in the garden behind the house."

Judge Dee folded his arms. Again he marvelled at the uncanny stillness that hung over this place.

Suddenly he heard the sounds of running feet.

Ma Joong and Sergeant Hoong came rushing into the hall.

"Your Honour!", Ma Joong panted, "we have found the dead bodies of that old couple!"

"Well", Judge Dee said testily, "dead people can do no harm. Let us go and have a look!"

They led the judge through a dim corridor. It gave on to a fairly large garden surrounded by old pine trees. In the middle stood an octagonal pavilion.

Ma Joong pointed silently to a flowering magnolia tree in a corner.

Judge Dee went down the stairs of the terrace and walked through the tall grass. On a bamboo couch, right under the magnolia tree he saw the remains of two people.

The bodies must have been lying there for several months. The bones were sticking up through the ragged, decaying robes. Strands of grey hair were attached to the bare skulls. They lay side by side, their arms crossed on their breast.

Judge Dee bent over and scrutinized the bodies intently.

"It seems to me", he said, "that the two old people died a natural death. I think that when one of them had succumbed to weakness and old age, the other just lay down there too and died.

I shall have the constables carry these bodies to the tribunal for an autopsy. But I don't expect any exciting discoveries."

Ma Joong shook his head disconsolately.

"If there is any information to be obtained here", he remarked, "we must get it all by ourselves!"

Judge Dee walked over to the pavilion.

The intricate lattice work of the window openings proved

that formerly it had been a very elegant place. Now there was left nothing but the bare walls, and one large table.

"Here", Judge Dee said, "the old Governor used to paint and read his books. I wonder where that gate in the back fence leads to."

They left the pavilion and strolled over to the wooden gate. Ma Joong pushed it open. They found themselves in a paved yard.

In front, a large stone gate loomed against the green foliage. The curved roof was decked with blue-glazed tiles. On left and right there rose a wall of thick shrubbery and closely planted trees. Judge Dee looked up at the inscribed stone slab inserted in the plaster over the gate.

He turned round and said to his companions:

"This is apparently the entrance to the Governor's famous maze. Look at that stanza written there:

> *A winding path goes round and round*
> *For over a hundred miles;*
> *Yet the road to one's heart*
> *Is shorter than one-thousandth of an inch.*

The sergeant and Ma Joong looked up intently. The inscription was written in very cursive style.

"I can't identify a single letter!", Sergeant Hoong exclaimed.

Judge Dee did not seem to have heard him. He stood there gazing enraptured at the inscription.

"That is the most magnificent calligraphy I have ever seen!", he sighed. "Unfortunately the signature is so covered with moss that I can hardly read it. Yes, that is it. 'The Hermit clad in Crane Feathers'. What a curious name!"

The judge thought for a moment. Then he continued:

"I cannot remember ever having heard of a person of that name. But whoever he be, that man is a superb calligrapher! Seeing such writing, my friends, one understands why the ancients praised great calligraphy by comparing it to 'the tension of a crouching panther, and the wild force of dragons sporting among rain and thunder'."

Judge Dee passed through the archway, still shaking his head in admiration.

"Give me handwriting that a man can read!", Ma Joong whispered to the sergeant.

In front rose a row of age-cold cedar trees. The space between their heavy trunks was filled with large boulders and thorny shrubs. The tree tops met on high, screening out the sunlight.

The air was foul with the smell of decaying leaves.

On the right, two gnarled pine trees on either side of the path formed a natural gateway. At the foot of one stood a stone tablet with the inscription "Entrance". Beyond it a dim, damp tunnel went straight on for a while, then disappeared in a curve.

As he was looking into this green tunnel Judge Dee suddenly felt an uncanny fear.

Slowly he turned. On the left he saw the opening of another tunnel. A number of large boulders were piled up among the cedar trees. One stone was marked "Exit".

Ma Joong and Sergeant Hoong stood behind the judge. They did not say a word. They too felt the weird, threatening atmosphere of this place.

Judge Dee again looked into the entrance. The tunnel seemed to exhale a cold current of air. The judge felt chilled to his very bones. Yet the air was completely still. Not a leaf moved.

Judge Dee wanted to avert his gaze but the dim tunnel held him hypnotized. He felt a compelling desire to enter. He thought that he could see the tall figure of the old

Governor standing in the green dimness beyond the curve, beckoning him.

With a great effort the judge mastered himself. In order to free himself from this evil atmosphere he forced his gaze to the ground, covered with a thick layer of decaying leaves.

Suddenly his heart stood still. In the middle of a muddy stretch, right in front of his feet, he saw the imprint of a small foot, pointing towards the tunnel. This eerie signpost seemed to order him to enter.

Judge Dee heaved a deep sigh, then turned round abruptly. He said casually:

"Well, we had better not venture into this maze without adequate preparations!"

So speaking he passed under the archway, crossed the paved yard and walked back into the garden. Never had the warm sunlight been so welcome to him.

Judge Dee looked up at a huge cedar tree that rose high over the pines. He said to Ma Joong:

"I would like to have at least a general idea of the size and shape of this maze. We need not go inside for that. If you climb this tree you should be able to obtain a view of the entire area."

"That is easily done!" Ma Joong exclaimed.

He loosened his girdle and took off his outer robe. Then he jumped and just caught the lowest branch. He pulled himself up. Soon he had disappeared among the thick foliage.

Judge Dee and Sergeant Hoong sat down on a fallen tree. Neither of them spoke.

They heard a crashing sound above them. Ma Joong jumped down. He looked ruefully at a tear in his under garment.

"I climbed up right to the top, Your Honour", he said. "From there I could overlook the maze. It is circular in form and extends well over an acre, right up to where the mountain slope begins. But I could discover nothing of its design. The tree tops meet nearly everywhere, I could see only short stretches of the path. Here and there a light haze hangs over it. I would not wonder if inside there were a number of stagnant pools."

"Did you see nothing like the roof of a pavilion or a small house?", inquired Judge Dee.

"No", Ma Joong replied, "I saw only a sea of green tree tops!"

"That is curious", Judge Dee mused. "Since the Governor spent so much of his time in that maze, one would expect him to have had some small library or studio inside."

The judge rose and straightened his robes.

"Let us now have a closer look at the mansion itself," he said.

They passed once more the garden pavilion and the two still figures under the magnolia tree. Then they ascended the terrace.

They inspected a number of larger and smaller empty rooms. Most of the woodwork had rotted away, the bricks showed through the plaster.

As the judge was entering a dim corridor, Ma Joong who had been walking ahead of him called out:

"Here is a closed door, Your Honour!"

Judge Dee and Sergeant Hoong walked up to him. Ma Joong pointed to a large wooden door that was in excellent state of repair.

"This is the first door we find in this place that closes properly!", the sergeant observed.

Ma Joong put his shoulders against it and nearly fell inside. The door swung open smoothly on well-oiled hinges.

Judge Dee stepped inside.

The room had only one window, barred with a solid

iron grating. It was empty but for a rustic bamboo couch in a corner. The floor was swept clean.

Sergeant Hoong entered the room too and walked over to the grated window.

Ma Joong hurriedly stepped out.

"Since our adventure under the bronze bell"*, he called to Judge Dee from outside, "I have become very chary of closed spaces! While Your Honour and the sergeant are inside, I shall stand guard here in the corridor and see that no well-wisher slams that door shut on you!"

Judge Dee smiled bleakly.

With a glance at the barred window and the high ceiling he remarked:

"You are quite right, Ma Joong! Once that door is locked we would not easily escape from this room!"

Feeling the smooth bamboo of the couch that did not show one speck of dust, he added:

"Someone has been living here until quite recently!"

"Not a bad hiding place", the sergeant commented. "This may have served as the lair of a criminal!"

"A criminal or a prisoner", Judge Dee said pensively.

He then ordered Sergeant Hoong to seal the door.

They inspected the other rooms but did not discover anything. As noon was approaching, Judge Dee decided to go back to the tribunal.

* See 'The Chinese Bell Murders'.

Eighteenth Chapter

JUDGE DEE DECIDES TO CONSULT AN OLD HERMIT;
MA JOONG CATCHES HIS MAN IN THE DRUM TOWER

ONCE they were back in the tribunal Judge Dee immediately had Headman Fang called in. He ordered him to proceed with ten constables and two stretchers to the country mansion to fetch the remains of the old gatekeeper and his wife.

Then the judge had his luncheon served in his private office.

While he was eating he called for the Head of the Archives. This was a man over sixty who had been recommended to the judge by the master of the Guild of Silk Merchants. He was a retired silk dealer who had lived all his life in Lan-fang.

As Judge Dee was emptying his bowl of soup, he asked:

"Have you ever heard of an old scholar in this district who uses the pen name of 'Hermit clad in Crane-feathers'?"

The archivist asked:

"I suppose that Your Honour means Master Crane Robe?"

"That might well be the same man", Judge Dee said. "He must live somewhere outside the city."

"Yes", the other replied, "that is Master Crane Robe, as he is generally called. He is a hermit who has been living in the mountains outside the south gate as long as I can remember. No one knows how old he is."

"I would like to meet him", the judge said.

The old archivist looked doubtful.

"That is a difficult proposition, Your Honour!" he remarked. "The old master never leaves his mountain valley and he refuses to see visitors. I would not know that he is still alive were it not that last week I heard that two fuel gatherers had happened to see him working in his garden. He is a very wise and learned man, Your Honour. Some even say that he has discovered the Elixir of Life, and soon will leave this world as an Immortal."

Judge Dee slowly smoothed his long beard.

"I have heard many a story", he said, "about such recluses. Usually they turn out to be nothing but extremely lazy and ignorant men. However, I have seen a specimen of this man's calligraphy, which is absolutely superior. He may be an exception. How is the road out there?"

"Your Honour will have to walk the greater part of the way", the archivist replied. "The mountain path is so steep and narrow that even a small sedan chair could not pass."

As the judge thanked the archivist Chiao Tai came in. He was looking worried.

"I trust that there is nothing wrong in the Chien mansion, Chiao Tai?", asked the judge anxiously.

Chiao Tai sat down and started twirling his short moustache. Then he said:

"It is very hard, Your Honour, to explain how one notices a change in the attitude of a body of soldiers. I suppose that it is mainly intuition. For the last two days I have felt there was something wrong with the men.

I checked with Corporal Ling and found that he too has been worrying. He tells me that some soldiers seem to spend more money than they would be able to account for."

Judge Dee had been listening intently.

"This sounds serious, Chiao Tai!", he said slowly. "Listen to a queer story of Ma Joong!"

Ma Joong once more told what he had heard in the Northern Row.

Chiao Tai shook his head.

"I fear that this means trouble, Your Honour! Our ruse of creating an imaginary regiment inspecting the border works two ways. On the one hand it enabled us to oust Chien Mow and subdue his men. On the other it may have convinced barbarian tribes planning to raid the city that they have to act now or never, before a garrison arrives."

Judge Dee tugged at his whiskers.

"A barbarian attack on his town would be the last straw!", he exclaimed angrily. "As if we had not enough difficulties on our hands already! I suspect that that mysterious trouble-maker who directed Chien Mow is at the back of this! How many men do you think we can trust?"

Chiao Tai looked thoughtful. After a while he said:

"I would not count on more than fifty in all, Your Honour!"

All were silent.

Suddenly Judge Dee crashed his fist on the desk.

"It yet may not be too late!", he exclaimed. "That remark of yours about a ruse working two ways, Chiao Tai, has given me an idea.

Ma Joong, we must immediately apprehend that Uigur ruffian you were to meet last night. Can you arrest that man without attracting the attention of the people out there?"

Ma Joong looked pleased. He put his large hands on his knees and said with a smile:

"Broad daylight is not the most suitable time for such an undertaking, Your Honour, but of course it can be done!"

"Go there immediately with Chiao Tai!", the judge ordered. "But remember that this is to be a secret arrest. If you find that you cannot apprehend him without someone knowing it, you must leave him alone and come back here!"

Ma Joong nodded. He rose and beckoned Chiao Tai to follow him.

They went to the quarters of the guards and sat down in a corner. There they held a whispered consultation. Then Ma Joong left the tribunal alone.

He walked round the tribunal compound and sauntered along the main street leading to the north city gate. He stood about for a moment in front of a small eating house. Then he entered.

Ma Joong had been there once before. The manager greeted him by his name.

"I want my luncheon in a small room upstairs!", Ma Joong announced and climbed the stairs.

On the second floor he found an empty corner room. When he had ordered his luncheon, the door opened and Chiao Tai came in. He had entered the restaurant by the backdoor.

Ma Joong hurriedly took off his upper gown and his cap. While Chiao Tai wrapped these up in a bundle Ma Joong ruffled his hair and bound a dirty rag round his head. He tucked the slips of his undergarment in his girdle and rolled up his sleeves. With a hasty farewell he left the room.

Tiptoeing down the stairs he went into the kitchen.

"Have you not a spare oil cake lying about, you fat bastard?", he barked at the cook who was sweating over the kitchen fire.

The cook looked up. When he saw that uncouth ruffian he hastily gave him a flour cake that had stuck to the pan.

Ma Joong muttered something, grabbed the cake and left the kitchen by the backdoor.

Upstairs Chiao Tai had started on his luncheon. Seeing the familiar brown robe and the pointed black cap of the tribunal the waiter who served him did not realize that this was not the same man who had entered the restaurant.

Chiao Tai planned to leave when the manager would be busy.

In the meantime Ma Joong had strolled to the market near the Drum Tower.

He loitered for a while among the stalls of the street venders, then walked over to the tower.

The dark area under the stone arches that formed the base of the Drum Tower was deserted. On rainy days itinerant merchants often used the sheltered space under the arches for displaying their wares but now they preferred the bright sunlight outside.

Ma Joong looked over his shoulder. When he saw that no one paid any attention to him he quickly stepped inside. He climbed the narrow stairway that led to the second floor.

This was a kind of loft with large windows on all four sides. In hot weather people sometimes came up there to catch the breeze but now there was no one about. The step ladder to the third floor was barred by a wooden gate. There was no lock on it. It was closed by an iron bolt with a strip bearing the large red seal of the tribunal pasted over it.

Ma Joong calmly broke the seal and wrenched the gate open. Then he climbed up to the third floor.

The huge round drum stood on a platform in the middle of the wooden floor. It was covered with a thick layer of dust that had blown in through the open arches. The drum is sounded only in times of emergency to warn the population. Evidently it had not been used for many years.

Ma Joong nodded. He quickly went down again. He looked round the corner of one of the arches. When he saw that no one observed him he slipped out and made for the Northern Row.

In broad daylight the quarter looked even more miserable than at night. There was no one about. Apparently the inmates were sleeping off the night before.

Ma Joong wandered about for a while but he failed to locate the house he had visited.

He pushed open a door at random. A slovenly clad girl was lying on a wooden couch.

Ma Joong gave the couch a kick. The girl slowly scrambled up. She gave Ma Joong a sullen look and started to scratch her head.

Ma Joong said gruffly:

"Orolakchee!"

Suddenly the girl became active. She jumped from the couch and disappeared through the screen at the back. She emerged again dragging along a dirty small boy. Pointing to Ma Joong she rapidly talked to the urchin. Then she said something to Ma Joong. He nodded eagerly although he had not understood a word.

The urchin beckoned to Ma Joong. He rushed out into the street, Ma Joong following on his heels.

The boy slipped into the narrow space between two houses. Ma Joong had difficulty squeezing his large frame through. When he passed underneath a small window-opening of about two feet square he reflected that if somebody inside would choose this moment to crush his skull there was very little he could do about it.

A nail ripped his robe. Ma Joong stood still and ruefully looked at the large tear. Then he shrugged his shoulders; after all this was an additional touch to his disguise.

Suddenly he heard a soft voice calling from above:

"Yoong Bao, Yoong Bao!"

He looked up. The girl Tulbee was looking out of the small window just above his head.

"How are you, my wench?", Ma Joong said pleasantly.

Tulbee seemed very excited. She started to whisper some words looking fixedly at Ma Joong with her large eyes.

Ma Joong shook his head.

"I don't know what is your trouble, my girl, but I am in a hurry just now. I'll come back later!"

As he made to go on Tulbee stuck her bare arm through the window and clutched the collar of Ma Joong's robe. She pointed in the direction the urchin had gone to, shaking her head emphatically. Then she drew her forefinger across her throat.

"Yes, that they are cutthroats I know!", Ma Joong said with a smile. "But don't you worry, I can take care of myself!"

Tulbee quickly drew him near to the window. For a moment her cheek touched his. There was a slight smell of lambsfat about her but Ma Joong still thought it was rather pleasant.

Then he softly loosened her arm and went on. When he emerged from the passage the urchin came to meet him. He jabbered excitedly, apparently he had feared that he had lost Ma Joong.

They scrambled over a heap of refuse, then climbed over a broken down wall.

The boy pointed to a neat plaster hut standing all by itself among tumble-down shacks. Then the urchin ran away.

Ma Joong now recognized the small house he had visited the night before with The Hunter. He knocked on the door.

"Come in!", a voice shouted from inside.

Ma Joong opened the door. He stood stock still.

A tall, spare man was standing with his back against the wall opposite. Ma Joong kept his eyes riveted on the long, evil-looking knife that rested on the palm of the man's right hand. It was poised for the throw.

After a tense moment the man said:

"So it is you, Yoong Bao! Sit down!"

He put the knife back in a leather sheath and sat down on one of the low footstools. Ma Joong followed his example.

"Last night", Ma Joong began, "The Hunter directed me to come here, and . . ."

"Shut up!", the other interrupted, "if I had not known all about you, you would be dead now. I never miss when I throw my knife!"

Ma Joong thought to himself that that was probably very true. The Uigur spoke excellent Chinese, Ma Joong took him for a minor chieftain.

Ma Joong smiled ingratiatingly.

"I was told that you, Sir, could help me to a job with a little money in it!"

"You are a traitor", the other said disdainfully, "and traitors think only of money. Yet you may be useful. But before I give you my instructions I want to make one point very clear. It will be good for your health to avoid even a semblance of double-dealing. At the slightest sign you will find a knife in your back!"

"Certainly, Sir!", Ma Joong said hurriedly. "You know my situation. I . . .".

"Enough!", the other said imperiously, "Listen carefully, I never repeat my instructions.

Three tribes are assembling in the plains over the river. Tomorrow, at midnight, they will occupy this city. We could have taken this town any time we liked, but we want to avoid excessive bloodshed. Your Chinese authorities are self-satisfied and lazy, and this is a distant outpost. If the fall of this town does not create too much interest in the capital, the authorities will not be in too much of a hurry to send an army here. Fortunately for us the route to the west no longer passes through this town. So the central authorities need not worry that we shall interfere with the tribute caravans from the western tributary kingdoms. By the time they decide to take action we shall have established our kingdom here and be in a position to ward off any attack.

The point is that we want to take this town by surprise. Everything has been prepared for taking over the tribunal and killing the magistrate and his men. But we need a few more Chinese to dispose of the guards on the gates."

"Ha!", Ma Joong exclaimed, "that is very fortunate! It so happens that I have a friend here who is the very man for you. He was a sergeant in our regular army who had to desert and hide himself because he got into trouble with the new magistrate here. That fellow Dee is a nasty man!"

"You Chinese are always afraid of those magistrates!", the Uigur said with a sneer. "I am not afraid of any of them! A couple of years ago I slit the throat of one with my own hands!"

Ma Joong gave his host an admiring look.

"Well", he said, "you had better contact my friend. He is a firstclass swordsman and knows all about the passwords and military routine."

"Where is he?", the other asked eagerly.

"Not far from here, Sir!", Ma Joong replied. "We found a perfect hiding place for him. He only goes out at night, during the daytime he sleeps on the third floor of the Drum Tower."

The Uigur laughed.

"That is not a bad idea!", he said. "Nobody would look for him there! Go and bring him here!"

Ma Joong looked doubtful. He said with a frown:

"As I just remarked, Sir, he cannot risk going out by daylight. Could not we go there ourselves? It is quite near!"

The Uigur shot Ma Joong a suspicious look. He thought for a while. Then he rose, transferring his knife from his girdle to his sleeve.

"I hope for you, my friend", he said, "that you are not planning some trick. You walk ahead. At the first suspicious move I shall throw my knife in your back and nobody will even guess where it came from!"

Ma Joong shrugged his shoulders.

"There is no need for all those warnings", he remarked. "Don't you know that we are entirely in your hands? One word to the tribunal and my friend and I are lost!"

"So long as you don't forget that, my friend!", the other said.

They went out into the street, the Uigur following Ma Joong at some distance.

As Ma Joong entered the market place he saw Chiao Tai standing with his back to a stone memorial tablet. His arms folded in his sleeves, he leisurely surveyed the crowd. His pointed cap, his brown robe with the black sash together with his air of authority clearly marked him as an officer of the tribunal.

Ma Joong halted in his steps.

This was where Ma Joong had to take his chance. Every moment the expected to feel the knife of the Uigur landing in his back.

Yet he could not move too quickly for he had to make sure that Chiao Tai saw him. With cold sweat on his brow Ma Joong carefully played his role.

He made as if he hesitated for a moment. When Chiao Tai lifted his hand and slowly smoothed his moustache, Ma Joong turned round and made a detour behind the stone tablet.

As soon as he was safely under the dark arch of the Drum Tower the Uigur joined him.

"Did you see that bastard leaning against the stone tablet?", Ma Joong whispered excitedly. "That is an officer of the tribunal!"

"So I saw", the other said dryly. "Hurry up!"

Ma Joong climbed the stairway to the second floor. He waited till the Uigur had come up too. Pointing to the broken seal on the gate Ma Joong said:

"Look! That is where my friend went up!"

The Uigur pulled his knife from the sheath. He ran his thumb along its hair-sharp blade.

"Climb up!", he ordered.

Ma Joong shrugged his shoulders resignedly. Slowly he ascended the narrow ladder, the Uigur following behind.

As Ma Joong had his shoulders through the floor opening he exclaimed:

"Well, well! The lazy dog is sleeping!"

So speaking he quickly went up the last steps. Pointing at the drum he said:

"Look at the fellow!"

The Uigur came up quickly.

When his head was on a level with the floor Ma Joong suddenly gave him a fearful kick right in the face.

With a gasp the Uigur fell down the steep ladder.

Ma Joong let himself slide down as fast as he could. At the bottom of the step ladder he could just dodge a vicious knife thrust. The Uigur was lying on the floor leaning on his left arm. Apparently he had broken a leg, and blood gushed from a nasty gash on his shaven head. But his eyes shone with a green light and he held his knife in a firm grip.

Ma Joong decided there was no time for the finer points. He quickly stepped behind the other. Before the Uigur could scramble round, Ma Joong had placed a kick. The Uigur's head crashed against the side of the ladder. The knife clattered to the floor. He lay quite still.

Ma Joong picked the knife up and put it in his girdle. Then he bound the Uigur's hands behind his back. He felt the other's leg; it seemed broken in more than one place.

Ma Joong went down. He left the tower and strolled nonchalantly out into the market place, heading for the stone tablet.

As he was about to pass in front of the tablet Chiao Tai stepped forward.

"Halt!", he shouted and gripped Ma Joong's arm.

Ma Joong shook his arm free and gave Chiao Tai a sullen look.

"Keep your dirty hands off me, you dogshead!", he barked.

"I am an officer of the tribunal", Chiao Tai said curtly. "I am sure that His Excellency the Judge would like to ask you a few questions, my man!"

"Me?", Ma Joong exclaimed indignantly, "I am an honest citizen, Constable!"

A crowd of idlers had gathered round them, eagerly following this incident.

"Will you come along, or must I knock you down first?", Chiao Tai asked threateningly.

"Shall we let ourselves be bullied by these running-dogs of the tribunal?", Ma Joong asked the crowd.

He noticed to his secret satisfaction that no one made a move.

Ma Joong shrugged his shoulders.

"All right", he said, "the tribunal has nothing on me!"

Chiao Tai bound his hands on his back.

Ma Joong turned round.

"Listen", he said, "I have a sick friend. Let me give that flour-cake peddler here a few coppers to take some food to him. The man cannot move!"

"Where is that fellow?", Chiao Tai asked.

Ma Joong hesitated a while. Then he said reluctantly:

"Well, to tell you the truth, last night he went up the Drum Tower over there to enjoy the fresh air. He fell down the steps and broke his leg. He is lying now on the second floor."

The crowd guffawed.

"I think", Chiao Tai said, "that the tribunal would like to see that patient of yours!" Turning to the crowd he added: "Let someone run to the warden and call him here with four men, a stretcher and a few old blankets!"

Soon the warden came running along with four sturdy fellows carrying bamboo poles.

"Warden, look after this ruffian!", Chiao Tai ordered.

He beckoned two of the men and went to the Drum Tower.

Chiao Tai climbed the stairs with the blankets over his shoulder. The Uigur was still unconscious. Chiao Tai quickly pasted a piece of oil paper over his mouth. Then he rolled him in one of the blankets and wrapped the other round the Uigur's head and shoulders. He called down the stairs. The warden's men came up to carry the limp form down.

The Uigur was laid on the improvised stretcher. The procession set out for the tribunal, Chiao Tai leading the way dragging Ma Joong along.

They entered by the side gate. As soon as they were inside Chiao Tai said to the warden:

"Put the stretcher down here. You and your men can go!"

As Chiao Tai locked the gate behind them Ma Joong slipped his hands out of the loose ropes. Together with Chiao Tai he carried the stretcher to the jail. They laid the Uigur on the couch in a small cell.

While Ma Joong bandaged the wounded man's head, Chiao Tai cut open his baggy trousers and attached a rough splint to the broken leg.

Ma Joong hurried out to report to the judge.

Chiao Tai locked the door of the cell. He then stood

with his back to the door. When the warden of the jail came along, Chiao Tai told him that he had caught a violent ruffian; he would inquire his name as soon as he had calmed down.

Judge Dee's private office was empty but for Tao Gan, who sat dozing in a corner.

Ma Joong shook him awake and asked excitedly:

"Where is His Excellency?"

Tao Gan looked up.

"The judge went out with Sergeant Hoong shortly after you and Chiao Tai had left", he replied testily. "What is all the excitement? Did you catch that Uigur fellow?"

"Better than that", Ma Joong said proudly, "we caught the murderer of Magistrate Pan!"

"That will cost you a round of wine tonight, brother!", Tao Gan said contentedly. "Well, His Excellency ordered me to go and invite Yoo Kee to visit the tribunal later this afternoon. I suppose that the judge wants to question him about the death of the old caretaker of the country mansion and his wife. I had better be off!"

Nineteenth Chapter

A RECLUSE DISCOURSES ON THE PURPOSE OF LIFE;
JUDGE DEE LEARNS THE OLD GOVERNOR'S SECRET

AFTER Ma Joong and Chiao Tai had left, Judge Dee took a paper from the pile on the desk. He looked at it but did not seem to absorb its contents.

Sergeant Hoong knew that the judge was worried.

Judge Dee impatiently threw down the document. He said:

"I don't mind telling you, Sergeant, that if Ma Joong and Chiao Tai do not succeed in catching that man, we shall find ourselves in a most dangerous position!"

"They have done more difficult jobs than that, Your Honour!", the sergeant said reassuringly.

Judge Dee made no comment. For half an hour he concentrated on various official documents.

At last he put down his writing brush.

"It is no use sitting waiting here any longer", he said curtly. "Evidently Ma Joong and Chiao Tai have seen a chance to arrest their man without attracting attention. The weather is fine, let us go and see whether we can find that Master Crane Robe!"

Sergeant Hoong knew from long experience that action always was the best sedative when the judge was harassed. He quickly went out to order two horses.

They left the tribunal by the main gate, heading south. They galloped over the marble bridge and passed through the southern city gate.

After they had ridden for some time along the main road, a peasant directed them to a narrow path that led to the mountains. It ended at the foot of a steep ridge.

Judge Dee and the sergeant jumped down from their horses. Sergeant Hoong handed a few coppers to a wood gatherer and asked him to look after the horses for an hour or so. Then they began the ascent.

A strenuous climb took them to the top of the pine-clad ridge. Judge Dee paused there a while to regain his breath. Looking down on the verdurous valley that spread out at his feet he lifted his arms and enjoyed the cool mountain breeze that blew through his wide sleeves.

When Sergeant Hoong too had rested himself they slowly descended by the winding path.

As they went down into the valley, the air became curiously still. The murmur of a brook was the only sound they heard.

They crossed the river by a narrow stone bridge. A side path led to a low thatched roof that was partly visible in the midst of the green foliage. The path took them through dense undergrowth to a crudely made bamboo gate.

Inside they found a small garden. On both sides stood flowering plants of well-nigh a man's height. The judge thought that he had never seen such a profusion of magnificent flowers.

The plaster walls of the small house were overgrown with vine; they seemed to sag under the load of the thatched roof, green with moss. A few rickety wooden steps led up to a single door of unpainted boards. It stood ajar.

Judge Dee meant to call out that there were visitors but somehow or other he felt reluctant to break the quiet atmosphere. He pushed aside the plants that grew by the side of the house.

He saw a rustic verandah made of bamboo poles. A

very old man clad in a ragged robe was watering a row of potted flowers. He had a large round straw hat on his head. The delicate fragrance of orchids hung in the air.

Judge Dee pushed the branches further apart and called out: "Is Master Crane Robe at home?"

The old man turned round. The lower half of his face was concealed by a thick moustache and a long white beard, the rest was covered by the broad rim of the hat. He did not answer but made a vague gesture in the direction of the house.

Then he put down his watering pot and disappeared behind the house without saying a word.

Judge Dee was not very pleased with this casual reception. He curtly told Sergeant Hoong to wait outside.

As the sergeant sat down on the bench near the gate, Judge Dee ascended the steps and entered the house.

He found himself in a large, empty room. The wooden floor was bare and so were the white plaster walls. The furniture consisted of a rough wooden table and two footstools in front of the low, broad window, and a bamboo table against the back wall. It looked like the interior of a peasant's house. But everything was scrupulously clean.

There was no sign of the host. Judge Dee felt annoyed and began to regret that he had come all this way.

With a sigh he sat down on one of the footstools and looked out of the window.

He was struck by the fine view on the rows of flowering plants that stood on racks in the verandah outside. Rare orchids blossomed in porcelain and earthenware bowls; their fragrance seemed to pervade the entire room.

As he was sitting there Judge Dee felt the immense tranquillity of his surroundings slowly soothe his harassed mind. Listening to the soft humming of an invisible bee, time seemed to be standing still.

Judge Dee's irritation evaporated. He placed his elbows on the table and leisurely looked around. He noticed that above the bamboo table a pair of paper scrolls had been stuck up on the plaster wall. They bore a couplet written in powerful calligraphy.

Judge Dee idly scanned the lines:

"There are but two roads that lead to the gate of
Eternal Life:
Either one bores his head in the mud like a worm,
or like a dragon flies up high into the sky."

The judge reflected that these lines were rather unusual; they could be interpreted in more than one way.

The couplet was signed and sealed but from where he sat the judge could not read the small characters.

A faded blue screen at the back was pulled aside and the old man entered.

He had changed his ragged robe for a loose gown of brown cloth and his grey head was uncovered. He carried a steaming kettle in his hand.

Judge Dee hastily rose and bowed deeply. The old man nodded casually, and leisurely sat down on the other footstool, with his back to the window. After a moment's hesitation the judge sat down too.

The old man's face was all wrinkled up like the skin of a crab apple. But his lips were red like cinnabar. As his host bowed his head while pouring the boiling water in the tea pot his long white eyebrows screened his eyes like a curtain so that the judge could not see them.

Judge Dee waited respectfully for the old man to speak first.

When he had replaced the lid on the tea pot his host folded his arms in his sleeves and looked straight at the judge. Under his bushy brows his piercing eyes were keen like those of a hawk.

He spoke in a deep, sonorous voice:

"Excuse this old man's remissness. I rarely entertain visitors!"

As he spoke the judge noticed that his teeth were even and of a pearly white.

Judge Dee answered:

"I beg your forgiveness for this sudden visit. You . . ."

"Ha, Yoo!", the old man interrupted him. "So you are a member of the famous Yoo family!"

"No", the judge corrected him hastily, "my family name is Dee. I . . ."

"Yes, yes", his host mused, "it is a long time since I saw my old friend Yoo. Let me see now, it must be eight years since he died. Or was it nine?"

Judge Dee reflected that the old man was apparently in his dotage. But since his host's mistake seemed to lead him straight to the object of his visit, he did not again try to correct it.

The old man poured the tea.

"Yes", he continued pensively, "a man of great purpose, the old Governor Yoo. Why, it must be seventy years ago now that we studied together in the capital. Yes, he was a man of great purpose who laid his plans far in the future. He was going to eradicate all evil, he was going to reform the Empire . . ."

The old man's voice trailed off. He nodded a few times and sipped his tea.

Judge Dee said diffidently:

"I am greatly interested in Governor Yoo's life here in Lan-fang."

His host did not seem to have heard him. He slowly went on sipping his tea.

The judge also brought the cup to his lips. After the first sip he knew that this was the most delicious tea he had ever

MASTER CRANE ROBE AND JUDGE DEE

tasted. Its mellow aroma seemed to pervade his entire body.

His host said suddenly:

"The water was taken from where the brook springs from the rocks. Last night I placed the tea leaves in the bud of a chrysanthemum. I took them out this morning when the flower opened in the sun. These leaves are saturated with the essence of the morning dew."

Then, without any transition, he continued:

"Yoo set out on his official career and I went away to roam over the Empire. He became a prefect, then a governor. His name rang through the marble halls of the Imperial palace. He persecuted the wicked, protected and encouraged the good, and went a long, long way towards reforming the Empire. Then, one day, when he had nearly realized all his ambitions, he found that he had failed to reform his own son.

He resigned from all his high offices and came to live here a life of retirement, tending his fields and his garden. So we met again, after more than fifty years. We had reached the same goal by different roads."

The old man suddenly chuckled softly like a child as he added:

"The only difference was that one way was long and tortuous, the other short and straight!"

Here his host paused. Judge Dee debated with himself whether he should ask for some explanation of that last remark. But before he could speak his host went on:

"Shortly before he passed away, he and I were discussing this very point. Then he wrote down that couplet on the wall there. Go and admire his calligraphy!"

Judge Dee obediently rose and went to look at the paper scrolls on the wall. Now he could read the signature: "Penned by Yoo Shou-chien of the Abode of Tranquillity."

The judge knew now for certain that the testament they had found in Mrs. Yoo's scroll picture was a forgery. The signature resembled the one added to the alleged last will, but it was definitively not the same hand. Judge Dee slowly stroked his beard. Many things had become clear to him.

As he sat down again the judge said:

"If I may respectfully say so, Governor Yoo's calligraphy is excellent, but yours, Sir, is in the inspired class. Your inscription on the gate to the Governor's maze struck me as . . ."

The old man seemed not to have listened. He interrupted the judge saying:

"The Governor was so full of purpose that a life time was not enough for exhausting his energy. Even when he had settled down here he could not stop. Some of his plans for righting old wrongs were not even meant to bear fruit until years later, when he himself would be dead! Wanting to be alone, he built that astonishing maze. As if he could ever be alone, with all his schemes and plans buzzing around him like angry wasps!"

The old man shook his head. He poured another cup of tea.

Judge Dee asked:

"Did the old Governor have many friends here?"

His host slowly tugged one of his long eyebrows. Then he chuckled and said:

"After all those years, and after all he had seen and heard, Yoo still studied the Confucianist Classics. He sent me a cartload of books out here. I found them most useful. They made excellent kindlings for my kitchen stove!"

Judge Dee was going to offer some respectful objections to this derogatory remark on the Classics, but his host ignored him. He continued:

"Confucius! Now that was a purposeful man for you! He spent his entire life rushing all over the Empire, always arranging things, always giving advice to whomsoever cared to listen to him. He buzzed about like a gadfly! He never paused long enough to realize that the more he did the less he achieved, and the more he acquired the less he possessed. Yes, Confucius was a man full of purpose. So was Governor Yoo . . ."

The old man paused. Then he added peevishly:

"And so are you, young man!"

Judge Dee was quite startled by this sudden personal remark. He rose in confusion. With a deep bow he said humbly:

"Could this person venture to ask a question . . ."

His host had risen also.

"One question", he gruffly replied, "only leads to another one. You are like a fisherman who turns his back on his river and his nets and climbs a tree in the forest to catch fish! Or like a man who builds a boat of iron, makes a large hole in the bottom and then expects to cross the river! Approach your problems from the right end and begin with the answers. Then, one day, perhaps, you will find the final answer. Good-bye!"

Judge Dee was going to bow his farewell but his host had already turned his back on him and was shuffling back to the screen at the end of the room.

The judge waited till the blue screen had dropped behind his host's back. Then he went out.

Outside he found Sergeant Hoong sleeping with his back against the garden gate.

The judge woke him up.

The sergeant passed his hand over his eyes. He said with a happy smile:

"It seems to me that I have never slept so peacefully! I

dreamt of my childhood when I was still four or five years old, things I had completely forgotten!"

"Yes", Judge Dee said pensively, "this is a very strange abode . . ."

They climbed the mountain ridge in silence.

When they were standing once more under the pinetrees on the top, the sergeant asked:

"Did the hermit give Your Honour much information?"

Judge Dee nodded absent-mindedly.

"Yes", he replied after a while, "I learned many things. I know now for certain that the testament we found concealed in the Governor's picture is a forgery. I also learned what was the reason why the old Governor suddenly resigned all his offices. And I know now the other half of General Ding's murder."

The sergeant was going to ask for some further explanation. But noticing the expression on Judge Dee's face he remained silent.

After a brief rest they descended the slope. They mounted their horses and rode back to the city.

Ma Joong was waiting in Judge Dee's private office.

As he started on his report of how he and Chiao Tai had caught the Uigur, the judge shook off his pensive mood and listened eagerly.

Ma Joong assured the judge that no one knew about the arrest. He related in great detail his conversation with the Uigur chieftain, omitting only his unexpected meeting with the girl Tulbee and her warning; he assumed, quite correctly, that Judge Dee would not be interested in that romantic interlude.

"That is excellent work!", Judge Dee exclaimed when Ma Joong had finished. "Now we have the trump card in our hands!"

Ma Joong added:

"Tao Gan is now entertaining Yoo Kee in the reception hall. They are drinking tea together. When I looked in there a few moments ago Tao Gan was fretting because Yoo Kee is talking so fast that he can't get in a word!"

The judge looked pleased. He said to Sergeant Hoong:

"Sergeant, go to the reception hall and tell Yoo Kee that to my great regret I am unavoidably detained by urgent business. Offer him my apologies and inform him that I shall see him as soon as I am free!"

When the sergeant made to go the judge asked:

"Did you, by the way, succeed in finding out the whereabouts of Mrs. Lee, that friend of the Governor's widow?"

"I ordered Headman Fang to see to that, Your Honour", replied the sergeant. "I thought that since he is a local man he might obtain quicker results than I."

The judge nodded. Then he asked Ma Joong:

"What are the results of the autopsy on the old couple we found in the garden of the Governor's mansion?"

"The coroner confirmed that they died a natural death, Your Honour", Ma Joong replied.

Judge Dee nodded. He rose and started changing into his official robes. While he was placing the winged judge's cap on his head he suddenly said:

"If I am not mistaken, Ma Joong, you reached the ninth and highest grade in boxing about ten years ago, did you not?"

The tall fellow squared his shoulders. He replied proudly:

"Indeed, Your Honour!"

"Now think back", Judge Dee ordered, "and tell me how you felt towards your master when you were still a beginner, say of the second or third grade!"

Ma Joong was not accustomed to analyse his feelings. He knitted his brows and thought furiously. After a while he answered slowly:

"Well, Your Honour, I was deeply devoted to my master. He certainly was one of the finest boxers of our time and I admired him greatly. But when I boxed with him and he eluded my cleverest blows without the slightest effort, playfully hitting me anywhere he liked despite my frantic defence, I still admired him but at the same time I hated him because of his infinite superiority!"

Judge Dee smiled wanly.

"Thank you, my friend!", he said. "This afternoon I went to the mountains south of this city and there met a person who greatly disturbed me. Now you have put into words exactly what I did not dare to formulate so clearly for myself!"

Ma Joong had no idea what the judge was talking about but he felt flattered by the praise. With a broad smile he pulled aside the screen leading to the court hall. The judge passed through and ascended the dais.

Twentieth Chapter

A REBEL CHIEFTAIN CONFESSES UNDER TORTURE;
A MYSTERIOUS STRANGER IS AT LAST IDENTIFIED

THREE beats on the gong announced the opening of the afternoon session of the tribunal.

No one knew that anything but routine matters would be dealt with, so only a few dozen spectators had drifted into the court hall.

As soon as Judge Dee had seated himself behind the bench and opened the session, he gave a sign to Headman Fang. Four constables went to the entrance of the court hall and remained standing there on guard.

"Because of important reasons of state", Judge Dee announced, "no one shall leave this court before the session is closed!"

A murmur of astonishment rose from the audience.

Judge Dee took up his vermilion brush and filled out a slip for the warden of the jail.

Two constables brought in the Uigur. He walked with difficulty, they had to support him by his arms.

In front of the dais he let himself down on one knee; the splinted leg he stretched out in front with a groan of pain.

"State your name and profession!", Judge Dee ordered.

The man lifted his head. Deep hatred shone from his burning eyes.

"I am Prince Ooljin, of the Blue Tribe of the Uigurs!", he snapped.

"Among you barbarians", the judge said coldly, "a man

calls himself a prince as soon as he has twenty horses! But that is neither here nor there.

The Imperial Government in its infinite grace has deigned to accept the Khan of the Uigurs as a vassal and he has duly sworn allegiance to His Majesty taking a solemn oath with Heaven and Earth as witness.

You, Ooljin, have been scheming to attack this town. You have betrayed your own Khan and you are guilty of rebellion against the Imperial Government.

Rebellion is a most serious crime, it is punished with the extreme penalty in a severe form. Your only hope for having this punishment somewhat mitigated lies in telling the complete truth; this means that you must also reveal who are the Chinese traitors who promised to collaborate with you in the execution of your nefarious scheme."

"You call such a Chinese a traitor", the Uigur shouted, "I call him a just man! Some Chinese recognize that what they have taken from us must be given back. Dit not you Chinese encroach on our pastures, your peasants ploughing our good grasslands and transforming them into rice fields? Have we not been driven away farther and farther to the desert where our horses and cattle die on our hands?

I shall not reveal the names of those Chinese who realized the awful wrong that your people have done to us, the Uigur tribes!"

The headman was going to hit him but the judge raised his hand.

Leaning forward in his chair he said quietly:

"It so happens that I have no time for preliminaries. Your right leg is already broken, you cannot walk anyway. So it won't inconvenience you much if your other leg should be broken too."

Judge Dee gave a sign to the headman.

Two constables threw the Uigur on his back on the floor

and stood with their feet on his hands. Another brought a wooden trestle of about two feet high.

The headman lifted Ooljin's left leg and bound the foot to the trestle. He looked up at the judge.

As Judge Dee nodded, a sturdy constable struck the knee with a heavy rounded stick.

The Uigur let out a hoarse scream.

"Take your time", the judge ordered the constable, " don't hit too fast!"

The constable struck a blow on the shin, then two on the thigh.

Ooljin screamed and cursed in his own language. When his shin was struck again he yelled:

"One day our hordes shall invade your accursed country, we shall raze your walls and burn your cities, we shall kill your men and make your women and children our slaves . . ."

His voice became a wild scream as the constable hit him another vicious blow. As he raised the stick again for the final blow that would break the leg, Judge Dee held up his hand.

"Yoo will realize, Ooljin", he said casually, "that this interrogation is mere routine. I just want you to confirm what your Chinese confederate told me when he reported on you and your tribesmen and gave away the entire plot!"

With a superhuman effort the Uigur tore away one of his hands from under the feet of the constable. Raising himself on his elbow he shouted:

"Don't try to catch me with brazen lies, you dog official!"

"Well", Judge Dee observed coldly, "of course a Chinese is much too clever for you stupid barbarians. He made it appear as if he was on your side. And when the time came, he reported everything to the authorities. Soon the government shall appoint him to a lucrative post as a reward for his valuable information. Don't you see how you and your ignorant Khan were made fools of?"

. As he began to speak the judge gave a sign to Ma Joong. Then Yoo Kee was led before the dais.

When he saw the Uigur lying on the floor Yoo Kee's face turned ashen. He wanted to run away but Ma Joong grabbed his arm in a vice-like grip.

As soon as the Uigur saw Yoo Kee, he spat out a string of curses.

"You son of a dog!", he yelled, "You vile traitor! Cursed be the day on which an honest Uigur resolved to work for a double-dealing Chinese cur like you!"

"Your Honour, this man is crazy!", Yoo Kee shouted.

Judge Dee ignored him. He calmly addressed the Uigur:

"Who are your accomplices in this man's mansion?"

Ooljin gave the names of the two Uigur warriors hired by Yoo Kee ostensibly as fencing masters. Then he shouted:

"And let me tell you that there are also Chinese traitors! That dogshead Yoo may have fooled me but I assure you that those other Chinese bastards were prepared to do everything just for the money!"

He then enumerated the names of three Chinese shop-keepers and four soldiers.

Tao Gan carefully noted down their names.

Judge Dee beckoned Chiao Tai to his side. He said in a whisper:

"Go immediately to your quarters in Chien's mansion and place those four soldiers under arrest. Then go with Corporal Ling and twenty men to Yoo Kee's mansion and arrest the two Uigurs there. You will then apprehend the three Chinese shopkeepers. Finally you will arrest The Hunter and his confederates in the Northern Row!"

As Chiao Tai hurried away Judge Dee said to Ooljin:

"I am not an unjust man, Ooljin. I won't stand for a

Chinese receiving a reward because he betrayed you after he had instigated and abetted your crime. If you want to prevent this man Yoo Kee from getting away with his treacherous deeds, you had better tell how Magistrate Pan was murdered!"

The Uigur's eyes blazed with unholy glee.

"Here is my revenge!", he shouted. "Listen, you official! Four years ago that man Yoo Kee gave me ten silver pieces. He told me to go to the tribunal and tell the new magistrate that that very night he could catch Yoo Kee in a secret conference with an emissary of the Uigur Khan, near the ford. Magistrate Pan came along with one assistant. The latter I knocked down as soon as we were outside the city gate. I myself cut the magistrate's throat and dragged his body to the river bank."

Ooljin spat in the direction of Yoo Kee.

"Now what about your reward, you dog?", he yelled.

Judge Dee nodded to the senior scribe. He read aloud his notes of what the Uigur had said. Ooljin agreed that it was a true account of his confession. The document was handed to the Uigur and he impressed his thumbmark on it.

Then Judge Dee spoke:

"You, Ooljin, are an Uigur prince from over the border and your crime of sedition concerns the external relations of our Empire. I am in no position to find out if and how deeply your Khan and the chieftains of the other tribes are implicated in this scheme of rebellion. It is not within my competence to pass judgement on you. You shall be conveyed immediately to the capital. There your crime shall be dealt with by the Board for Barbarian Affairs."

He gave a sign to the headman. Prince Ooljin was laid on a stretcher and carried back to the jail.

"Bring the criminal Yoo Kee before me!" Judge Dee ordered.

226

A CRIMINAL CONFESSES HIS NEFARIOUS SCHEMES

As Yoo Kee was pressed to his knees in front of the dais, Judge Dee said sternly:

"Yoo Kee, you are guilty of high treason. This is a crime against the state for which the law prescribes a terrible punishment. Yet perhaps the great name of your late father and a recommendation from me might bring the authorities to mitigate somewhat the fearful fate that awaits you. Therefore I advise you to confess now and give a full account of your crime!"

Yoo Kee did not reply. His head hung low and he breathed heavily. Judge Dee gave a sign to the headman to leave him alone.

At last Yoo Kee looked up. He said in a toneless voice, quite different from his accustomed animated way of talking:

"Beyond the two Uigurs, I have no accomplices in my mansion. I would have told my servants at the very last moment that we were going to take over the town. The four soldiers received a gift in money. Tomorrow, on the hour of midnight, they would light a signal fire on the highest watchtower in the Chien mansion. They were told that this would be the sign for a band of ruffians to create a disturbance and that that was the cover under which the two large goldsmiths' shops of this city would be looted. In fact, however, the fire would be the sign for the Uigur tribes over the river to attack. Ooljin and his Chinese helpers would then have opened the Watergate, and . . ."

"Enough!", Judge Dee interrupted him. "Tomorrow you shall have full opportunity for telling the entire story.

Now I only want you to answer one question. What did you do with the testament you found concealed in your late father's scroll picture?"

A look of surprise flashed over Yoo Kee's haggard face. He replied:

"Since the original testament stated that the property was to be divided equally between me and my half brother Yoo Shan, I destroyed it. Instead I inserted into the lining of the scroll a paper that I had written myself and that would establish beyond all doubt that I was the only rightful heir."

"You see", the judge said disdainfully, "that every one of your black deeds is known to me! Lead the criminal back to jail!"

Not long after the judge had closed the session, Chiao Tai came to his private office and reported that all the criminals had been duly placed under arrest. In the Northern Row there had been some trouble, The Hunter had resisted his arrest but he had been knocked down by Corporal Ling.

Judge Dee leaned back in his chair. Sipping a cup of hot tea he said:

„Ooljin and the six Uigurs must be conveyed to the capital. Let Corporal Ling select ten soldiers, and set out on horseback tomorrow morning. If they change horses at the nearest military post, they should be in the capital within a week. The three shopkeepers and the soldiers who accepted the bribe, I shall judge here."

Looking at his four lieutenants sitting in a half circle in front of his desk, Judge Dee continued with a smile:

"I think that with the arrest of the leaders we have nipped this plot in the bud!"

Chiao Tai nodded eagerly.

"The Uigur tribesmen", he said, "are not to be despised as warriors in a pitched battle in the open field. They are fine horsemen and their archers shoot with deadly accuracy. But they have neither the experience nor the equipment necessary for laying siege to a walled city. When tomorrow night they don't see the signal fire on the watch tower, they will not dare to attack!"

Judge Dee nodded.

"I leave it to you, Chiao Tai", he said, "to make the necessary preparations to meet any eventuality."

With a bleak smile the judge added:

"You cannot complain that you are not kept busy here, my friends!"

"The other day when we were approaching Lan-fang", Sergeant Hoong said with a smile, "Your Honour observed that our task here would be interesting because we would meet here unusual problems! That surmise has indeed come true!"

Judge Dee wearily passed his hand over his eyes.

"I find it difficult to believe", he said, "that it is only one week since we arrived here in Lan-fang!"

Putting his hands into his wide sleeves he continued:

"Looking back upon the last few days I think that Chien Mow's mysterious visitor worried me more than anything else. It was evident that he was the brain behind the tyrant's activities. I knew that as long as he was free anything might happen!"

"How did Your Honour discover that it was Yoo Kee?", Tao Gan asked. As far as I can see there was no clue at all to the stranger's identity!"

Judge Dee nodded.

"It is true", he replied, "we did not know much. Yet there were two indirect clues. First, we knew that he must be a man conversant with the internal and external affairs of the Empire. Second, that he probably lived in the vicinity of Chien Mow's mansion.

I must confess that at first I strongly suspected Woo Feng of being our man. Woo is exactly the kind of reckless fellow who would venture on such a wild scheme. And his family background would have given him sufficient knowledge of affairs of state to guide Chien Mows' actions."

"Moreover", Sergeant Hoong interrupted, "there is Woo's queer predilection for barbarian art!"

"Exactly!", said Judge Dee. "However, Woo lived far from Chien Mow's mansion and it seemed unlikely to me that he would be able to leave his quarters regularly in an elaborate disguise without the garrulous host of the Eternal Spring Wineshop coming to know of it. Lastly, Ma Joong's talk with The Hunter proved that the plans of the conspirators were not affected by Woo's arrest."

Judge Dee pulled his hands from his sleeves and leaned with his elbows on the table. Looking at Chiao Tai he continued:

"You, Chiao Tai, suggested the solution to me!"

Chiao Tai looked his astonishment at this unexpected statement.

"Yes", the judge went on, "it was you who, in connection with our imaginary army, pointed out to me that a ruse could work two ways! It suddenly dawned on me that Yoo Kee's elaborate preparations for defending himself against a barbarian attack could as well be explained as preparations for taking part in such a raid!

Once that my suspicions had been aroused I found that Yoo Kee fitted the part of Chien Mow's secret adviser very well. First, Yoo Kee is of course thoroughly conversant with political affairs, he grew up in the house of one of the greatest statesmen of our time. Second, his house is within walking distance of Chien Mow's mansion, he would soon see the black flag that Chien used to hoist on his gate when he wanted Yoo Kee to visit him that day.

Then I started to ask myself a few questions. Why should a man who is afraid of a barbarian raid purchase a mansion in the most dangerous spot, in the southwest corner of the city near the Watergate? And that while he already possessed a mansion near the East Gate, a safe location where he can flee to the mountains at the first sign of danger? And why did Chien Mow take no measures against Yoo Kee when the latter took Chien's best fencing master away?

There could be only one answer: Yoo Kee was Chien's adviser, it was he who organized the plan for establishing an independent kingdom here on the border.

Lastly, Chien Mow told me so himself!"

"When was that, Your Honour?", Sergeant Hoong and Ma Joong exclaimed at the same time. Tao Gan and Chiao Tai stared at the judge in utter amazement.

Judge Dee looked at his lieutenants with a quizzical smile.

"When Chien Mow was dying", he replied, "we all thought that he tried to start a sentence with 'You...'. I should have known better! A dying man who can hardly speak does not try to formulate a complicated sentence. He only wanted to pronounce one name, the name of the murderer of Magistrate Pan. And that name was Yoo Kee!"

Tao Gan crashed his fist on the desk. He gave the others a meaningful look.

"I must add", Judge Dee continued, "that it was old Master Crane Robe who suggested this to me. At the very beginning of our conversation he misheard 'Yoo' for 'You'. At least I thought that he had misheard... Looking back on that strange conversation I suspect that every word of the old master was said with a purpose and had a very special meaning..."

Judge Dee's voice trailed off. He fell silent and for a few moments pensively stroked his beard. Then he looked at his lieutenants and continued in a brisk voice:

"Tomorrow I shall close the case against Yoo Kee. The charge of high treason is the most serious one that can be made, it disposes of his murdering Magistrate Pan.

In the same session, I shall close the murder of General Ding!"

The last announcement gave Judge Dee's lieutenants their second shock that evening. They all spoke together.

Judge Dee raised his hand.

"Yes", he said, "I have finally found the solution of that queer and complicated case. The man who actually killed the General signed his name to the deed!"

"So it was, after all, that impudent rascal Woo!", Sergeant Hoong said excitedly.

"Tomorrow", Judge Dee said calmly, "you will know how General Ding met his death."

He sipped his tea. Then he went on:

"Today we have made much progress. Yet there still remain two vexing problems. The first is a practical and urgent one, namely the disappearance of White Orchid. The second is a less urgent one, but all the same it needs our full attention. I mean the riddle of Governor Yoo's picture.

Unless we can establish that Mrs. Yoo and her son Yoo Shan are the rightful owners of half of the Governor's property, they will forever be as destitute as they are now. For since Yoo Kee will be indicted on the charge of high treason, the government will confiscate all his possessions.

Unfortunately, Yoo Kee destroyed the testament he found in the Governor's scroll picture. So that proof is gone. Yoo Kee's confession does not alter the fact that the old Governor on his deathbed bequeathed the picture to Mrs. Yoo and her son, and 'all the rest' to Yoo Kee. The higher authorities, and especially the Board of Finance will base themselves on that oral will, and confiscate all Yoo Kee's property. Thus unless I solve the riddle of that picture, Mrs. Yoo and Yoo Shan will receive nothing!"

Tao Gan nodded. He slowly played with the three long hairs that sprouted from his left cheek. Then he asked:

"At the beginning we did not know that Yoo Kee was concerned with this plan for taking the city. We only knew that he was the defendant in an inheritance suit. Why did Your Honour right from the beginning take such a great interest in the case Yoo versus Yoo?"

Judge Dee answered with a smile:

"Since I am explaining, I may as well tell you the background of my special interest in that case.

I must state that I have always been deeply interested in the personality of Governor Yoo Shou-chien. Many years ago when I was preparing myself for my second examination, I copied out all the reords I could lay hands on of the criminal cases solved by Governor Yoo when he was still a district magistrate. Poring over those I made it my ambition to learn his brilliant deductive methods. Later I carefully studied his inspired memorials to the Throne and tried to absorb his burning passion for justice and his deep devotion to the state and the people. He was for me the shining example, the ideal of the perfect servant of the state.

How I longed to meet him in person! But that was of course quite impossible since he was a Governor and I but a struggling young candidate.

Then Governor Yoo suddenly resigned. This inexplicable action of my hero perturbed me greatly. I have been wondering about it ever since.

When I found in the archives here in Lan-fang the file Yoo versus Yoo, it seemed to me as if at last I would have an opportunity of coming nearer to the idol of my youth, that I would meet him, as it were, in the spirit. The riddle of his testament seemed to me a challenge from beyond the grave . . ."

Judge Dee paused and looked intently at the scroll picture hanging on the wall opposite.

As he pointed at it he continued:

"I am firmly resolved to find the secret of that scroll! Since Yoo Kee's confession, the old Governor's message has become more than a challenge. I feel it is my solemn duty to the Governor's memory to see to it that the widow and the son of the man I worshipped obtain what is rightfully theirs. All the more so since I sent his eldest son to the execution ground."

The judge rose and stood himself in front of the picture. His lieutenants left their seats and also gazed once more at the mysterious landscape.

Folding his hands in his sleeves Judge Dee said slowly:

" 'Bowers of Empty Illusion'! How deeply it must have shocked the old Governor when he found that his eldest son had inherited his father's brilliant mind, but nothing of his noble character!

I know every brush stroke of this picture by heart. I had hoped that the old country mansion would have given me some clue, yet I cannot . . ."

Suddenly the judge stopped. Bending forward he looked over the entire picture from top to bottom. As he straightened himself he slowly tugged at his whiskers. Then he turned round. His eyes were shining.

"I have found it, my friends!" he exclaimed. "Tomorrow, this riddle also will be solved!"

JUDGE DEE CLOSES THE CASE OF THE MURDERED GENERAL;
CHIAO TAI RELATES THE STORY OF A MILITARY DISASTER

THE next day, when Judge Dee opened the morning session
of the tribunal hundreds of people were crowding the
courtroom. The news of Yoo Kee's arrest had spread all
over the town and the wildest rumours were circulating
with regard to the arrest of the Uigur chieftain.

Judge Dee slowly surveyed the crowd, and pondered for
a while as to how he should start the questioning. He reflected that Yoo Kee excelled in dissimulation and secret
planning; he was wont to direct affairs from behind a
carefully constructed screen. Often such persons break
down completely once they have been forced to come out
into the open.

The judge wrote Yoo Kee's name on a slip and handed it
to Headman Fang.

As Yoo Kee was brought in Judge Dee saw that his
surmise had been correct. Yoo Kee had changed overnight
into a different person. The cloak of easy joviality that he
had so carefully worn had fallen off. There was left nothing
but a listless, broken man.

Judge Dee said quietly:

"At yesterday's session we went through the formalities.
You can now begin immediately with your confession!"

"Your Honour", Yoo Kee spoke in a toneless voice,
"when a man has been left no hope either in this world or the
next there is no reason why he should not tell the whole truth."

Yoo Kee paused for a moment. Then he suddenly said bitterly:

"I know that my father hated me. Well, I hated him too although I admit that I feared him! While he was still alive I had already made the firm resolution that I would become a greater man than he. He had been a governor, I was to be a sovereign ruler!

For years I made a careful study of the border situation. I realized that if the barbarian tribes could be united and given some guidance they could easily overrun the entire border region. With Lan-fang as capital I could found a kingdom astride the border. While keeping off the Chinese authorities by promises of submission and lengthy negotiations about vassalage, I would steadily enlarge the kingdom to the west by attracting more and more barbarian chieftains; thus while my power would be growing in the west, my attitude to the Chinese authorities in the east would gradually stiffen until I would be so strong that no one would dare to attack me."

Yoo Kee heaved a sigh, then went on:

"I was confident that I had sufficient diplomatic skill and knowledge of Chinese internal politics to execute this scheme. But I lacked military experience. In Chien Mow I found a useful tool. He was a determined and ruthless man, but he knew he was not qualified to act as a political leader. I encouraged him to establish himself as the local ruler here and showed him how he could consolidate his position against the central authorities. He acknowledged my leadership. After our plans had materialized, I would have appointed Chien Mow as my Generalissimo. At the same time I used Chien's activities to test the reaction of the central authorities. Everything succeeded, the central government seemed to acquiesce in the irregular situation here. So I resolved to take the next step and establish contact with the Uigur tribes.

Then that interfering fool, Magistrate Pan arrived. Through an unfortunate accident a letter I had written to an Uigur chieftain fell into his hands. I had to act quickly. I ordered Orolakchee, a cousin of the Khan and my confidential agent, to lure Pan to the river and kill him. Chien Mow was angry, he feared that the government would retaliate. But I instructed him how he could cover up this crime, and nothing untoward happened."

Judge Dee was going to interrupt Yoo Kee but on second thoughts he decided that it was better to let him tell his story in his own way. Yoo Kee went on in the same toneless voice:

"I would have come out into the open then were it not that the Khan received information of big Chinese victories over the barbarians in the north. He started to waver and finally withdrew his support. Then I engaged in complicated negotiations with minor chieftains, and finally succeeded in uniting three powerful tribes. They would attack the city if I guaranteed that the Watergate would be open and that the main points inside the town would be occupied by my men.

When the date had been fixed, Your Honour arrived with a regiment of the regular army for inspecting the border, Chien Mow was arrested and his men dispersed. I feared that my plans had leaked out and that in the near future a strong garrison would be sent to Lan-fang. I decided to take immediate action.

Tonight three Uigur tribes will gather in the plain. When at midnight they see the signal fire on the watchtower, they will ford the river and enter the city by the Watergate.

That is all!"

The crowd started to talk excitedly. They realized that they had narrowly escaped being overrun by cruel barbarian horsemen.

"Silence!", shouted Judge Dee.

Then he ordered Yoo Kee:

"State how many men these three tribes can put under arms!"

Yoo Kee thought for a while, then he replied:

"About two thousand trained mounted archers, and a few hundred footmen."

"What part were the three Chinese shopkeepers to play in this scheme?" asked the judge.

"I never met them", Yoo Kee answered, "it was my fixed policy to remain in the background as much as possible. I ordered Orolakchee to enlist the help of about one dozen Chinese to guide the Uigur warriors to the tribunal and the gates. He located those men and guaranteed their support."

Judge Dee gave a sign to the senior scribe. He read out his record of Yoo Kee's statement, and Yoo Kee affixed his thumbmark to it.

Then the judge spoke in a solemn voice:

"Yoo Kee, I pronounce you guilty of the crime of high treason. It is possible that the higher authorities will mitigate to some degree the severity of the extreme penalty in deference to the meritorious services of your late father, and because you confessed without pressure. But it is my duty to warn you that the Code prescribes for high treason the punishment of execution by the process called 'lingering death', that is, being cut to pieces alive.

Lead the criminal away!"

Then Judge Dee addressed the court:

"I have arrested all the leaders of this nefarious scheme. The barbarians will not dare to attack tonight when they do not see the signal fire. I have issued orders, however, to make the necessary preparations for any eventuality. In the course of today you will receive instructions from your wardens what to do. The barbarians have never been able to take a walled city so there is nothing to fear!"

The spectators broke out in cheers.

Judge Dee hit his gavel on the bench. Then he announced: "I shall now hear the case Ding versus Woo."

He filled out a slip with his vermilion brush. Soon Woo Feng was led before the dais by two constables.

As soon as Woo was kneeling the judge took from his sleeve a cardboard box and pushed it over the edge of the bench. It fell down with a thud in front of Woo.

He looked at it curiously. It was the box discovered in the sleeve of the murdered General. The corner the mouse had gnawed off had been neatly repaired.

The judge asked:

"Are you familiar with that box?"

Woo looked up.

"This", he replied, "is the kind of box they sell sweet plums in. I have seen hundreds of them on sale on the market of the Drum Tower. Occasionally I have bought one myself. Thus, although I am indeed familiar with such boxes in general, I have never seen this particular one. The congratulatory inscription on top evidently means that it was offered to someone as a present."

"You are quite right", Judge Dee said, "it is an anniversary present. Do you mind tasting the plums inside?"

Woo gave the judge a bewildered look. Then he shrugged his shoulders and replied:

"Not in the least, Your Honour!"

He opened the box. Nine plums were neatly arranged on a layer of white tissue paper. Woo poked them with his forefinger. When he had found a soft one he put it in his mouth. He ate it and spat the stone on the floor.

"Does Your Honour wish me to eat more?", Woo asked politely.

"This is quite sufficient!", Judge Dee said coldly. "You may stand back!"

Woo rose and looked around at the constables. They made no move to grab him and lead him back to the jail. So he retreated a few paces and remained standing there. He looked curiously at the judge.

"Let Candidate Ding come forward!", Judge Dee ordered.

As Ding knelt in front of the bench Judge Dee spoke:

"Candidate Ding, I have now discovered who killed your father. This case proved to be a singularly complicated one, I don't pretend to have disentangled all its ramifications. Your father's life was threatened from more than one side, and more than one attempt was made to kill him. This court, however, is concerned only with the one attempt that succeeded. The accused Woo has nothing to do with that. Hence the case against Woo Feng is herewith dismissed!"

A murmur of astonishment rose from the crowd. Candidate Ding remained silent, he did not repeat his accusation of Woo.

Woo cried out:

"Your Honour, has White Orchid been found?"

When the judge shook his head Woo turned round without another word and unceremoniously elbowed his way through the spectators to the door of the court hall.

Judge Dee took a red-lacquered writing brush from the bench.

"Rise, Candidate Ding", he ordered, "and tell me what you know about this brush!"

As he spoke the judge held out the writing brush to Ding, the open end of the shaft pointing straight at the young man's face.

Candidate Ding looked dumbfounded. He took the

brush from Judge Dee's hands and turned it round in his fingers. When he had read the engraved inscription he nodded his head.

"Now I see the inscription I remember, Your Honour! Some years ago when my father was showing me some rare old jade pieces he also took out this writing brush. He told me that it was an advance gift for his sixtieth birthday from a very exalted personage. My father did not reveal his name but he said that that person had told him that since he feared his end was near he wished to present that brush in advance; my father was not to use it until he had actually celebrated his sixtieth birthday.

My father valued this writing brush highly. After he had shown it to me he put it back into the locked box where he kept his jade collection."

"That writing brush", Judge Dee said gravely, "is the instrument that killed your father!"

Candidate Ding looked bewildered at the brush in his hands. He scrutinized it carefully and peered inside the hollow shaft. Then he shook his head doubtfully.

Judge Dee had followed intently his every move. Then he said curtly:

"Give that brush back to me. I shall demonstrate how the deed was done!"

When Candidate Ding had handed back the brush, Judge Dee kept it in his left hand. With his right he took a small wooden cylinder from his sleeve and held it up so that every one could see it.

"This", he said, "is an exact replica in wood of the hilt of the small knife that was found in General Ding's throat; it is just as long as the entire dagger including the blade. I shall now insert it into the hollow shaft of this brush."

The stick fitted exactly into the shaft. But when it had gone in for half an inch, it stuck.

242

Judge Dee handed the brush to Ma Joong.

"Press this stick further down!", he ordered.

Ma Joong placed his large thumb over the protrudin' end of the stick. With evident difficulty he pressed it down till it had disappeared into the shaft.

He looked expectantly at the judge.

"Stretch out your arm and release your thumb as quickly as you can!" ordered, the judge.

The wooden stick shot up in the air for about five feet, then clattered down on the stoneflags.

Judge Dee leaned back in his chair. Stroking his beard he said slowly:

"This writing brush is an ingenious instrument of death. Its hollow shaft contains a number of thin coils of what I presume to be southern rattan. After he had inserted these coils the person who made this instrument pressed them down as far as they would go with a hollow tube. He poured melted resin of the lacquer tree down that tube and held the coils down till the resin had completely dried. Then he removed the tube and replaced it by this."

Judge Dee opened a small box and with great care took from it the knife that had been found in the dead General's throat.

"You will see", he continued, "that its tubular hilt fits exactly into the shaft of this brush, while its hollow blade fits its curved inside. Even if one peered into the shaft, the knife would be invisible.

Some years ago a certain person presented this writing brush to the General and therewith pronounced his death sentence. He knew that when the General would use this brush, he would sooner or later burn its tip in a candle to discard the superfluous hairs, as we all do when we start writing with a new brush. The heat of the flame would soften the resin, the coils would be released and the poisoned knife would shoot out of the shaft. It was a ten to one chance that it would hit the victim in the face or throat. Afterwards the coils would be invisible because they would have stretched out along the inside to the hollow shaft."

While Judge Dee was speaking Candidate Ding had first shown an expression of utter bewilderment. Slowly this expression had changed to one of incredulous horror. Now he cried out:

"Who, Your Honour, contrived this diabolical device?"

"He signed his name to the deed", Judge Dee said quietly. "But for that fact I would never have solved this riddle. Let me read out to you the inscription:

'With respectful congratulations on the completion of six cycles. The Abode of Tranquillity.' "

"Who is that? I have never heard that studio name!", Candidate Ding cried out.

Judge Dee nodded.

"It was known only to a few intimate friends", he replied. Yesterday I found out that it is the pen name of the late Governor Yoo Shou-chien!"

Loud exclamations rose from the audience.

When the excitement had subsided Judge Dee spoke:

"It so happens that on the same day both the father and the son appear in this tribunal, the son alive and the father in spirit.

You, Candidate Ding, will probably know better than I what deed of your father motivated old Governor Yoo to condemn him to death and to execute the sentence himself in this singular way. However this may be, I cannot proceed against the dead. I, the magistrate, herewith declare the case closed!"

Judge Dee let his gavel descend on the bench. He rose and disappeared through the screen behind the dais.

While the spectators filed out of the court hall they talked excitedly about the unexpected solution of the General's murder. They were full of praise for Judge Dee for having found out this ingenious device. A few elderly men with experience in court matters, however, were doubtful. They could not understand the significance of the incident of the box with plums and remarked to each other that evidently there was more to this case than met the eye.

When Headman Fang entered the quarters of the guards he found Woo waiting for him.

Woo bowed deeply for the headman and said hastily:

"Please allow me to take part in the search for your daughter!"

Headman Fang looked at him thoughtfully. Then he answered:

"Since you, Mr. Woo, were prepared to suffer severe torture for my daughter's sake, I shall welcome your assistance. I have an order to carry out just now. Wait here for a few moments, when I am back I shall tell you everything about our first unsuccessful search."

Cutting short Woo's protests, the headman walked to the gate and surveyed the crowd that was streaming out. He saw Candidate Ding who was just stepping out into the street. Headman Fang overtook him and said:

"Mr. Ding, His Excellency would like to see you for a moment in his private office."

Judge Dee was sitting behind his desk with his four lieutenants gathered round him. The judge had ordered Tao Gan to saw the shaft of the writing brush in two. They had seen the clot of resin at the bottom of the shaft, and the thin rattan staves stretched out along its inside.

When Headman Fang had shown Candidate Ding in, Judge Dee turned to his lieutenants and said:

"Your presence is no longer required!"

They rose and left for the corridor. Chiao Tai, however, remained standing in front of Judge Dee's desk.

"Your Honour", he said stiffly, "I beg to be allowed to stay!"

Judge Dee raised his eyebrows and shot a curious look at Chiao Tai's impassive face. Then he nodded and motioned to a footstool by the side of his desk.

Chiao Tai sat down and Candidate Ding made a move to follow his example. But as the judge did not ask him to be seated, after some hesitation the young man remained standing where he was. Then Judge Dee spoke:

"Candidate Ding, I refrained from denouncing your late father in public. Were it not for some special reason which I shall specify presently, I would not denounce him before you who are his only son.

I know exactly why your father was compelled to resign. The confidential documents relating to that case happened to pass through the Office of Records and Compilation in the capital when I was working there. There were no details, for not a single eye-witness to your father's black deed survived the disaster. Commander Woo, however, collected sufficient secondary evidence to show beyond doubt that your father was responsible for the massacre of one entire regiment of our Imperial army.

When political considerations prevented the authorities from indicting your father, Governor Yoo decided that he himself would execute him as he deserved. The old Governor was a fearless man, he would have killed your father openly were it not that that would have involved the Governor's own family. Therefore he decided that the deed would be done after he had placed himself beyond the pale of human justice.

I would not make bold to pass judgement on the Governor's actions, a man like he can never be measured by ordinary standards. I only wish to make it perfectly clear to you that I know all the facts."

Candidate Ding did not answer. It was evident that he knew of his father's crime. He had bent his head and stood there looking silently at the floor.

Chiao Tai was sitting quite still. He looked straight in front of him with unseeing eyes.

Judge Dee silently stroked his long beard for a few moments. Then he said:

"Having thus disposed of your father's case, Candidate Ding, I now come to you yourself!"

Chiao Tai rose.

"I beg to be excused, Your Honour!"

Judge Dee nodded. Chiao Tai left the room.

The judge did not speak for a while.

At last Candidate Ding looked up fearfully. He shrank back as he saw the burning eyes of the judge bore into his.

Gripping the arms of his chair the judge leaned forward and said contemptuously:

"Look at your magistrate, you miserable wretch!"

The young man looked at him with deadly fear in his eyes.

"You despicable fool!", Judge Dee spat in a voice trembling with wrath, "you thought you could deceive me, your magistrate, with your foul plot!"

With an effort the judge mastered himself. When he spoke again his voice was steady. But it had a merciless metal ring that made Candidate Ding cringe with fear.

"It was not Woo Feng who planned to kill your father with poison. It was you, his only son!

Woo's arrival in Lan-fang supplied you with the idea for covering the crime you were contemplating. You started rumours about Woo, you spied on him. It was you who, sneaking into Woo's studio when he was out or in the midst of one of his drinking bouts, abstracted a piece of paper bearing an impression of his seal!"

Candidate Ding opened his mouth.

Judge Dee crashed his fist on the desk.

"Be silent and listen!", he barked.

"On the night of your father's anniversary you had the box with poisoned plums ready in your sleeve. When your father left the hall you, his dutiful son, escorted him to his library. The steward walked behind you.

Your father unlocked the door. You knelt down and wished him good night. The steward stepped inside and lighted the two candles on the desk. Then you took the box from your sleeve and silently presented it to your father. Probably you bowed. The inscription on top of the box made any explanation superfluous. Your father thanked you and put the box in his left sleeve.

At that very moment the steward stepped out again. He thought he saw your father put the key back into his sleeve, and he thought that the words of thanks he heard your father say referred to your wishing him good night. But there is an unexplained interval of two minutes or so, the time during which the steward lighted the two candles. Why should your father have been standing there with the key in his hand? Of course he had put it back in his sleeve as soon as he had unlocked the door. It was the box with the poisoned plums that the steward saw him putting in his sleeve. The instrument with which a depraved son planned to kill his own father!"

Judge Dee's eyes bored like daggers into Ding's. The young man had started to tremble all over, but the could not avert his eyes from Judge Dee's compelling gaze.

"You did not murder your father", the judge continued in a low voice. "Before he had even opened the box, the hand of the dead Governor struck."

JUDGE DEE CONFRONTS A CRIMINAL WITH THE EVIDENCE

Candidate Ding swallowed several times. Then he cried out in an unnatural voice:

"Why, why should I want to kill my own father?"

The judge rose. He took up the roll with his notes on the Ding case. Standing in front of Candidate Ding he said in a terrible voice:

"You utter fool! You dare to ask this question? You dare to ask why, while in your sordid scribblings you not only clearly mentioned the depraved woman who was the cause of your hatred for your father, but also betrayed your sinful relations?"

Throwing the roll into Ding's face the judge continued:

"Re-read what you wrote in your miserable poem about 'breasts white as snow', and 'the moon that is not marred by its spots'. It so happened that a maid servant reported to me that the fourth wife of your father has an unsightly mole on her left breast. You are guilty of the descipable crime of adultery with one of your father's wives!"

A deep silence reigned in the room.

When the judge spoke again his voice was tired.

"I could accuse in the tribunal you and your paramour of this shameful adultery. But the main purpose of the law is to restore the damage caused by a criminal act. In this case there is nothing to restore. What we can and shall do, however, is to prevent the rot from spreading further.

You know what gardeners do when a branch of a tree is rotten to the core. They cut that branch off so that the tree itself may live. Your father is dead, you are his only son, and you have no children yourself. You will realize that this line of the Ding clan must be cut off. That is all, Candidate Ding!"

Candidate Ding turned round. He left the office walking as a man in a dream.

A knock sounded on the door.

Judge Dee's face lit up as he saw Chiao Tai come in. "Sit down, Chiao Tai!" he said with a tired smile.

Chiao Tai seated himself on a footstool, his face pale and drawn. He began without any preliminary, speaking in a toneless voice, as if reading aloud an official report.

"Ten years ago, in the autumn, General Ding Hoo-gwo with seven thousand men met with a slightly superior force of barbarians across the northern border. If he had offered battle he would have had an even chance to win.

But he did not want to risk his life. He opened secret negotations and bribed the barbarian general to withdraw. Then the barbarian insisted that his warriors could not return to their tents without several hundred enemy heads to show their prowess in battle.

General Ding ordered the sixth battalion of the left wing to detach themselves from the main army and take up an advanced position in a valley. It counted eight hundred men led by Commander Liang, one of the most gallant officers of the Imperial army, and eight captains.

As soon as the battalion had entered the valley two thousand barbarians swooped down on them from the mountains. Our men fought bravely but their valour was of no avail against such superior numbers. The entire battalion was massacred. The barbarians cut off as many heads as they could, stuck them on their spears and rode away.

Seven captains had been hacked to pieces. The eighth had been stunned by a spear blow on his helmet and left for dead under his horse. He came to when the barbarians had left and found himself the only survivor."

Chiao Tai's voice had become strained. Perspiration streamed down his haggard face. He continued:

"That captain found his way back to the capital and there accused General Ding before the Board of Military

Affairs. He was told that the affair was closed and that he should forget all about it.

Then that captain threw away his army uniform. He swore that he would not rest till he had found General Ding and cut off his head. He changed his name, joined a band of chivalrous highwaymen, and for some years roamed all over the Empire searching for General Ding. Then, one day, he met a magistrate travelling to his post. That man taught him the meaning of justice, and . . ."

Chiao Tai's voice faltered. A strangled sob rose from his throat.

Judge Dee looked at him affectionately. He said gravely:

"Fate decided, Chiao Tai, that your good sword would not be soiled by a traitor's blood. Another man decided that General Ding should die and executed his sentence.

What you have just told me shall remain strictly between ourselves. But I shall not keep you here against your will. I have known all along that your heart is in the army. How would it be if under some pretext or other I sent you to the capital? I shall give you a confidential letter of recommendation to the head of the Board of Military Affairs. You will certainly be appointed a commander over a thousand!"

A bleak smile crossed Chiao Tai's face.

"I much prefer", he said quietly, "to wait until in due time Your Honour has been appointed to high office in the capital. I beg to be allowed to continue serving Your Honour until my services are no longer required."

"So be it!", the judge said with a happy smile. "I am grateful to you for your decision, Chiao Tai. I would have missed you greatly!"

Twentysecond Chapter

JUDGE DEE EXPLAINS THE MURDER OF GENERAL DING;
HE REVEALS THE SECRET OF THE SCROLL PICTURE

In the meantime Headman Fang.had had a long talk with
Woo.

Evidently Woo was interested in nothing but White
Orchid's disappearance. He had completely forgotten his
days in jail and the whipping he had received in the tribunal. For a few moments he listened absent-mindedly to the
headman's explanation of how General Ding had met his
end. Then he interrupted peevishly:

"I have not the slightest interest in that accursed Ding
clique. What I want to know is how we shall go about
locating your eldest daughter! You realize, by the way,
that I intend to approach a middle-man about our marriage
as soon as she is found!"

The headman bowed in silence. Secretly he was very
proud that such a distinguished young man wanted to
marry his daughter. But he was shocked by his casual
reference to these matrimonial plans. As most middle-class
householders, Fang was a stickler for formality, and it is a
fundamental rule of propriety that the prospective groom
shall not touch upon this subject directly with the father of
the bride until a middle-man has approached him. It was
his strict sense of propriety that had made the headman tell
his daughter Dark Orchid to gather information about
Mrs. Lee, as Sergeant Hoong had ordered. Fang did not
like to execute that order himself for he reasoned that it

might reflect on Mrs. Lee's good name if a man made inquiries about her.

Headman Fang hastily changed the subject, saying:

"I expect that His Excellency will tomorrow evolve a new plan for the search. In the meantime you, Mr. Woo, could perhaps paint four or five real portraits of my missing daughter, to be circulated among the wardens of the other quarters of this town."

"That is an excellent idea!", Woo exclaimed enthusiastically, "I shall go back home and set to work immediately!"

He jumped up but the headman laid a restraining hand on his arm. He said diffidently:

"Would it not be better, Mr. Woo, if before leaving the tribunal you requested to see His Excellency? You have not yet taken leave of him properly, and perhaps you might thank him for clearing you of suspicion."

"Later, later!", Woo said airily and rushed away.

Judge Dee had partaken of a frugal luncheon in his private office with Sergeant Hoong attending upon him.

The sergeant saw that the judge looked tired. He ate in silence.

When the meal was over Judge Dee lingered over his tea. At last he said:

"Sergeant, call my other lieutenants. I want to tell all of you the full story of the General's murder."

When his four lieutenants were gathered in front of him, Judge Dee settled back in his armchair and told them the substance of his private conversation with Candidate Ding.

Tao Gan shook his head in perplexity. Heaving a deep sigh he said:

"Your Honour, it seems to me that never before have we been confronted with such a mass of complicated problems!"

"Superficially it looks that way", the judge replied. "In fact it was only the local background that complicated everything. Now the confused threads are gradually becoming untangled and a clear pattern emerges.

We have but three real cases. First, General Ding's murder. Second, the case Yoo versus Yoo. Third, the disappearance of Fang's daughter.

Our measures against Chien Mow, our discovery of Yoo Kee's scheme, and the solution of Magistrate Pan's murder, must be viewed as local background. They are separate issues and have nothing to do with the substance of our three cases."

Sergeant Hoong nodded. After a while he remarked:

"I have been wondering all along why Your Honour did not proceed immediately against Woo. At first all evidence pointed strongly to his guilt."

"At our very first meeting", the judge answered, "Candidate Ding behaved in a suspicious way. When I and Ma Joong met him in the street, he could not conceal his consternation when I disclosed my identity. Since I have the undeserved reputation of a detector of crimes, Ding evidently thought for a moment of abandoning his plan of poisoning his father and throwing the blame on Woo. Then he decided that his scheme was flawless and that after all he could take his chance. He invited us to a tea house and dished out his story of Woo's designs on General Ding's life."

"That bastard Ding fooled even me!", Ma Joong exclaimed angrily.

Judge Dee smiled and went on:

"Then the General was killed. Young Ding had not the slightest idea of what could have happened. I checked that again this morning. You saw that I suddenly produced the fatal writing brush, pointing the open end of the shaft right at Ding's face. If it had been Ding who had tampered with that brush after the Governor had presented it to the General, Ding would certainly have betrayed himself.

As it was, Candidate Ding must have been as puzzled by this mysterious murder as we. He must have had an anxious half hour, trying to find out what had happened. Had his paramour had a hand in the killing? Was it someone who had found out about his murder plot and who would in due course ask for a substantial reward for having executed his scheme for him? Then Ding decided that his original plan of making Woo the culprit must be carried out anyway. With Woo's guilt established, Ding need not be afraid of the real murderer intimidating or blackmailing him. Thus he came rushing in here and accused Woo. Ding, however, did not realize that the false trail he had so carefully constructed was extremely poor."

"That is beyond me, Your Honour!", Tao Gan interrupted. "That box of poisoned plums pointed straight to Woo!"

"Too much so", the judge replied. "It was badly overdone and moreover based on a wholly mistaken evaluation of Woo's character. Woo is an over-clever and excitable young man of a type that, I must confess, is not very sympathetic to me. But he undoubtedly is a great artist. Such persons are usually rather vague and casual about the routine of daily life, but they show a tremendous capacity for concentration as soon as it regards things they are really interested in. If Woo chose to poison some one he would certainly never use gamboge, and never overlook such a blatant clue as his seal on the paper inside the box."

Tao Gan nodded.

"The final proof of Woo's innocence", he said, "was his willingness to eat the new plums I had put inside that box."

"Exactly!", Judge Dee said. "However, let us keep to the chronological order of developments. When Ding had reported the murder, I immediately went to see Woo. I wanted to compare the personalities of accuser and defendant. I forthwith decided that Woo was hardly the type to commit a premeditated murder, let alone because of such a far-fetched motive as suggested by Ding.

I assumed that the actual killing had been done by a third person. I could well imagine that a man who had committed such a black crime as General Ding would have many enemies, and I took it that Ding utilized this fact for discrediting Woo. As to Ding's reason for persecuting Woo I assumed that they were rivals in love. The recurring portrait of a girl in Woo's paintings and Ding's love letters convinced me that both young men were in love with the same girl.

Our discovery of the box with poisoned plums strengthened me in my conviction that Ding was scheming against Woo. I assumed as a matter of course that Ding had taken due precautions that the poison would be discovered before his father ate the plums. I reasoned that a man would never risk his father's life in order to get rid of a rival in love."

"Yes", Sergeant Hoong interrupted, "I now understand why Your Honour ruled out Woo as the culprit."

"Indeed", Judge Dee replied, "I considered Ding as a treacherous and mean character. This prepared me for the next development, namely when I discovered that Woo and Ding were *not* in love with the same girl. This fact reduced the connection between Woo and Ding to the latter's false accusation. But why then had Ding accused Woo at all? The only possible answer was that Ding himself had killed his father and planned to use Woo as scapegoat.

Then I formed the theory that Ding had prepared two murder weapons. One had been actually used, but I had yet to discover it. The other was the box of poisoned plums, a second weapon that Ding held in reserve in case the first would fail to work. This being so, it was of the utmost importance to find Ding's motive for this hideous parricide.

Could it have something to do with the girl Ding was so passionately in love with? I sent Dark Orchid back to the Ding mansion to collect more data."

Here Judge Dee paused and slowly drank a cup of tea. Deep silence reigned in the room. Then the judge continued:

"At the same time, however, I was worrying about a curious inconsistency. Since Ding had made such elaborate preparations to ensure that his second weapon, the box of plums, would be traced to Woo, it was evident that he would have taken good care that also his first weapon pointed straight at Woo. I cudgeled my brain but failed to find in the actual murder the slightest clue pointing to Woo.

Therefore I decided to return to my first theory, namely that the real killing had been done by an unknown third person, whose deed happened to coincide with Ding's despicable poison plot. As a rule I do not like coincidences, but I had to admit that this case pointed forcibly to the fact that a coincidence had occurred."

"It was a coincidence", Chiao Tai remarked, "brought about by the fact which Your Honour mentioned a few moments ago, namely that General Ding had many enemies. And after all it was indeed because of the General's betrayal of his own men, that the old Governor killed him!"

Judge Dee nodded and went on:

"This conclusion did not bring me any nearer to the solution of the actual murder, but it helped me in so far that I could now rule out both Ding and Woo as suspects. When I had discovered Ding's motive for wishing to kill his father, that part of the case was solved."

Sergeant Hoong interrupted:

"So that was that Your Honour meant by referring to half of the murder being clear! Your Honour had then connected Dark Orchid's report about the General's fourth wife having an unsightly mole on her breast, with the reference in Ding's poem!"

"Exactly", Judge Dee said. "As to the other half of this case, the real killing of the General, I confess that I would probably never have solved that riddle if the old Governor had not signed his name to his deed.

The only conclusion I had arrived at was that the General must have been killed by some mechanical device, for it was absolutely impossible for the killer to have entered or left that sealed room. But I would never have discovered the secret of the writing brush. I am no match for the old Governor's brilliant mind! You will have noticed that after the knife had left the shaft, the coils straightened out along the inside; I would not have seen them even if I had peered inside the shaft.

When during my visit to old Master Crane Robe I learned that 'The Abode of Tranquillity' was the pen name of the old Governor, I remembered having seen that name engraved on the shaft of the brush General Ding had been writing with when he was killed. I thought of Tao Gan's suggestion about the blow-pipe and realized that the hollow shaft of a writing brush could serve the same purpose. The displaced candle taught me that there was some mechanical device inside the brush that was released as soon as the brush was heated. The rest was easy."

"What shall we do if Candidate Ding does not kill himself?", asked Chiao Tai.

"I shall accuse him and his paramour in this tribunal of adultery and torture them until they confess!", Judge Dee answered calmly.

Slowly smoothing his long beard the judge looked at his lieutenants. When no one asked more questions he continued:

"Now I come to our second case, the old Governor's testament."

His lieutenants turned round and looked at the picture on the wall.

"The written testament concealed in the lining", the judge said, "was a false clue deliberately planted there by the old Governor to delude Yoo Kee. The Governor's scheme was successful, for when Yoo Kee had found that document, he did not destroy the scroll but handed it back to Mrs. Yoo. The landscape picture itself contains the real clue, which is much more subtle!"

Judge Dee rose and walked over to the picture. His lieutenants hastily left their seats and stood by his side.

"I vaguely suspected", the judge began, "that there existed some connection between this landscape and the Governor's country estate. That was the main reason why I went out there myself."

"Why should there be any connection?", Tao Gan asked eagerly.

"For the simple reason", Judge Dee replied, "that those were the only two things which the old Governor wished to be preserved at all costs. He took clever precautions to ensure that this scroll picture should not be destroyed after his death, and he gave strict instructions to Yoo Kee that nothing was to be changed on his country estate.

At first I thought that this landscape picture was a disguised map of the country house, indicating the location of a secret wall safe where we would find the Governor's real testament. But during my visit out there I failed to discover the slightest resemblance. Only last night I found the connecting link!"

Judge Dee looked with a smile at his lieutenants. They hung on his lips.

"If you study this landscape carefully", he said, "you will notice some queer points in its composition. There are a number of houses, scattered among the cliffs. Every one of them can be reached by the mountain path, except the largest and most elaborate building here on top right! It lies on the river, but there is no road at all! I concluded that that building must have a special significance.

Now look at the trees! Is there nothing about them that strikes you as peculiar?"

Tao Gan and Sergeant Hoong scrutinized the picture closely. Ma Joong and Chiao Tai had given up. They looked at the judge with fond admiration.

When the sergeant and Tao Gan shook their heads the judge continued:

"All the houses are surrounded by clusters of trees, painted rather carelessly. Only the pine trees are drawn in detail; each trunk stands out clearly against the background.

Now you will notice that there is numerical sequence in those pine trees. Two at the top of the mountain where the path begins, three further down, four where the path crosses the river, and five near the large house on top right. I concluded that these pine trees are landmarks that indicate a route to be followed. The two pine trees on top are the link that connects this picture with the country estate: they represent the pair of pine trees that we saw at the entrance of the maze!"

"Thus this landscape is a guide map to the maze, showing how one reaches a small house or pavilion that the Governor had built inside!", Tao Gan exclaimed.

Judge Dee shook his head.

"No", he said, "not exactly. I agree that it indicates a route to a pavilion inside the maze. Since the Governor went there nearly every day, it is evident that somewhere inside there must be a pavilion where he could read and write. I also agree that this elaborate building represents that pavilion. But I don't agree that it can be reached by following the path of the maze.

The old Governor planned his abode inside the maze as a real secret. He would never leave important documents there if anyone who had sufficient courage and patience to search the maze and follow its regular path could find it.

Why did the Governor make such a sharp distinction between the first and the second half of the route. Why indicate the second half by a mountain river?"

"To make it more difficult!", Tao Gan replied promptly.

"No", Judge Dee said, "the Governor took special pains to indicate that the place marked by the four pines is an important point. Instead of the regular mountain path, from there on one 's course is indicated by the river. The bridge is a further indication that here there occurs an important change.

I am convinced that at this point one leaves the regular path of the maze, and enters a secret short cut that leads to the hidden pavilion, located not on the real path, but somewhere in between its curves."

Tao Gan nodded his agreement.

"What a perfect hiding place!", he exclaimed. "It is safer than any stronghold! If one does not know the key to the secret short cut, one could explore the maze for weeks on end and never find the pavilion. But the Governor and everyone who knew the secret could reach it probably in a few minutes!"

"Yes", Judge Dee said, "your last point is very important. The Governor would not like to walk for half an hour or so along the winding path of the maze every time he went inside. This consideration suggested to me the existence of a secret short cut.

Let us now follow the route indicated on this picture!"

The judge pointed with his forefinger to the small house on top of the mountain, with one pine tree on either side.

"Here", he said, "is the entrance of the maze. We

descend those steps hacked out in the rock, and follow the path downward. The first fork has no meaning, it does not matter whether one turns right or left. Coming to the second fork, three pine trees along the side of the path indicate that we must keep to the left.

Then we arrive at the river. This is the point where we leave the regular path of the maze. The entrance to the secret short cut is marked by four pine trees; I presume that in the maze we shall find the entrance between the second and third tree, right in the middle, just as the river in this picture.

Somewhere along this secret path we shall find five pine trees in two groups of two and three. The Governor's hidden pavilion must be located there!"

As he spoke the judge placed his forefinger on the large house on top right of the picture. He went back to his desk and sat down.

"If I am not greatly mistaken", Judge Dee concluded, "we shall find in that pavilion a safe or an iron chest with the Governor's confidential papers, including his testament!"

"Well", Ma Joong said, "it is all a little beyond me, but I am all for a try! However, there still is our third case, the disappearance of White Orchid!"

Judge Dee's face clouded. As he sipped his tea he said slowly:

"That is a most distressing case! We have not yet come one step nearer to finding that girl. I regret this all the more because I have taken a liking to our headman. He is that type of honest, decent tradesman, a class our country is justly proud of . . ."

The judge wearily passed his hand over his forehead. Then he continued:

"After dinner tonight we shall consult here together about ways and means for locating that girl. With our other cases disposed of we shall be able to concentrate on this last riddle.

Let us now go out to the country house and verify whether my theory about the secret short cut through the maze is correct. If we find the Governor's will, I can forward it to the higher authorities appended to my official report on Yoo Kee's treason. The Board of Finance will then have to except Yoo Shan's part when they declare the Yoo property confiscated.

Chiao Tai, you will need all the afternoon for organizing the defence of the town, in case the barbarians attack tonight. But you, Sergeant, shall accompany me with Ma Joong and Tao Gan!"

Twentythird Chapter

An hour later the country estate of the old Governor presented a scene of great activity.

Constables of the tribunal were everywhere. Some were clearing the garden path, others were making an inventory of the old furniture inside the mansion, others again were exploring the back garden.

Judge Dee was standing in the paved courtyard in front of the stone gate giving access to the maze. He was issuing his final instructions to Sergeant Hoong, Ma Joong and Tao Gan. Twenty constables were gathered around them.

"I don't know", Judge Dee said, "how long the road will prove to be. I assume that it will be relatively short, but we cannot be sure. As we walk along one constable will detach himself from our group every twenty feet or so. He will remain standing there so that he can shout to the man in front and behind. I would not like to get lost in this maze!"

Turning to Ma Joong the judge added:

"You will walk ahead with your spear. I don't believe all those stories about mantraps in this maze, but the place has been growing wild for years, and dangerous animals may have made their lairs here. Let everybody be careful!"

Then they passed underneath the stone archway and entered the maze.

In the dim tunnel they were met by the dank smell of

265

rotting leaves. The path was narrow but two men could easily walk abreast. On both sides closely planted trees and overgrown boulders formed an impenetrable wall. The trees were of all kinds, but not one single pine tree was in sight. The branches met overhead, linked together by thick clusters of vine that often hung so low that Judge Dee and Ma Joong had to stoop in order to pass underneath. The tree trunks were covered with extraordinarily large fungi. Ma Joong hit one with his spear. An evil-smelling cloud of white dust burst from it.

"Be careful, Ma Joong!", the judge warned him. "Those things may be poisonous!"

At the first left turn the judge halted. He pointed with a contented smile at three gnarled pine trees standing close together right in the curve.

"That is our first landmark!", he observed.

"Look out, Your Honour!" Ma Joong shouted.

Judge Dee quickly jumped aside.

A spider as large as a man's hand dropped to the ground with a dull thud. Its hairy body was spotted yellow, its eyes shone with an evil green light.

Ma Joong crushed it with the butt of his spear.

Judge Dee drew his neckcloth tight.

"I would not like to have one of those fall on my neck!", he observed dryly. Then he walked on.

The path seemed to double back. After twenty feet or so it made a sharp right turn.

"Halt!", Judge Dee called out to Ma Joong. "There is our next landmark!"

Alongside the path, four pine trees stood in a row.

"Here", Judge Dee said, "we must leave the regular path and enter the secret short cut. Explore the space between the second and third pine tree!"

Ma Joong poked with his spear among the thick under-

growth. Suddenly he jumped, pushing the judge unceremoniously back.

A red adder of about two feet long crept over the rotting
leaves and disappeared with amazing quickness in a hole
under the tree.

"A hospitable place!", Ma Joong growled. "That reptile
was not included in the landscape picture!"

"That is why I told you to put on your thick hunting
leggings!", Judge Dee remarked. "Have a good look!"

Ma Joong squatted and peered under the branches. As
he straightened himself he said:

"Yes, there is a path here. But it is so narrow that a man
can hardly pass. I shall go first and push the overhanging
branches apart!"

He disappeared among the dense foliage. Judge Dee
drew his robes tight about him and followed with Sergeant
Hoong and Tao Gan walking behind him. The constables
looked doubtfully at Headman Fang. Drawing his short
sword he called out to his men:

"Don't hesitate! If there are any wild animals we shall
take care of them!"

The passage proved only a few fathoms long. After a
brief struggle with the thorny branches they came out on
the main path again.

On left and right there was a sharp curve. Judge Dee
first turned left. He saw a long, straight stretch ahead.

He shook his head.

"It must be the opposite direction", he said. "I don't
think that a short cut would include such a long straight
section of the path."

He turned back to the spot where they had come out on
the path. When they had rounded the corner they found
themselves in a short passage.

"Here we are!", Judge Dee exclaimed excitedly. He

pointed to left and right. Three pine trees stood on one side of the path, two on the other.

"According to the Governor's picture", Judge Dee said to his companions, "the hidden pavilion must be very near. I assume that there is a path between that pair of pine trees. The three opposite would seem to be there only to make a total of five!"

Ma Joong eagerly plunged into the shrubs that filled the space between the two trees. They heard him curse fiercely.

He emerged again, his leggings soaked in mud.

"There is nothing there but a stagnant pool!" he said disgustedly.

Judge Dee frowned.

"There must be some path round that pool", he said impatiently. "Up till now everything checked!"

Headman Fang gave a sign to the constables. They drew their swords and started hacking the undergrowth away. The edge of a black pool appeared. Bubbles were still rising on the spot where Ma Joong had plunged in. A foul smell polluted the air.

Judge Dee stooped and peered under the overhanging branches. Suddenly he shrank back.

A queerly shaped head rose slowly from the water. Its yellow eyes looked at them with a fixed stare.

Ma Joong gasped and raised his spear. But the judge laid a restraining hand on his arm.

Slowly a huge salamander crawled out of the pool. Its slimy body was more than five feet long. Once on the bank it slithered away quickly among the waterplants.

All had received a bad fright.

"I prefer six Uigurs to that animal!", Ma Joong said feelingly.

But the judge seemed very pleased. He said with evident satisfaction:

"I have often read in our old books about those large salamanders. This is the first time I have actually seen one!"

Then he scrutinized what was visible of the bank of the pool. It did not look very promising, there was nothing but a mass of mud-covered waterplants. The judge then surveyed again the black water.

"Do you see that stone there?", he suddenly said to Ma Joong. "Evidently that is the first of a row of stepping stones leading across. Let us go ahead!"

Ma Joong tucked the slips of his robe in his girdle. The others followed his example.

He stepped on the flat stone and explored the surrounding area with his spear.

"Here is the next stone!", he called out, "directly in front left!"

He pushed the low branches apart and made a step forward. Then he suddenly halted. Judge Dee who was following close behind collided with him. The judge would have fallen into the water if Ma Joong had not steadied him.

Ma Joong silently pointed at a broken branch. He whispered in Judge Dee's ear:

"That branch was broken by a human hand, and not so long ago either. Look, the leaves have not yet dried. Someone passed along here yesterday, Your Honour! He slipped on this stone and when trying to steady himself grabbed this branch!"

Judge Dee looked at the branch and nodded.

"He may be quite near, we had better be prepared for an attack!", he replied in a low voice. Then the judge passed the word to Sergeant Hoong who was standing on the stone close by, and he in his turn informed Tao Gan and Headman Fang.

"I prefer any human being to that slimy beast!", Ma

Joong muttered. Testing the balance of his spear he went ahead.

The pool proved not very large but they lost much time because they had to locate the stepping stones one by one; some of them were just under the surface of the water. A person who knew the pattern, however, could cross the pool in a few minutes.

When they were on solid ground again Ma Joong and Judge Dee crouched. The judge parted the branches a little.

There was a fairly large clearance, hemmed in by trees and huge boulders. In the middle stood a round pavilion built of stone, under a high cedar tree. The windows were shuttered but the door stood ajar.

Judge Dee waited till all the constables had crossed the pool. Then he shouted:

"Surround the pavilion!"

As he spoke he sprang forward, ran to the pavilion and kicked the door open. Two large bats flew out with flapping wings.

The judge turned round. The constables had fanned out and were searching the bushes. Judge Dee shook his head.

"There is no one here", he said. "Let the headman and the constables make a thorough search of this clearance!"

Then he went inside again, Ma Joong and his two other lieutenants following him. Ma Joong pushed the shutters open.

In the dim, greenish light Judge Dee saw that the pavilion was bare but for a stone table in the centre and a marble bench against the back wall. Everything was covered by a thick layer of dirt and mould.

On the table stood a box of about one foot square. Judge Dee bent over it. He brushed the dirt off with the tip of his sleeve. The box was made of green jadeite, beautifully carved with dragons and clouds.

The judge carefully lifted the cover. He took out a small roll wrapped up in a piece of faded brocade.

As he held it up for his companions to see he said in a solemn voice:

"This is the Governor's testament!"

Slowly Judge Dee unwrapped it. He unrolled the scroll and read aloud:

'This is the last will and testament of Yoo Shou-chien, Member of the Imperial Academy, ex-Governor of the Three Eastern Provinces, etc.

Revered Sir and Colleague, to you who have solved the riddle of my picture and who have penetrated to the heart of my maze, I herewith make my bow!

One sows in spring and reaps in autumn. When twilight is setting over one's declining years it behoves a man to look back and weigh his deeds as they shall be weighed in the Hereafter.

I thought that I had attained success. I suddenly found nothing but miserable failure. I strove hard to reform the Empire and I failed to reform my son Yee Kee, my own flesh and blood.

Yoo Kee is a man of wicked nature and inordinate desires. Since I foresaw that after my death he would sooner or later bring about his own downfall, I married again in order to fulfil my duty to my Ancestors and to ensure that our house would not perish should Yoo Kee die in prison or on the execution ground.

Heaven blessed this marriage with my second son Yoo Shan of whom I have great expectations. It is my duty to see that Yoo Shan shall continue to prosper after my death.

If I divide my property equally between my sons Yoo Kee and Yoo Shan, I endanger the latter's life. Hence on my deathbed I shall make it appear as if I leave everything to Yoo Kee. But here I write down my real intention over my seal and signature and state that it is my will that if Yoo Kee reforms he and Yoo Shan shall each receive half; should Yoo Kee be guilty of some crime, everything shall go to Yoo Shan.

I shall hide in the picture scroll a written testament to that effect for Yoo Kee to discover. If he faithfully executes this last will, all will be well and Heaven will have had mercy on my house. Should Yoo Kee in his wickedness destroy that testament he will deem that my picture had yielded up its secret and leave it in the hands of my faithful young wife, till you, my wise colleague, read its hidden meaning and find the present document.

I beseech August Heaven to grant that when you read this document the hands of Yoo Kee shall not be stained with blood. Should he, however, have committed a dark crime I hold you responsible for forwarding the enclosed plea to the competent authorities.

May Heaven bless you, my wise colleague, and have pity on my house!

Signed and sealed: Yoo Shou-chien.'

"This confirms what we found in every detail!", Sergeant Hoong exclaimed.

Judge Dee nodded absent-mindedly. He was engrossed in the enclosure, a loose sheet of thick ornamental paper that had been rolled up together with the scroll.

Then he read its content aloud:

'Yoo Shou-chien, who never once pleaded the cause

PLAN OF THE GOVERNOR'S MAZE

of himself or his own, now after his death humbly pleads for such mercy as can be extended within the limits of the law for his eldest son Yoo Kee who became a criminal through the incompetent guidance of his old father who always loved him despite his faults.'

Silence reigned in the dimly lit pavilion. The only sounds heard were the shouts of the constables outside.

The judge slowly rolled up the scroll. Deep emotion thickened his voice as he said slowly:

"His Excellency Yoo truly was a noble man!"

Tao Gan was scratching the table with his fingernail.

"There is an engraved design here!", he remarked.

He pulled out his knife and started scraping off the dirt. Sergeant Hoong and Ma Joong set to work also. Gradually a circular design became visible.

Judge Dee leaned forward.

"This", he said, "is a map of the maze. Look, the course of the winding path forms four stylized characters in archaic script: 'Bowers of Empty Illusion'. That is the same motto as we found inscribed on the landscape picture! This was the keynote of the old Governor's thoughts after he had resigned from official life. Empty illusion!"

"The short cut is also indicated here!", Tao Gan said eagerly. "The location of the pine trees is shown by dots!"

Judge Dee again peered at the map. He traced the design with his forefinger.

"What an ingenious maze this is!", he exclaimed. "Look, if one enters by the regular entrance and always turns right at every fork, one will arrive at the exit after having gone through the entire maze. And if, conversely, one enters by the exit, the same will happen if one always takes the left turn. But unless one knows the secret short cut, one will never discover this hidden pavilion!"

"We must obtain permission from Mrs. Yoo to have this maze cleaned, Your Honour", the sergeant remarked. "Then it will become one of the famous sights of this district, just like the pagoda in the lotus lake!"

At that moment Headman Fang came in.

"Whoever was here left again before we came, Your Honour!", he reported. "We searched all through the undergrowth, but found nothing."

"Let your men also examine the trunks of the trees and look among the branches", Judge Dee ordered. "Our unknown sightseeer may have hidden himself up there!"

As the headman went out again, Judge Dee looked curiously at Tao Gan. Tao Gan had squatted on the broad bench and was peering intently at the layer of dirt covering it.

Shaking his head he said:

"If I did not know better, Your Honour, I would say that this dark spot here looks uncommonly like blood!"

Judge Dee felt a cold fear grip his heart.

He quickly stepped forward and rubbed his fingers over the spot Tao Gan indicated. He went to the window and looked at his hand. He saw dark red smears.

Turning round to Ma Joong the judge ordered curtly: "Look under that marble bench!"

Ma Joong poked his spear in the dark cavity underneath. A large toad came hopping out.

He went down on his knees and peered under the bench.

"There is nothing but cobwebs and dirt!", he reported.

In the meantime Tao Gan had looked in the empty space behind. He turned round with a pale face.

"There is a body lying behind the bench!" he said in a trembling voice.

Ma Joong jumped on the bench. Together they pulled up the mutilated body of a girl. She was completely naked and covered with dried blood and mud. Where the head had been, there was only the ragged stump of the neck.

They laid their gruesome find on the bench. Ma Joong loosened his neckcloth and covered up the loins. Then he stood back, his eyes wide with horror.

Judge Dee bent over the remains of what once must have been a shapely young girl. He noticed the ugly knife wound under the left breast and some badly healed scars on the arms. Slowly he turned the body over. The shoulders and hips were marked by thin welts.

As he straightened himself his eyes blazed with anger. He said in a tense voice:

"This girl was killed here only yesterday. The body is quite stiff, but no decay has set in."

"How did she come here?", Ma Joong asked aghast. "She must have been naked already when she crossed the maze! Look, the thorns scratched her thighs and her legs are covered with mud from the pool. It is she who slipped on one of the stepping stones and when trying to steady herself broke that branch!"

"The main problem is who brought her here!", said the judge curtly. "Call Headman Fang!"

As the headman entered the judge ordered:

"Roll this body in your gown, Headman. Order the constables to cut a few tall branches to make a stretcher!"

The headman took off his upper gown and bent over the bench.

Suddenly he uttered a hoarse cry. He was staring with bulging eyes at the mutilated body.

"This is White Orchid!", he said in a strangled voice.

Everyone exclaimed at once.

Judge Dee raised his hand.

"Are you quite certain, Headman?", he asked quietly.

"Once when she was only seven years old", the headman sobbed, "she fell over a kettle with boiling water and scalded her left arm. Do you imagine I am not familiar with that scar?"

He pointed to a white scar that marred the beauty of the shapely arm. Then he threw himself over the body sobbing as if his heart would break.

Jude Dee folded his arms in his wide sleeves. Knitting his thick eyebrows he remained for a while in deep thought.

Suddenly the judge asked Sergeant Hoong:

"Sergeant, did you find out where Mrs. Lee lives?"

The sergeant silently pointed to the prone figure of Headman Fang.

Judge Dee laid his hand on the headman's shoulder.

"Where is the house of Mrs. Lee?", he asked tensely.

Without looking up the headman answered:

"This morning I told Dark Orchid to go and find out."

Judge Dee turned round quick as lightning. He pulled Ma Joong close to him by his sleeve and whispered something in his ear.

Ma Joong rushed out of the pavilion without another word.

Twentyfourth Chapter

A YOUNG GIRL GOES TO VISIT A FAMOUS ARTIST;
A CRIMINAL IS CAUGHT IN AN UNEXPECTED PLACE

THAT morning Dark Orchid had left the tribunal to go and find out Mrs. Lee's address as her father had ordered her.

She walked at a brisk pace along the main street leading to the eastern city gate. She had been worrying for days about her elder sister. She hoped that the walk would help to clear her thoughts.

She loitered for half an hour or so among the stalls of the street venders on the crossing, then she went on to the shopping centre near the East Gate. Her father had told her that Mrs. Lee was an artist, so Dark Orchid entered the first shop of paper and brushes she saw.

The owner knew Mrs. Lee. He said that for many years she had been a regular customer. She was still alive, he put her age at about fifty. He added that Dark Orchid could save herself the trouble of going to Mrs. Lee's house because for the last month or so she had not taken on any new girl students.

Dark Orchid replied that she only wished to see Mrs. Lee about a distant relative. The owner of the shop explained to her how she could find the house. It was only a few streets away.

Dark Orchid reflected that she could now return to the tribunal and report to her father. But the sun was shining, she felt loath to go back so soon. She decided to walk to the address indicated and have a look at Mrs. Lee's house.

It was located in a quiet, middle-class neighbourhood. As she looked at the well-kept houses with neat black-lacquered frontdoors, Dark Orchid thought that this probably was a quarter favoured by well-to-do retired shopkeepers.

About halfway down the street she found the name 'Lee' on the gate of a fair sized house.

Standing in front of the door studded with copper nails, Dark Orchid could not resist the temptation to knock.

There was no answer. This excited the girl's curiosity and made her all the more determined to have a peep inside. She knocked again as loudly as she could. Then she put her ear against the door.

She heard the faint sounds of shuffling footsteps.

As she knocked once more the gate opened. A quietly-dressed middle-aged woman stood in the gateway, supporting herself on a silvertopped cane. She looked Dark Orchid up and down and asked coldly:

"Why do you knock on my door, young woman?"

Dark Orchid knew from the lady's dress and manner that she must be Mrs. Lee herself. She bowed deeply and said respectfully:

"My name is Dark Orchid, I am the daughter of Blacksmith Fang. I am trying to find a teacher who will deign to give guidance to my poor efforts at painting, and a paper shop directed me here. I made bold to come and pay my respects to you, Madam, although the shopkeeper informed me that you do not accept students any longer."

The elder woman gave Dark Orchid a thoughtful look. Suddenly she smiled and said:

"It is quite true that I do not accept students any more. But since you went to all the trouble to call on me, please come in and have a cup of tea!"

Dark Orchid bowed once more. She followed Mrs. Lee

as she limped across a small but well-kept garden to what evidently was the main room of the house.

While Mrs. Lee went away to fetch boiling water Dark Orchid looked round admiring the elegant surroundings.

The room was not large but scrupulously clean and furnished in excellent taste. The bench on which she was sitting was of rosewood, covered with pillows of embroidered silk. The carved chairs and dainty small tea-tables were also of rosewood. On a high table against the back wall a thin cloud of incense curled up from an antique bronze burner. Over it hung a long, narrow scroll picture portraying birds and flowers. The lattice window was pasted over with spotless white paper.

Mrs. Lee came back with a copper kettle.

She poured the boiling water in a tea pot of exquisite painted porcelain, and then she sat down on the other corner of the bench.

Over a cup of fragrant tea they exchanged the usual polite enquiries.

Dark Orchid thought that despite her slight limp Mrs. Lee must have been a handsome woman when she was young. Her face was regular although her features were somewhat heavy and her eyebrows thicker than is thought beautiful for a woman. She evidently enjoyed talking with the girl. Dark Orchid felt quite flattered.

It struck the girl as curious that there seemed to be no servants in the house. When she asked about this Mrs. Lee replied quickly:

"My house is rather small, I keep only one old woman who does the rough work for me. I am a bit peculiar in this respect, I hate to have a crowd of servants around me all the time. A few days ago she became ill, I sent her home to her husband. He is an old street vender who lives round the corner. In his spare time he looks after my garden."

Dark Orchid hastily apologized once more for her intrusion which must be all the more vexing since Mrs. Lee's maid was away. She rose to take her leave.

Mrs. Lee immediately protested. She said that she enjoyed a little company and quickly poured another cup of tea.

Presently she took Dark Orchid to an outhouse. Nearly all the floor space was taken up by a huge, red-lacquered table. On shelves against the wall there stood half a dozen brush holders with brushes of all kinds and sizes, and small jars containing various pigments. Rolls of paper and silk were stacked in an open porcelain jar on the floor. The window opened on a miniature garden thick with flowering plants.

Mrs. Lee made Dark Orchid sit down on a tabouret by the side of the table and started to show her paintings. As Mrs. Lee unrolled scroll after scroll, even Dark Orchid, who did not know much about painting, could see that her hostess was an accomplished artist. She did nothing but flowers, fruit and birds, but everything was drawn with astonishing accuracy and delicately coloured.

Dark Orchid felt greatly embarrassed by Mrs. Lee's kindness. She wondered whether she should not tell her that she had come only because the tribunal had ordered her to do so. Then she reflected that she did not know whether the judge wished this to be kept secret or not. Thus she thought she had better continue playing her role and take her leave as soon as a suitable opportunity arose.

When Mrs. Lee was rolling her pictures up again Dark Orchid rose and looked out of the window. She remarked casually on a few plants that were trampled down.

"That happened the other day when those yokels from the tribunal came to search this neighbourhood!", Mrs. Lee answered venomously. There was so much hatred in her voice that Dark Orchid turned round and gave her an astonished look. But Mrs. Lee's face was placid as ever.

Dark Orchid bowed and started on the polite phrases of thanks.

Mrs. Lee leaned out of the window and looked at the sun.

"Well, well!", she exclaimed, "who would have thought that it is past noon already! And now I must prepare my meal. How I hate that work! Here, you look a very capable young girl, I suppose it would be impertinent to ask you to lend me a hand?"

This was a request that Dark Orchid could not refuse without being intolerably rude. At the same time she thought that she could at least redeem her imposture a little by preparing a good meal for her kind hostess. She replied quickly:

"This person is extremely awkward in all things, but allow me at least to kindle the kitchen fire for you!"

Mrs. Lee looked pleased. She took Dark Orchid across the rear courtyard to the kitchen.

The girl took off her upper gown and bound up her sleeves. Then she rekindled the fire from the glowing embers. Mrs. Lee sat down on the low kitchen bench and started a long story about her husband who had died suddenly shortly after their wedding.

Dark Orchid found a bamboo box with noodles. She chopped a few onions and garlic, and took a dozen dried mushrooms from the string hanging outside the window.

While Mrs. Lee talked on, Dark Orchid put fat in the fryingpan and added the chopped vegetables and soy, stirring with the long iron spoon. At the right moment she put the noodles in the pan. Soon an appetizing smell filled the small kitchen.

Mrs. Lee fetched bowls, chopsticks and a platter with pickled vegetables. They sat down on the kitchen bench to eat.

Dark Orchid had a healthy appetite but Mrs. Lee ate very little. She put her bowl down when it was still half full. She laid her hand on the girl's knee and complimented her on her cooking. As Dark Orchid looked up from her bowl she surprised a look in Mrs. Lee's eyes that made her curiously uncomfortable. She reasoned with herself that it was ridiculous to be shy before another woman. But somehow or other she felt ill at ease. Imperceptibly she edged away a little.

Mrs. Lee rose. She came back with a pewter jug and two small cups.

"Let us have one cup to aid the digestion!", she said with a smile.

Dark Orchid forgot her embarrassment. She had never yet tasted wine. This seemed a very lady-like and exciting thing to do.

She sipped from her cup. It was the delicious scented liquor that is called Rose Dew; it is served cold and much stronger than the ordinary yellow wine which is always taken warm.

After Mrs. Lee had filled the girl's cup a few times, Dark Orchid felt very happy. Mrs. Lee helped her to put on her upper gown and took the girl back to the reception room. She made Dark Orchid sit down next to her on the couch and continued her story about her unlucky marriage.

Mrs. Lee drew her arm round Dark Orchid's waist. She intimated that married life has many disadvantages for a woman. Men were rough and had no understanding, one could never talk really intimately with them as one could with a person of one's own sex. The girl thought that there was much in what Mrs. Lee said. She felt very proud that the elder lady talked so confidentially with her.

After a while Mrs. Lee rose.

"How rude of me!", she exclaimed. "I made you work

in the kitchen without thinking about your comfort! You must be very tired. Why don't you rest a little in my bedroom while I do some work on my painting?"

Dark Orchid reflected that she ought to go home. But she did indeed feel tired and somewhat dizzy and she thought it would be interesting to see the dressing table of such an elegant lady.

As she was making some half-hearted protests, Mrs. Lee led her to a room at the back of the house.

The bedroom surpassed Dark Orchid's expectations. A delicate perfume emanated from a ball-shaped cloisonné censer that hung from the ceiling. The ebony dressing table bore a round silver mirror on a carved sandalwood stand. In front she saw over a dozen elegant small boxes of porcelain and red lacquer. The broad couch was of ebony, intricately carved and inlaid with mother of pearl. The bed curtains were of fine white gauze with designs woven in gold thread.

Mrs. Lee casually pulled aside a screen. Two marble steps led down to a small bathroom. Turning round she said:

"Make yourself comfortable, my dear! As soon as you have rested we shall have a cup of tea in my studio!"

Mrs. Lee left, closing the door behind her.

Dark Orchid took off her upper gown and sat down on the tabouret in front of the dressing table. She eagerly inspected the contents of the toilet boxes, sniffing the powders and salves. When she had satisfied her curiosity she turned to the four red leather boxes that stood in a pile by the side of the couch. The boxes were marked in gold lacquer with the characters of the four seasons. They contained Mrs. Lee's robes, Dark Orchid did not dare peep inside.

She pulled aside the screen and stepped down into the

bathroom. Next to the low wooden tub there stood a small bucket, and in a corner she saw the large wooden containers for cold and warm water. The lattice window had been pasted over with opaque oilpaper. The sunlight threw on it the shadows of the bamboo in the garden outside, so that the window looked like a delicate ink-painting of waving bamboo leaves.

Dark Orchid lifted the cover of the warm water container. The water was quite hot. Fragrant herbs floated on the surface.

She quickly slipped out of her robes, and poured a few buckets of hot water into the tub. When she was adding cold water she suddenly heard a sound behind her. The girl turned round quickly.

Mrs. Lee was standing in the doorway leaning on her cane. She said with a smile:

"Don't be afraid, young girl, it is only me! I thought that after all I would take a nap too. It is very sensible of you to take a bath first, it will make you sleep better!"

As she spoke Mrs. Lee looked at the girl with a queer fixed stare.

All of a sudden Dark Orchid felt very much afraid. She hastily stooped to pick up her clothes.

Mrs Lee stepped forward and jerked the under garment from Dark Orchid's hands.

"Were you not going to take a bath?", she asked in a strained voice.

Dark Orchid started to apologize in confusion. Suddenly Mrs. Lee drew the girl close to her. She said softly:

"You need not be prudish, my dear! You are very beautiful!"

A feeling of revulsion surged up in the girl's breast. She pushed the woman away with all her force. Mrs. Lee stumbled back. When she had steadied herself her eyes were blazing in her contorted face.

As Dark Orchid stood there trembling not knowing what to do Mrs. Lee's cane suddenly lashed out and struck the girl a sharp blow on her bare thigh.

The pain made Dark Orchid forget her fear. She quickly stooped to pick up the small bucket with the intention to throw it at Mrs. Lee's head. But she had not reckoned with Mrs. Lee's expert handling of her cane.

Before Dark Orchid's fingers had touched the bucket Mrs. Lee hit a vicious blow across her hips that made the girl jump aside screaming with pain.

Mrs. Lee laughed contemptuously.

"Don't try any tricks, my dear!", she said softly. "Remember that with this cane I can stab as well as strike! You are more difficult than your sister White Orchid, but you'll soon learn to behave!"

The unexpected reference to her sister made Dark Orchid forget her pain.

"Where is my sister!", she cried out.

"Do you want to see her?", Mrs. Lee asked with an evil leer. She did not wait for an answer but quickly went inside the bedroom.

Dark Orchid stood there paralysed with fear and anxiety. She heard Mrs. Lee chuckle behind the screen.

Then Mrs. Lee pulled the screen aside with her left hand. In her right she held a long, sharp knife.

"Look!", she said triumphantly and pointed to the dressing table.

Dark Orchid uttered a piercing scream of stark terror.

In front of the mirror stood the severed head of her elder sister.

Mrs. Lee quickly stepped down in the bathroom testing the edge of the knife on her thumb.

"You don't like me, foolish girl!", she hissed. "Therefore I shall kill you just as I killed your sister!"

DARK ORCHID SURPRISED WHILE TAKING A BATH

Dark Orchid turned round, screaming for help at the top of her voice. She had a vague idea to smash the lattice window and escape to the garden.

She shrank back as she saw a huge shadow darken the window.

The window was jerked from its frame and a colossal man jumped inside.

He gave the two women a quick look, then sprang over to where Mrs. Lee was standing. He dodged the knife thrust, caught her wrist and twisted it round. The knife clattered to the floor.

In the twinkling of an eye he had bound Mrs. Lee's hands behind her back with her own sash.

"Ma Joong!", cried Dark Orchid, "she killed my sister!"

"Cover yourself up, impudent girl!", he said gruffly. "I already know that this woman killed your sister!"

Dark Orchid felt a glowing blush rise to her face. While Ma Joong dragged Mrs. Lee to the bedroom, Dark Orchid hurriedly put on her clothes.

When she entered the bedroom Ma Joong had laid Mrs. Lee on the couch securely bound hand and foot. As he replaced White Orchid's severed head in the basket he said:

"Run and open the gate! The constables will be here soon, I came ahead on horseback."

"I don't take orders from you, you bully!", Dark Orchid snapped.

Ma Joong laughed loudly. She hurriedly left the room.

When dusk had fallen Judge Dee and his lieutenants gathered in his private office.

Woo came in and greeted the judge.

"The body of White Orchid has been deposited in the quarters of the guards", he said hoarsely. "Her head has been added to it. I have already ordered a coffin of solid wood."

"How is the headman?", the judge inquired.

"Now that he knows what happened to White Orchid", Woo replied, "he has calmed down, Your Honour. Dark Orchid is with him."

Woo bowed and went out again.

"That young man has sobered down considerably!", Judge Dee remarked.

"I can't understand what that fellow is hanging around here for!", Ma Joong said peevishly.

"I understand that he feels in some way responsible for White Orchid's tragic fate", Judge Dee observed. "That poor girl must have lived through hell while she was in Mrs. Lee's clutches. You saw the marks on her body."

"I still cannot understand", sergeant Hoong said, "how Your Honour discovered out there in the maze that there existed a connection between White Orchid and Mrs. Lee."

Judge Dee leaned back in his armchair. Slowly stroking his beard he said:

"The choice was not very great. The old Governor kept the secret of the short cut strictly to himself. Even his son Yoo Kee or his young wife had never been inside. Only a person with exceptional opportunities could have discovered it.

We knew that Mrs. Lee often drank tea in the garden pavilion with the Governor and Mrs. Yoo, discussing his paintings. I take it that Mrs. Lee once surprised the Governor when he was working on his landscape. Mrs. Lee has the trained eye of a painter, it would not be difficult for her to recognize that this was no ordinary landscape. Since she was familiar also with the situation at the entrance of the maze, she must have guessed its meaning without the Governor being aware of it."

"Probably she saw the picture at an early stage", Tao Gan observed, "when only the pine trees had been marked in. The Governor would have painted in the rest later."

Judge Dee nodded.

"Since Mrs. Lee has this abnormal interest in young girls", he continued, "she kept this knowledge to herself. She thought that it might come in useful in a time of crisis!

Somehow or other she lured White Orchid to her house. Fang's eldest daughter was a girl of a soft, pliable character, Mrs. Lee must have found it easy to subdue her. She kept her a captive in her house for a few weeks. The girl's visit to the deserted temple must have made Mrs. Lee uneasy. She must have taken White Orchid to the country mansion and locked her up in that room with the grated window. Thus when the constables searched the eastern quarter and inspected Mrs. Lee's house they did not find her. That visit, however, must have frightened Mrs. Lee. She decided to kill her captive. The hidden pavilion of the old Governor was the safest place for that cruel murder."

"If we had left the tribunal an hour or so earlier that morning when we went to visit the country estate for the first time", Tao Gan exclaimed, "we could have prevented this crime! Mrs. Lee must have left there shortly before our arrival!"

"Fate decided that just that morning Mrs. Yoo would come to see me", Judge Dee said gravely. "Later, when we inspected the entrance to the maze, I saw the footprint of Mrs. Lee or White Orchid. I did not speak about it at the time, for when I stood there looking into the maze an inexplicable terror took hold of me. The soul of that poor girl who had been brutally murdered there only half an hour or so before must have been hovering over me. I also thought I saw the ghost of the old Governor beckon me from the shadows . . ."

Judge Dee's voice trailed off. He shivered as he recalled those moments of stark terror.

For a while all were silent.

Then the judge took a hold on himself and said in a brisk voice:

"Well, fortunately Ma Joong was in time to prevent a second cruel murder.

"Let us now have our evening meal. Thereafter all of you had better rest a few hours. For all we know there may be a very exciting night ahead of us. It is difficult to predict what those barbarians will do!"

That afternoon Chiao Tai had with quiet efficiency organized the defence of the town. He had posted the best soldiers near the Watergate, and divided the rest over the walls of the city. On his orders the wardens had warned the population that the barbarians might attack the town that night. All able men had been busy assembling large stones and faggots of dry wood on the city wall, and making bamboo spears and iron tipped arrows. Three hours before midnight they would man the walls, every fifty men directed by one professional soldier.

Two soldiers had been posted on the Drum Tower. As soon as the Uigurs approached the river they would beat the huge drum with their thick wooden clubs. The dull roll of that drum would be the sign for lighting the torches on the walls. If the barbarians tried to scale them, they would meet a barrage of heavy stones and flaming faggots.

Judge Dee ate his evening meal in his own quarters. Then he slept for a few hours on the couch in his library.

One hour before midnight Ma Joong, clad in full armour, came to fetch him. Judge Dee put on a thin mailcoat under his robe and took down the long sword of his grandfather that hung on the wall next to his bookshelves. Having placed his official magistrate's cap on his head, he followed Ma Joong.

They rode on horseback to the Watergate.

Chiao Tai was waiting for them. He reported that Sergeant Hoong, Tao Gan and four soldiers were posted on the watchtower of the Chien mansion. They would see to it that not a spark of fire was visible there.

Judge Dee nodded and climbed the steep stone steps to the top of the Watergate. On the battlement a burly soldier, nearly as tall as Ma Joong, stood stiffly to attention. He was carrying a long pole with the Imperial standard on top.

The judge stood himself on the battlement. On his right he had the soldier carrying the Imperial standard, on his left, Ma Joong holding high the staff with the commander's insignia of Judge Dee.

The judge reflected that this was the first time that he was in charge of defending the Empire's boundary against a foreign attack. Looking up at the Imperial standard fluttering in the evening breeze he felt a deep pride glow in his breast. He folded his sword in his arms and looked out over the dark plain.

When the hour of midnight approached Judge Dee pointed to the distant horizon. Far away they saw flashes of light. The Uigurs were preparing to advance.

The lights gradually came nearer, then remained stationary. The barbarian horsemen had halted, waiting for the signal fire on the watchtower.

The three men stood there silently for over an hour.

Then suddenly lights flared up over the river. They became smaller and smaller, then disappeared altogether in the darkness.

Having waited in vain for the signal fire, the Uigurs had ridden back to their homesteads.

JUDGE DEE ON THE RAMPARTS OF LAN-FANG

Twentyfifth Chapter

TWO DEPRAVED CRIMINALS SUFFER THE EXTREME PENALTY;
JUDGE DEE LEARNS THE SECRET OF AN ABSTRUSE COUPLET

THE next day Judge Dee heard Mrs. Lee during the morning session of the tribunal.

She readily confessed her crimes.

Once, shortly before the Governor's death, Mrs. Lee had been drinking tea with Mrs. Yoo in the garden pavilion, waiting for the Governor. Mrs. Lee had been looking over some of his pictures and found a preliminary sketch of the landscape painting. She had seen from a few notes that the Governor had written in that this picture was a guide map to a short cut through the maze.

Mrs. Lee had felt greatly attracted to Mrs. Yoo, but as long as the Governor was alive she had not dared to reveal her feelings to her. After the Governor's burial Mrs. Lee had visited the country mansion but only found the old couple there; they did not know where Mrs. Yoo had gone after Yoo Kee had expelled her. Mrs. Lee made inquiries in the countryside, but Mrs. Yoo had instructed the peasants to tell no one on what farm she was hiding with her son.

Then, some weeks before, Mrs. Lee had revisited the old country mansion when she happened to be in that neighbourhood. When she found the dead bodies of the old couple she had explored the first two stages of the short cut. She found that the clues in the landscape picture of which she had kept careful notes were correct.

Mrs. Lee had met White Orchid in the market and persuaded the girl to accompany her to her house. Once there, she soon completely cowed the shy girl and kept her captive as a victim of her whims. She made White Orchid do all the housework, beating her with her cane at the slightest provocation.

When Mrs. Lee discovered that White Orchid had slipped out to the deserted temple and there met a strange man, she had been furious. She had dragged the frightened girl to an empty storeroom where the thick walls deafened all sound. Mrs. Lee had made the girl strip and lashed her arms to a pillar.

Then Mrs. Lee had started to interrogate her, repeating again and again the same question: had White Orchid betrayed her whereabouts to the stranger? Everytime the girl denied this. Mrs. Lee had cruelly beaten her with a thin rattan stick, hissing horrible threats at her all the time. Writhing under the vicious lashes, White Orchid had frantically cried for mercy. This further enraged Mrs. Lee. She had let the rattan descend with all her force on the bare hips of the screaming girl until her arm grew tired. By then White Orchid was nearly distracted by pain and fear, but she still persisted that she was innocent.

But Mrs. Lee feared that her secret had leaked out. The next morning she disguised White Orchid as a nun and took her to the Governor's country estate. There she locked the girl up in the room the old couple had been living in, taking away all her clothes to obviate every attempt at escaping. Mrs. Lee visited her every other day, bringing her a jug of water and a basket of dried beans and oil cakes. She had planned to bring the girl back from there as soon as White Orchid's escapade to the temple had proved harmless.

Then, however, the constables came to search for the girl in the eastern quarter. Mrs. Lee became alarmed. Very early the next morning she hastened to the country mansion. She had found her way to the hidden pavilion by the landmarks of the pine trees, compelling White Orchid to lead the way, mercilessly driving the girl on with her cane. In the pavilion she had made the girl lie down on the marble bench and then thrust her knife in her breast. A perverse instinct had moved her to cut off the head, the body she had pushed over the edge of the bench. Mrs. Lee had taken the severed head back with her in a basket. In her hurry Mrs. Lee had paid no attention to the box on the table.

Mrs. Lee related all this without any pressure. Judge Dee noticed that she took pleasure in telling everything and that she gloated over her cruel deeds. She also volunteered the information that thirty years ago she had murdered her husband by mixing poison in his wine.

Judge Dee felt a deep revulsion for this depraved woman. He was relieved when Mrs. Lee had affixed her thumbmark to her confession and could be led back to the jail.

At that same session Judge Dee heard the three Chinese shopkeepers who had been the Uigur's accomplices. They proved to have no clear idea about the real portent of the plot. They had thought it was a plan to create a brawl and loot a few shops under cover of the confusion.

The judge had them given fifty blows with the bamboo and sentenced them to wear the heavy wooden pillory for one month.

That afternoon the steward of the Ding mansion came rushing to the tribunal. He reported that Candidate Ding had hanged himself and that the fourth wife of the late General had swallowed poison. Neither had left an explanatory note. The general opinion was that they had become despondent over the General's tragic death. The woman's suicide was favourably commented upon by some old-fashioned people who thought it a proof of supreme devotion if a wife followed her deceased husband into the grave. They opened a subscription for the erection of a commemorative stone tablet.

During the following ten days Judge Dee devoted all his time to the liquidation of the affairs of Chien Mow and Yoo Kee. Some minor punishments were meted out to the two counsellors of Chien Mow, and those of his henchmen who had practised extortion. Mrs. Yoo had been informed of the contents of the Governor's last will. She would be summoned to the tribunal as soon as the final verdict of the central authorities had come in from the capital.

Sergeant Hoong had hoped that the judge would relax somewhat now that he had solved all three criminal cases and broken up the plot against the town. But to his disappointment he found that Judge Dee was still greatly worried about something. The judge was often in a bad temper, and occasionally revised a previous decision, which was a most uncommon thing for him to do. The sergeant could not imagine what was the cause of the Judge's worries, and Judge Dee vouchsafed no explanation.

One morning the clatter of horsehoofs and loud gongs resounded through the main street. Two hundred soldiers of the regular army entered Lan-fang with waving banners. This was the garrison force sent in response to Judge Dee's request.

Their commander was an officer who had seen active service against the barbarians of the north, an intelligent young man who impressed the judge very favourably. He presented an official letter from the Board of Military Affairs which gave Judge Dee full authority also over all military affairs of the district.

The garrison was quartered in the Chien mansion and Chiao Tai returned to the tribunal.

The arrival of the garrison somewhat heartened the judge. Soon, however, he relapsed into his morose mood. He buried himself in the routine affairs of the district and went out very little. The only time he left the tribunal was when he attended the burial rites for White Orchid.

Woo had arranged a magnificent funeral, he had insisted on defraying all the expenses himself. The painter had become a changed man. He had foresworn drinking, a decision which involved him in a bitter quarrel with his landlord, the owner of the Eternal Spring wineshop. The latter took this decision as a reflection on the quality of his stock. All winebibbers of that quarter sadly called this breach the end of a beautiful friendship.

Woo sold all his paintings and rented a small room in the compound of the Temple of Confucius. He spent most of his time studying the Classics, going out only to visit Headman Fang in the nearby tribunal. They seemed to have become staunch friends, Woo would talk with him for hours in the guards' quarters.

One afternoon when Judge Dee was sitting in his private office listlessly scanning some routine documents, Sergeant Hoong came in and handed him a large sealed envelope.

"This letter, Your Honour", he said, "was brought just now by a courier from the capital!"

Judge Dee's face lit up. He broke the seals and eagerly glanced through the papers inside.

As he folded the documents up again he nodded contentedly. Tapping the papers with his forefinger he said to the sergeant:

"This is the official verdict on Yoo Kee's treason, the killing of General Ding, and Mrs. Lee's murder. It will interest you that the conspiracy of the Uigur tribes has been settled on high government level, in negotiations between our Board for Barbarian Affairs and the Khan of the Uigurs;

Lan-fang is safe from further attacks! Tomorrow I shall close these cases. After that I shall be a free man!"

Sergeant Hoong did not quite understand Judge Dee's last remark. But the judge gave him no time for asking questions. He started immediately to issue orders for the morning session of the tribunal.

The next morning the personnel of the tribunal started preparations two hours before daybreak. Torches were lighted in front of the main gate, where a group of constables was making ready the cart for conveying the condemned to the execution ground outside the southern city gate.

Despite the early hour, a large number of citizens were assembled there. They looked with morbid fascination at these preparations. Then mounted lance knights came from the garrison headquarters and formed a cordon round the cart.

One hour before dawn a sturdy constable hit the large bronze gong at the gate three formidable blows. The guards opened the double doors, and the crowd filed into the courtroom, lighted by large candles.

The crowd looked on in respectful silence as Judge Dee appeared on the dais and slowly seated himself behind the bench. He was clad in full ceremonial dress of shimmering green brocade. A scarlet pelerin hung over his shoulders. This was the sign that he would pronounce capital punishments.

First Yoo Kee was led before the dais.

As he knelt on the flagstones in front of the bench, the senior scribe placed a document in front of the judge. Judge Dee drew the candle nearer and read slowly in a solemn voice:

"The criminal Yoo Kee is guilty of high treason. He should properly be submitted to the lingering death, being cut to pieces alive. In view of the fact that the criminal's father, His Excellency Yoo Shou-chien, has merited greatly of the State and the people, and in view of the fact that he has entered a posthumous plea for mercy for his son, this sentence is mitigated in so far that the said criminal shall first be killed and thereafter dismembered. In deference again to the memory of the late Governor Yoo, the criminal's head shall not be exposed on the city gate and his property shall not be confiscated."

Judge Dee paused and handed a paper to the headman.

"The criminal is allowed to read his late father's plea", he announced.

Headman Fang gave the paper to Yoo Kee who had been listening with an impassive face. When he had read this pathetic document, however, Yoo Kee burst out into heartbreaking sobs.

Two constables bound Yoo Kee's hands behind his back. Headman Fang took a long white board that had been prepared in advance and stuck it between the ropes on Yoo Kee's back. There his personal name Kee, his crime and his punishment were written out in large characters. The family name Yoo was omitted, in deference to the old Governor.

When Yoo Kee had been led away Judge Dee spoke:

"The Imperial Government announce that the Khan of the Uigurs has sent a special delegation to the capital headed by his eldest son, to offer apologies for the outrageous scheme evolved by Prince Ooljin, and begging to be allowed to renew his pledge of allegiance to the Throne. The Imperial Government have graciously accepted the apologies, and have handed over the said Ooljin and his four accomplices to the delegation, leaving it to the Khan to take appropriate action."

Ma Joong whispered to Chiao Tai:

"Translated into ordinary language 'appropriate action'

means that the Khan will flay Ooljin alive, boil him in oil and cut what is left into small pieces! The Khan does not take kindly to people who bungle his schemes!"

"The Khan's son", the judge continued, "has been invited to prolong his stay in the capital as an honoured guest of the Imperial Government."

The spectators started cheering. They knew that with his eldest son kept as hostage in the capital, the Khan would abide by his promises.

"Silence!" shouted the judge.

He gave a sign to the headman. Mrs. Yoo and her son Yoo Shan were led before the dais.

"Madam", Judge Dee said kindly, "you have taken cognizance already of the late Governor's original testament that was dicovered in his hidden studio in the heart of the maze. You shall now take full possession of all the property, also in the name of your son Yoo Shan. I am certain that under your guidance he shall grow up as the image of his illustrious father, and as a man worthy of the great name of Yoo!"

Mrs. Yoo and her son knocked their heads on the floor several times in succession to express their gratitude.

When they had stood back the senior scribe placed another document before the judge.

"I shall now read", Judge Dee spoke, "the official verdict on the case of General Ding!"

Caressing his whiskers he read out slowly:

„The Metropolitan Court has taken due notice of the facts pertaining to the death of General Ding Hoo-gwo. In the Court's opinion the fact that a certain name was found engraved on the writing brush which concealed the deadly weapon does not in itself provide conclusive proof that it was that same person who transformed the said writing brush into an instrument of death, nor that as such it was necessarily destined to kill the General. Accordingly the Court rules that General Ding's demise shall be entered into the records as death by accident."

"That is a neat example of jurisprudence!", Sergeant Hoong whispered into Judge Dee's ear as he rolled up the document.

The judge nodded imperceptibly and replied in a low voice:

"They evidently wanted to keep the Governor's name out of this!"

Then he took up his vermilion brush and filled out a slip for the warden of the jail.

Mrs. Lee was brought in by two constables.

During the period of waiting in jail, the horror of impending death had slowly taken possession of her. She had completely lost the attitude of self-glorification which she had displayed when confessing her hideous crimes. Her face was haggard, she looked with wide eyes at the scarlet pelerin on Judge Dee's shoulders and at the huge man who stood by the side of the dais with impassive face. He carried a naked sword over his shoulder, his two assistants stood behind him with knives, saws and coils of rope. As Mrs. Lee realized that those were the executioner and his helpers she tottered on her feet. Two constables had to assist her kneeling down in front of the dais.

Judge Dee read:

"The criminal Lee *née* Hwang is guilty of kidnapping girls for immoral purposes and premeditated murder. She shall be scourged and then executed by decapitation. The state renounces its claim on the said criminal's property which shall be conferred on the victim's family in lieu of blood money. The criminal's head shall be exposed on the city gate for three days, as a warning example."

Mrs. Lee started to scream. A constable gagged her with

a strip of oilpaper while two others bound her hands behind her back. Finally they stuck the placard stating her name, her crime, and her punishment among the ropes.

When Mrs. Lee had been led away the crowd of spectators prepared to leave the courtroom. Judge Dee hit his gavel on the bench and shouted for order.

"I shall now read", he announced, "the names of the temporary personnel of this tribunal."

He read out the names of Headman Fang and of the former outlaws whom he had engaged as constables and guards on the second day after his arrival in Lan-fang. They stood at attention facing the judge.

Judge Dee leaned back in his chair. Stroking his beard he thoughtfully surveyed the men who had faithfully served him during the critical days that lay behind. Then he spoke:

"Headman, you and the men under you were engaged under an emergency, but you have loyally served the tribunal. Since conditions have now returned to normal, I release you of your duties, with the understanding that those among you who wish to enter permanent service shall be welcome to do so."

"All of us", Headman Fang replied respectfully, "owe a debt of gratitude to Your Honour, and I myself more than anyone else. I would beg Your Honour to continue to employ me in my present position, were it not that I owe it to my daughter to leave a city where she is constantly reminded of the tragedy that struck our family.

"Candidate Woo Feng has offered me the position of chief steward in the mansion of one of his father's friends in the capital. I feel all the more inclined to accept that generous offer since I have learned through an intermediary that Candidate Woo intends to marry my second daughter Dark Orchid as soon as he has passed his second literary examination."

"What black ingratitude of the girl!", Ma Joong muttered indignantly to Chiao Tai. "I saved her life! And what is more, I saw her as only her husband ought to see her!"

"Shut up!", Chiao Tai whispered, "you had a nice view of the wench, that is sufficient reward!"

"I beg to be allowed", the headman continued, "to leave my only son here in Lan-fang. For nowhere in the Empire could he find such a master to serve as Your Honour. I beg Your Honour to accept him, despite his slender capacities, in the permanent service of the tribunal."

Judge Dee had been listening gravely. Now he spoke:

"Headman, your son shall continue to serve here as a constable.

"It rejoices me that August Heaven in its infinite mercy has so willed it that a dark crime will in due course result in the happiness of two families. When the red candles are burning on your daughter's wedding, the auspicious atmosphere of a new bright future will put a healing salve on the old wounds in her father's heart.

"I regretfully accept your resignation as from tomorrow!"

Headman Fang and his son knelt and knocked their heads on the floor several times in succession.

Three constables reported that they wished to return to their original trades. All the others requested to be engaged on a permanent basis.

When these formalities had been completed Judge Dee closed the session.

Outside the tribunal a dense crowd was waiting. Yoo Kee and Mrs. Lee had been placed in the open cart of the condemned. The placards with their names and crimes were there for all to see.

Then the gates opened and Judge Dee's palanquin was carried out into the street. Ten constables marched in front and ten behind. Ma Joong and Sergeant Hoong rode on the left, Chiao Tai and Tao Gan on the right. Four runners carrying placards marked "The Magistrate of Lan-fang" took up their position at the head. The guards sounded their copper hand gongs and the cortège moved along heading south.

The cart of the condemned surrounded by the military escort brought up the rear. The crowd followed behind.

As the cortège crossed the marble bridge, the red glow of dawn shone on the pagoda in the lotus pond.

The execution ground was situated just outside the southern city gate. Judge Dee's palanquin was carried through the gate in the palisade. As he descended the garrison commander came to meet him.

The commander led the judge to a temporary bench that had been put up there during the night. The soldiers formed a square in front.

The executioner stuck his sword in the ground and took off his jacket. The heavy muscles rolled on his naked torso. His two helpers climbed on the cart and led the two criminals to the centre of the execution ground.

They loosened Yoo Kee's ropes and dragged him to a pole with two cross bars that had been stuck in the ground. One bound his neck to the pole, the other fastened his arms and legs to the bars.

When they were ready the executioner selected a long, thin knife and stood himself in front of Yoo Kee. He looked up at the judge.

Judge Dee gave the sign.

The executioner plunged his knife straight into Yoo Kee's heart. He died without uttering a sound.

Then Yoo Kee's body was sliced to pieces. Mrs. Lee swooned when she saw them start on this horrible process, and several spectators hid their face in their sleeve.

Finally the executioner held the severed head up to the

judge who marked the forehead with his vermilion brush. It was thrown into a basket together with the remains of his body.

Mrs. Lee had been revived by burning strong incense under her nose.

The two assistants dragged her in front of the dais and threw her on her knees.

As she saw the executioner approach with the scourge Mrs. Lee burst out in frantic screams. In abject fright she begged him to spare her.

The executioner and his men were accustomed to such scenes, they paid not the slightest attention to her entreaties. One of the assistants loosened her hair. He took the long tresses in his hand and pulled her head forward. The other had ripped off her upper garment and bound her hands behind her back.

The executioner tested the balance of the scourge. This fearful instrument has thongs bristling with iron hooks, it is seen only on the execution ground for no one ever survives its blows.

When Judge Dee had given the sign the executioner raised the scourge. It fell down on Mrs. Lee's bare back with a sickening thud, lacerating the flesh from neck to waist. Mrs. Lee would have fallen on her face by the weight of the blow if the assistant had not taken a firm hold on her hair.

When Mrs. Lee had regained her breath she started screaming at the top of her voice. But the executioner struck again and again. The sixth blow laid the bones bare, blood oozed from the torn flesh. Mrs. Lee lost consciousness.

Judge Dee raised his hand.

It took some time before she had been revived.

Then the executioner raised his sword while his helpers pulled Mrs. Lee up on her knees.

A DEPRAVED CRIMINAL ON THE EXECUTION GROUND

As the judge gave the sign the sword swung down and severed the head from the body in one fearful blow.

Judge Dee marked the head with his vermilion brush. Then the executioner threw it into a basket. Later it would be exposed nailed by the hair to the city gate and remain hanging there for three days.

Judge Dee left the dais and ascended his palanquin. As the bearers hoisted the shafts on their shoulders, the first rays of the sun shone on the helmets of the soldiers.

Judge Dee's palanquin was first carried to the Temple of the City God, the military commander following behind in his open sedan chair.

There the judge reported to the tutelary deity the crimes that had been committed in his city and the capital punishments meted out to the evil-doers. Then the judge and the military commander burned incense and prayed.

They took leave of each other in the temple yard.

Once returned to the tribunal Judge Dee went straight to his private office. After he had drunk a cup of strong tea the judge told Sergeant Hoong that he could go and have his breakfast. Later in the day they would draft the report on the execution for the higher authorities.

Sergeant Hoong found Ma Joong, Chiao Tai and Tao Gan standing talking together in a corner of the main courtyard. As the sergeant joined them he found that Ma Joong was still grumbling about what he insisted on calling Dark Orchid's infidelity.

"I had taken it for granted all along that it was I who should marry that wench!", he said sourly. "She nearly knifed me during that attack on our party in the mountains. I really liked her!"

"Consider yourself lucky, brother!", Chiao Tai said consolingly. "That girl Dark Orchid has a mighty sharp tongue, she would have led you a terrible life!"

Ma Joong clasped his hand to his forehead.

"That reminds me!", he exclaimed, "I'll tell you what I'll do! I shall buy myself that girl Tulbee. That is a fine sturdy young woman, and she can't speak a word of Chinese! Won't that be nice and quiet in the house?"

Tao Gan shook his head. His long face was even more sad than usual when he said darkly:

"Don't you give yourself illusions, my friend! I assure you that in a week or two that woman will be talking your head off, and in fluent Chinese too!"

But Ma Joong was not to be discouraged.

"I'll go there tonight", he said, "and anyone who wants to go with me is welcome. You'll find fine girls there, and they don't conceal their charms either!"

Chiao Tai tightened his belt. He shouted impatiently:

"Can't you fellows talk about something more important than mere women? Come along, let us be off and have a real good breakfast! There is nothing better for an empty stomach than a few cups of warm wine!"

All agreed that those were wise words, they walked together to the main gate.

In the meantime Judge Dee had changed into his hunting dress. He ordered a clerk to have his favourite horse brought from the stables.

The judge swung himself on its back. He pulled his neck cloth up over his mouth and nose. Then he rode out into the street.

The streets were full of people standing about in groups. They were discussing the execution of the two criminals and paid no attention to this solitary horseman.

When the judge rode through the southern gate he spurred on his horse. On the execution ground the constables were still busy clearing away the temporary bench. They had raked clean sand over the blood stains.

Once he was in the fields Judge Dee slowed down. He inhaled the fresh morning air and looked at the peaceful scene. But even in these pleasant surroundings he found no rest for his troubled thoughts.

The scene on the execution ground had as always deeply shocked the judge. He was relentless as long as he was working on a case; but as soon as the criminal had been found and had confessed, Judge Dee always longed to dismiss the case from his thoughts. He hated his duty of supervising the execution with all its horrible, bloody detail.

The plan to resign from official life that had been at the back of the judge's mind ever since his conversation with Master Crane Robe had now developed into a compelling desire. The judge reflected that he was just past forty; it was not too late to begin a new life on the small farm that he possessed in his native province.

What was better than a quiet life in peaceful retirement, devoting himself to reading and writing and giving full attention to the education of his children? What was the use of spending his every waking hour on all the wickedness and the sordid schemes of criminal minds, while life had so many good and beautiful things to offer?

There were countless capable officials to fill his place. And could he not serve the state as well by composing, as he had often planned to do, treatises setting forth in easy language the lofty doctrines of the Classics so that everyone could understand them?

Yet Judge Dee felt doubtful. What would happen to the Empire if all officials took this same aloof attitude? Was it not his duty to give his sons a chance later to enter upon an official career? Could the sheltered life on a small farm prepare those youngsters sufficiently for their future?

As he spurred on his horse Judge Dee shook his head.

The answer to his problem lay in that difficult couplet he had seen on the wall of Master Crane Robe's abode:

"There are but two roads that lead to the gate of
Eternal Life:
Either one bores his head in the mud like a worm,
or like a dragon flies up high into the sky."

Ever since that strange visit these lines had been buzzing in his thoughts. Judge Dee sighed. He would leave it to the old master to decide for him. He would explain which of the two roads the judge should take.

When he had come to the foot of the mountain ridge Judge Dee jumped from his horse. He called a peasant who was working in his field nearby and asked him to look after the animal.

As the judge turned to begin the ascent, two wood gatherers came down the mountain path. They were an old couple, their faces were wrinkled and their hands as gnarled as the dry wood they were carrying on their backs.

The man halted in his steps. He put his load of faggots down. Wiping the perspiration from his forehead, he looked up at the judge and asked politely:

"Where might the gentleman be bound for?"

"I am on my way to visit Master Crane Robe", the judge answered curtly.

The old man slowly shook his head.

"You will not find him, my lord", he said. "Four days ago we found his house empty. The door was slamming in the wind and the rain had spoilt all his flowers. Now I and my old woman here use that house for storing our wood."

A feeling of utter loneliness assailed the judge.

"You can save yourself the trouble of going up there, my lord!", said the peasant and handed the reins back to Judge Dee.

As the judge took them absent-mindedly he asked the wood gatherer:

"What happened to the old master? Did you find his dead body?"

A sly smile rippled over the wrinkled face as the old man slowly shook his head.

"Men such as him", he replied, "don't die like you or me, my lord! They never really belong to this world to begin with. In the end they fly up into the azure vault of heaven like a winged dragon. They leave nothing but emptiness behind!"

The old man shouldered his burden and went his way.

Suddenly understanding flashed through Judge Dee's mind. This then was the answer!

He said with a smile to the peasant:

"Well, I belong very much to this world of ours! I shall continue boring my head into the mud!"

He swung himself in the saddle and rode back to the city.

THE END

A feature all old Chinese detective stories have in common is that the role of detective is always played by the magistrate of the district where the crime occurred.

This official is in charge of the entire administration of the district under his jurisdiction, usually comprising one walled city and the countryside around it for fifty miles or so. The magistrate's duties are manifold. He is fully responsible for the collection of taxes, the registration of births, deaths and marriages, keeping up to date the land registration, the maintenance of the peace etc., while as presiding judge of the local tribunal he is charged with the apprehension and punishing of criminals and the hearing of all civil and criminal cases. Since the magistrate thus supervises practically every phase of the daily life of the people, he is commonly referred to in Chinese as the 'Father-and-mother Official'.

The magistrate is a permanently overworked official. He lives with his family in separate quarters inside the compound of the tribunal, and often spends his every waking hour upon his official duties.

The district magistrate is at the bottom of the colossal pyramidal structure of ancient Chinese government organization. He must report to the prefect, who supervises ten or more districts. The prefect reports to the provincial governor, who is responsible for several prefectures. The governor in his turn reports to the central authorities in the capital, with the Emperor at the top.

Every citizen in the Empire, whether rich or poor and without regard for social background, could enter official life and become a district magistrate by passing the literary examinations instituted by the Government. In this respect the Chinese system was already a rather democratic one at a time when Europe was still under strict feudal rule.

A magistrate's term of office was usually three years. Thereafter he was transferred to another district, to be in due time promoted to prefect. Promotion was selective, being based solely on actual performance.

The magistrate was assisted by the permanent personnel of the tribunal, such as the scribes, the warden of the jail, the coroner, the constables, the guards and the runners. These, however, only perform their routine duties. They are not concerned with the detection of crimes.

This task is performed by the magistrate himself, with the assistance of three or four trusted lieutenants. These he selects at the beginning of his career and they accompany him to whatever post he goes. The lieutenants are placed over the other personnel of the tribunal. Unlike the latter they have no local connections and are, therefore, less liable to let themselves be influenced by private considerations in the execution of their official duties. For the same reason it is an old-established rule that no official shall ever be appointed magistrate in his own native district.

The present novel gives a general idea of ancient Chinese court procedure. When the court is in session, the judge sits behind the bench, with his lieutenants and the scribes standing by his side. The bench is a high table covered with a piece of red cloth that hangs down in front from the top of the table till the floor of the raised dais.

On this bench one always sees the same implements: an inkstone for rubbing black and red ink, two writing brushes, and a number of thin bamboo staves in a tubular holder.

These staves are used to mark the number of blows that a criminal should receive. If the constables are to give ten blows, the judge will take the corresponding number of markers and throw them on the floor in front of the dais. The headman of the constables will put apart one marker for every blow or blows given.

Next to these implements one will often see on top of the bench the large square seal of the tribunal, and the gavel. The latter is not shaped like a hammer as in the West. It is an oblong, square piece of hardwood of about one foot long. In Chinese it is significantly called *ching-t'ang-mu** 'Wood that frightens the hall'.

The constables stand in front of the dais, facing each other in two rows on left and right. Both plaintiff and accused must kneel on the bare flagstones between these two menacing rows, and remain so during the entire session. They have no lawyers to assist them, they may call no witnesses, so their position is generally not an enviable one. The entire court procedure was in fact intended to act as a deterrent, impressing on the people the awful consequences of getting involved with the law.

The magistrate's private office was usually located at the back of the court room, separated from the dais by a screen.

It is a fundamental principle of ancient Chinese law that no criminal can be pronounced guilty unless he has confessed to his crime. To prevent hardened criminals from escaping punishment by refusing to confess even when confronted with irrefutable evidence, the law allows the application of legal severities, such as beating with whip and bamboo, and placing hands and ankles in screws. Next

---

* In the novel itself all Chinese names are transcribed in such a way, that they can be easily pronounced. In this Postscript, however, I use the regular system of transcription used in most English sinological publications.

to these authorized means of torture magistrates often apply more severe kinds. If, however, the accused should receive permanent bodily harm or die under excessive torture, the magistrate and the entire personnel of his tribunal are punished, often with the extreme penalty. Most judges, therefore, depend more upon their shrewd psychological insight and their knowledge of their fellow men than on the application of torture.

All in all the old Chinese system worked reasonably well. Sharp control by the higher authorities prevented excesses, and public opinion acted as another curb on wicked or irresponsible magistrates. Capital sentences had to be ratified by the Throne and every condemned criminal could appeal to the higher judicial instances, going up as high as the Emperor himself. Moreover, the magistrate was not allowed to interrogate any accused or witness in private, all his hearings of a case including the preliminary examination had to be conducted in the public sessions of the tribunal. A careful record was kept of all proceedings and these reports had to be forwarded to the higher authorities for their inspection.

Readers of 'Dee Goong An' have inquired how it was possible that the scribes accurately noted down the court proceedings without the use of shorthand. The answer is that the Chinese literary language in itself is a kind of shorthand. It is possible, for instance, to reduce to four written ideographs a sentence that counts say twenty or more words in the colloquial. Moreover there exist several systems of running handwriting, where characters consisting of ten or more brush strokes can be reduced to one scrawl. While serving in China I myself often had Chinese clerks make notes of complicated negotiations conducted in Chinese and found their record of astonishing accuracy.

In most Chinese detective novels the magistrate is engaged

in solving three or more totally different cases at the same time. This interesting feature I have retained in the present novel. In my opinion Chinese crime stories in this respect are more realistic than ours. A district had quite a numerous population. It is therefore only logical that often several criminal cases had to be dealt with at the same time.

In this novel I have followed the Chinese time-honoured tradition of adding at the end of the story a detailed description of the execution of the criminals. Chinese sense of justice demands that the punishment meted out to the criminal should be set forth in full detail. I also adopted the custom of Chinese writers of the Ming Dynasty of describing in their novels men and life as they were in their own time, although the scene of their plots is often laid in former centuries. The same applies to the illustrations of this novel, which reproduce customs and costumes of the Ming period (A.D. 1368-1644) rather than those of the T'ang Dynasty.

I may add that 'Judge Dee' is one of the great ancient Chinese detectives. He was a historical person, one of the well known statesmen of the T'ang dynasty. His full name was Ti Jen-chieh and he lived from 630 till 700 A.D. Later he became a Minister of the Imperial Court and through his wise counsels exercised a beneficial influence on affairs of state. It is chiefly because of his reputation as a detector of crimes, however, that later Chinese fiction has made him the hero of a number of crime stories which have only very slight foundation in historical fact.

I borrowed three plots from three different 16th century
Chinese collections of crime and mystery stories. In the
original none of these three plots bears any relation to
Judge Dee or 'Dee Goong An'. Since, however, through my
translation of 'Dee Goong An', the reader has become
familiar with Judge Dee and his four assistants, those three
plots have now been re-written as one continuous story
centering round that famous ancient Chinese master-
detective. Judge Dee could be introduced into this story
without much difficulty, for the magistrate-detective figures
in all old Chinese crime novels. The type is more important
than the name, in fact it makes little difference whether a
crime is solved by 'Judge Pao', 'Judge Peng', 'Judge Shih'
or 'Judge Dee'.

The 'Case of the Sealed Room' was suggested by an
anecdote concerning Yen Shih-fan, a notoriously wicked
statesman of the Ming period who died in 1565 A.D. It is
said that he invented a special writing brush capable of
ejecting a deadly missile when heated near a candle (cf.
A. Waley's introduction ot the English translation of 'Chin
P'ing Mei', page VIII). The original story states that Yen
Shih-fan used this 'loaded writing brush' as a defensive
weapon, to be used should one of his many enemies surprise
him writing in his library and if no other weapon was at
hand. I described such a 'loaded brush' as a weapon of
attack and wrote a new story around it dealing with delayed
vengeance, a motif not uncommon in Chinese novels. It
should be added that when a new writing brush is to be
used, the writer must first burn off the superfluous hairs

around the point. To do this he holds it to a flame keeping the shaft horizontal to his eye. There is thus a good chance that a missile projected from the end of the brush will hit his face. Even if the wax holding the coiled spring inside the shaft should not melt during the actual trimming process, the writer will still have little chance of survival once he begins to use his brush, since his head would usually be bent over the paper and therefore be in the direct line of fire. This is indeed what happened to General Ding in the present novel.

Quite another motif is worked out in the 'Case of the Hidden Testament'. This case is based on a well-known ancient Chinese plot. A brief version occurs in the *T'ang-yin-pi-shih*, a collection of ruling cases compiled in 1211 A.D.; cf. my translation entitled 'T'ang-yin-pi-shih, Parallel Cases from under the Peartree, a 13th century manual of Jurisprudence and Detection' (Sinica Leidensia Vol. X, Leiden 1956), page 177, Case 66-B. Another brief version is found in the famous 16th century collection of crime stories *Lung-t'u-kung-an* which describe the exploits of the master-detective Pao-kung who lived during the Sung Dynasty. There the story bears the title of *Ch'e-hua-chou* 'The Taking apart of the Scroll Picture'. A more elaborate version is given in the popular 17th century collection of Chinese stories *Chin-ku-ch'i-kuan;* it is inserted there as the third tale, entitled *T'eng-ta-yin-kuei-tuan-chia-szu* 'Magistrate T'eng's marvellous solution of the Inheritance Suit'. In the original story the real testament is found hidden in the scroll's mounting, the clues contained in the picture itself are an embellishment I have added. I also added the new plot of the maze mystery which – as far as I know – does not occur in ancient Chinese detective stories although mazes are occasionally mentioned in the description of Chinese palaces. The design of the maze reproduced in the present story is in reality that of the cover of a Chinese incense burner. It is an old Chinese custom to place a thin plate of copper with a cut-out and continuous design, on top of a vessel filled to the brim with incense powder. When the powder is lighted at one end of the design, it slowly burns on like a fuse following the design. During past centuries, there were published in China a number of books reproducing various designs of this kind, usually representing some auspicious phrase, and often of great ingenuity. The design utilized in the present story was borrowed from the *Hsiang-yin-t'u-k'ao*, a book on this subject published in 1878.

The plot of the girl with the severed head is a quite common one in old Chinese crime stories; cf., for instance, my translation of the *T'ang-yin-pi-shih*, Case 64–A. I worked it into a story centering round sapphism, an aberration described in a number of Chinese novels and plays. The best known example is the love story of the girl Ts'ao Yü-hua and Mrs. Fan Yün-chien, in the 17th century play *Lien-hsiang-pan*, by the famous artist and playwright Li Yü. Cruelty of women towards women servants etc. is amply illustrated in Chinese 'romans de moeurs'; I mention as an example Chapter VIII of the well known novel *Chin-p'ing-mei*. The frequent occurence of sapphism, and occasional cases of sadism among women in ancient China must doubtless be ascribed to the polygamic family system, where a number of women were obliged to live in constant and close proximity. Students of sociology will find this problem discussed at some length in my book 'Erotic Colour Prints of the Ming Period' (Tokyo 1951, Vol. I, p. 146–148). I selected this motive for inclusion in the present novel partly because it enabled me to create unexpected developments and partly in order to show how surprisingly 'modern' old Chinese plots can be.

The exposure of the three monks who falsely reported the theft of a golden statue, in Chapter VII of the present novel, is based on a story in the *T'ang-yin-pi-shih*, the collection of criminal cases mentioned above. This particular case will be found on page 159 of my translation, Case 57–B.

The 'framework' of the present novel, viz. a tale of a distant town where a local bully has usurped power, also is a common situation in Chinese novels. Sometimes a clever magistrate outwits and deposes the usurper, sometimes it is the usurper who is the hero of the story. He takes over from a corrupt magistrate, and subsequently is officially confirmed in his position by a grateful government.

Finally, the role played by 'Master Crane Robe' in this novel (see Chapter XIX) is a much-chastened version of the 'deus ex machina' found in many old Chinese detective novels; they introduce a supernatural being (sometimes the King of the Nether World himself come down to earth in human shape) which helps the magistrate to solve a baffling crime by means of occult powers. This element is, of course, unacceptable to the modern reader. In the present novel, therefore, I represent Master Crane Robe as a high-minded Taoist recluse, leaving it open as to whether the clues Judge Dee discovered during their conversation were the result of a lucky accident, or of the master's inside knowledge of Governor Yoo's affairs, or, again, of the master's unusual mental powers. I chose as background of their conversation the contrast between Confucianism and Taoism. As is well known, Confucianism and Taoims are the two basic ways of thought that have dominated Chinese philosophy and religion ever since approximately the 4th century B.C. Confucianism is realistic and very much of this world, Taoism is romantic and wholly unworldly.

Judge Dee, as an orthodox Confucianist scholar-official, venerates the Confucianist Classics which attach supreme importance to such accepted moral values as justice, righteousness, benevolence, duty, etc. Master Crane Robe, on the other hand, advocates the Taoist principle of the relativity of all accepted values, and a life of non-action 'jenseits vom Guten und Bösen', in complete harmony with the primordial forces of nature. These two conflicting views are epitomized in the couplet of Governor Yoo about the worm and the dragon. This couplet I quoted from a Buddhist work on Ch'an (Japanese: Zen) philosophy. The Ch'an sect of Buddhism often comes very close to Taoism.

R. H. VAN GULIK